WHEN HIS B(                        \
MAN WHO HAS ᴄᴏᴀꜱᴛᴇᴅ ᴛʜʀᴏᴜɢʜ ʟɪꜰᴇ ᴏN
THE FADING MEMORY OF HIGH SCHOOL
HEROICS, RISKS EVERYTHING TO SAVE HIM.

*The FBI? What had Billy done now? And why did they think I
was involved? I had to take a breath and replay in my head
what she had just said. The FBI wanted to talk to Billy. That
was really bad. But if they couldn't have Billy, then The Federal
Bureau of Investigation wanted me. Darwin Burr was wanted by
the FBI. That was a hundred times worse than bad. When I got
stopped by a small town cop for speeding a couple years ago I
was so nervous it took me five minutes to find my car
registration. There was no way I could talk to a real FBI agent.*

They had a parade for Darwin Burr years ago when his team
won the state title.

He's coasted through life on that memory. Still lives in
Claxton, Illinois — but the bucolic farm town now simmers
with racial tension. He has a cushy job working for his
wheeler-dealer, boyhood friend, Billy Rourke. He has a
country house, a healthy 401K, and still drinks for free at
Clarkie's Bar.

His wife Daina, who escaped from Latvia and never looked
back, disdains Darwin's lack of ambition. She's consumed by
her job helping Claxton's underclass and has little time for
Darwin or their daughter, Astra.

When Billy arranges for Darwin to assist Astra's high school basketball coach —the mysterious and flirtatious Fariba Pahlavi — Darwin stops coasting. He discovers a passion for coaching. And Fariba.

Just as Darwin is getting back in the game, Billy vanishes, the FBI wants Darwin's help to find him, and Darwin learns his wife's secret past has put her life in jeopardy.

Darwin knows Billy's guilty, but he can't betray his friend, and he's falling in love with Fariba, but can't abandon his wife. He has no good choices, no winning shot, and in this world heroes don't get parades.

"...The moral and ethical questions raised by his own actions, and by the actions of those closest to him, are part of what keep these pages turning: the reader is keenly interested in finding out what choices Darwin will make. A great read by a writer who just keeps getting better and better".—*Sands Hall. Author of the memoir, FLUNK. START. Reclaiming My Decade Lost in Scientology, and of the novel, Catching Heaven*

"... Len Joy knows men, and as a woman reader, I like getting inside men's heads. Strange as they are, they have troubles and desires and they make mistakes, oh boy, and when they figure that out, they have feelings, too. No fancy stuff. No mumble jumble interiority. This is Do Something, Find Out What Happens, Deal With It...Len Joy is ... solid Americana."—*Sandra Scofield - National Book Award Nominee*

"Len Joy combines lyrical language, unflinching insight, and a kind of rough-edged masculinity to unique effect. His work is a nuanced study of small town life and the deceptive allure of the American dream."— *Abby Geni, Author of the novels, THE WILDLANDS and THE LIGHTKEEPERS*

# BETTER DAYS

## Len Joy

**Moonshine Cove Publishing, LLC**
Abbeville, South Carolina U.S.A.

Copyright © 2018 by Len Joy

ISBN: 978-1-945181-44-3
Library of Congress PCN: 2017957014

Front cover design by Yva Draghichi; interior and back cover by Moonshine Cove Staff; "Better Days" by Bruce Springsteen. Copyright © Bruce Springsteen (Global Music Rights.) Reprinted by permission. International copyright secured. All rights reserved.

## About the Author

Len Joy lives in Evanston, Illinois. Recent work has appeared in *Annalemma, Johnny America, Pindeldyboz, LITnIMAGE, Hobart, 3AM Magazine, Righthand Pointing, Dogzplot, Slow Trains, 21Stars Review, The Foundling Review* and *The Daily Palette (Iowa Review)*.

His first novel, AMERICAN PAST TIME, was published by Hark! New Era Publishing in April 2014. It was described by Kirkus Reviews as "a well-crafted novel and darkly nostalgic study of an American family through good times and bad." Pamela Erens, ("The Virgins" and the just released "Eleven Hours") wrote that, "Len Joy has an eye for the humble, utterly convincing details of family life. This is America seen neither through the gauze of nostalgia nor with easy cynicism but rather with a clear-eyed tenderness."

He is a nationally ranked age-group triathlete and is a member of TEAM USA which represents the USA in International triathlon and duathlon competition.

http://lenjoy.blogspot.com

https://www.facebook.com/American-Past-Time-A-Novel-246412282215014/

For Suzanne

Well my soul checked out missing as I sat listening
To the hours and minutes tickin' away
Yeah, just sittin' around waitin' for my life to begin
While it was all just slippin' away.
I'm tired of waitin' for tomorrow to come.

# BETTER

# DAYS

# Chapter 1
*(Saturday, October 22, 2005)*

Last October, a few weeks before everything went to hell, Daina told me I lacked ambition. I didn't argue with her. We'd been married twenty-five years and on the subject of Darwin Burr, Daina was the world's leading authority. I always figured she had enough ambition for both of us.

We met in Chicago in the spring of '79 at *Faces* on Rush Street. Billy Rourke, who had been my best friend since he moved to Claxton when we were ten, convinced me there were better places for a couple of twenty-two year old guys to spend a Friday night than Clarkie's Bar in downtown Claxton. We started making the sixty mile drive to Chicago.

Daina and I were married the next spring. Billy was my best man. That same year, AutoPro, the nationwide auto parts retailer, opened a distribution center in Claxton. Billy got a job in the shipping department and they hired me as an assistant store manager for one of their ten thousand stores.

Billy Rourke, with the quick comeback, the bullshit stories, the stupid jokes, was a natural for the frat-boy corporate culture of AutoPro. When Fred Langdon dropped dead from a heart attack on Christmas Eve in 1985, the corporate bosses surprised everyone by making Billy the general manager of the Claxton distribution center. I was the store manager for the AutoPro store out on Dillon Highway. Billy transferred me into the DC as his assistant. And that's what I've been for the last twenty years.

AutoPro became the largest employer in Claxton. Billy sponsored softball teams, bowling leagues, flag football and the summer basketball leagues where my team dominated for fifteen years until my sore knees made me give it up. If someone needed funding for their walkathon or Toys for Tots or church camp, Billy took care of them. When we were growing up, Billy was sort of a joke. But not anymore. In Claxton, Billy Rourke was The Man.

My official job was to make sure that the fifty million dollars of auto parts we shipped each month made it to the right AutoPro stores. My unofficial job, which as far as Billy was concerned was more important, was to be Billy's golf partner when he was being wined and dined by AutoPro's suppliers. For a vendor, Billy's support could mean the difference between being a twenty thousand and a twenty million dollar account. Most of the vendor sales reps had one job — keep Billy happy.

After I passed up a couple opportunities for new assignments, Daina became convinced Billy was bad for my "career," so conversations about Billy always ended up being Daina-lectures. Daina escaped from Latvia when she was nineteen and had this American dream notion that I should be trying to get ahead. The thing was, I didn't know what "ahead" was. Running the distribution center wasn't bad work, and while Billy could be a pain in the ass, if he pissed me off, I could tell him to fuck off and he wouldn't fire my ass. Most bosses, at least at AutoPro, wouldn't let you do that.

Billy took care of me. I got regular increases, max bonus, and pocket money just for my signature on some of his real estate deals. In one of his early deals I ended up with two wooded acres, a half-mile off Hoover Road, five miles south of Claxton. With Billy financing I built my dream home — a brick fortress with four bedrooms, three full baths, gleaming oak floors, granite countertops, ceramic tiled bathrooms and a paved driveway with a basketball hoop.

Billy tried to convince the county that the unnamed gravel road that led to the house needed to be paved, but back then he didn't have as much influence. He did put up his own road sign — Rourke Road — at the intersection with Hoover Road, so he could tell it from the half dozen other roads that were simply turnoffs for hunters and snowmobilers. But kids stole the sign years ago and he never replaced it.

It was a beautiful location, especially in the fall when all the trees turned colors. And quiet — my only neighbor was reclusive Ed Mackey who lived a mile down the road.

I owned the house free and clear and I had nearly two million dollars in my 401k (all invested in AutoPro, which had been a highflying stock the last two decades). Thanks to Billy and AutoPro I was in good shape to retire at 55.

Daina's remarks about my lack of ambition came up while I was waiting for Billy to pick me up for a golf match. We were being entertained by Bob Collins, senior sales manager for SunCal Oil Company and some guy named Blainey who had tried to make it on the PGA tour and now was SunCal's designated golfer. SunCal was one of Billy's major suppliers.

It didn't take long for suppliers to figure out that a golf outing at Pheasant Run or Cog Hill could help them build their relationship with Billy Rourke. Billy sucked at golf, but he loved the game. He had the best equipment the vendors could provide, but he could barely break a hundred. It killed him that I thought the game was boring.

"Goddamn it, Darwin," he said after an unusually tight match. "You've got a fucking five handicap. If you practiced a little, you'd be scratch. We'd never lose."

"We don't lose now," I told him. "None of these guys are stupid enough to beat us." That always got him agitated. He hated the idea we weren't winning on our merits. Or my merits. But that was Billy. He had no problem encouraging a supplier to "loan" him state-of-the-art golf clubs and golf balls and invite him to play on the most exclusive golf courses, but he couldn't countenance someone taking a dive. I was glad I wasn't one of his suppliers.

I was buttoning my AutoPro golf shirt and admiring my physique in the bedroom mirror. Don't look a day over thirty, I lied to myself. I stared out the window at my forest. The maples had turned red and orange and yellow, while the oak trees stubbornly refused to change colors and most of the elm trees had given up and dropped their leaves. In the driveway, my daughter Astra was shooting baskets. Girls varsity basketball practice started today.

I had been working with Astra on her game all summer. She had developed a decent three point shot, could dribble with either hand and played tenacious defense. She'd been a second string jayvee player as a Freshman, but this year because of budget cuts there wasn't going to be a jayvee team. If Astra didn't make the Varsity she'd be out of luck.

Astra was blonde and pretty like her mom, but had been gangly and self-conscious about her braces when she started high school. But now the braces were off and she had grown up a lot in the last year. Making the varsity would do wonders for her confidence. One thing I learned from Billy was that confidence was as important as ability. Maybe more.

I was brought back to reality by the sound of Daina coming up the stairs. "Darwin? Darwin!" The double Darwin call. She wasn't coming upstairs to wish me good luck on my golf match. " Did you see this "Management Opportunity Posting" the company sent you? You put your name in, yes?" She marched into the bedroom clutching one of those useless *AutoPro* HR bulletins.

"Hey babe, how do I look? These pants make my ass look fat?" I struck my best boy-toy pose, but she had smelled "management opportunity" and was locked in like a cruise missile.

"Ass looks great. What about job? Listen, 'AutoPro has a position available for Territory Sales Manager in the Midwest Region. AutoPro seeks to fill this position from qualified associates within the AutoPro family.' Darwin, this is management opportunity?"

"Those bulletins are just HR bullshit. Jack Donley's not going to hire some clerk from Distribution. This shirt go with my pants?"

"It's white shirt. Goes with everything. Why do you always diminish yourself? You run that distribution center. You could do this job."

"I just have to hang with Billy five more years and I'm home-free. I don't want to work for some prick like Donley. Besides, where's Billy ever going to find a clerk with a five handicap? He'd lose every match." I grabbed for her ass, but she knocked my hand away.

"Five more years." She spit the words at me. "Look at you. You're in prime of life. You think you will stop work and play games like child? I don't understand you Americans. You are schoolboy hero. That's supposed to be enough? You play games as boy. You play games at work. Now you want to play games all the time? You have no ambition."

It amazed me that Daina could sustain her passion for the same goddamn argument month after month, year after year. It must have been something in her Latvian heritage. The determination that drove her to claw her way over the Iron Curtain, brought her to America where she learned English, passed her GED and completed her nursing training in five years, now compelled her, after a full day on the job as a public health nurse, to take courses at the community college so she'd be qualified to take her boss's job when he retired in three years.

The kitchen door slammed announcing Billy's arrival. "Hey Dar, get your ass in gear. The battle awaits. Daina, this coffee smells great. Must be a special Russian blend, eh?" He knew confusing Russians with Latvians was a surefire way to piss off Daina. I grabbed my golf shoes and headed for the door, hoping to escape.

"I've got to run, babe. You working tonight?"

"Without you, Billy lost. You know that." She followed me out of the bedroom.

I stopped on the landing and pulled her toward me, nuzzling the soft hairs on her neck. She tried to resist, but not much. "Daina, Daina, if Billy let me move on I'd have to start working again. I'll be home by five."

As expected, we won our golf match. At the club bar, Bob Collins counted out ten crisp hundred dollar bills for Billy, and as a special kicker for "continued success," handed him a box of Cohiba Habanas.

On the drive home, Billy, puffing on a fat cigar, was feeling exceptionally good about himself. He had actually parred three holes today and nearly broke 90. Of course Collins had a generous policy on "Gimmes" for Billy. He exited the interstate and turned onto Hoover Road. "I'm playing poker tonight at the Club," Billy said. "Want to join me? Easy money."

"I can't afford your poker games. Besides, Daina gets jealous when I spend too much time with you."

"Ha! Daina should be grateful. If it weren't for me she'd have never met the legendary Darwin Burr."

Billy had told the story at least a thousand times of how he spotted Daina sitting alone at the main bar in *Faces* sucking on a swizzle stick. With shocking white-blonde hair and pale blue eyes she was so icy-hot most guys were afraid to talk to her. I know I was. But not Billy. With his red hair and freckles, Billy looked like a young Mickey Rooney with a beer gut. He was not anyone's version of good-looking. But what he lacked in the looks department he made up for with confidence.

He walked over and started telling her some bullshit story. I figured she'd shoot him down, but the next thing I know they're on the dance floor. He kept her out there fifteen minutes and when they finally walked off, Billy steers her over and introduces me.

"Daina, this here's the legendary Darwin Burr. He's the... oh my god. Will you listen to that? *Get Ready* by *Rare Earth*. That song is Mr. Darwin Burr's most fav-o-rite song of all time. It would mean so much to him if he could have this dance with you."

Billy pulled that kind of shit all the time. He was a good dancer, because even though he was shaped like a bowling pin, he had no inhibitions. I danced liked the Tin Man. He was setting me up just to bust my balls, but this time it didn't work.

Daina smiled at me like she wanted to do more than dance. She leaned into me on tiptoes and whispered in my ear, "You big man, Darvin. Take me for valk, yes?" She'd had a few drinks and it was the seventies. Things were different back then.

Daina liked sex. I wasn't used to that. The girls back in Claxton didn't have Daina's enthusiasm. The first weekend I stayed at her apartment we had sex seven times. That beat my old record for weekend sex by six.

Toward the end of that first summer we were taking a shower and she was scrubbing my chest with her special imported-from-Latvia loofah when she asked me, "Vhy does Billy always call you 'the legendary Darvin Burr'?"

"You mean you danced with him for two hours and he never told you about the state championship?"

"Not two hours. Two dances. Vut championship?" she said as she kneeled down and started soaping my balls.

"My high school basketball team were Illinois state champions back in '75. I made the winning shot. It was a big deal. Hey! Keep doing that. Feels great." Daina had stopped her soaping and was staring up at me, with the perplexed look she had whenever I used some word she hadn't learned yet. "We were champions. Number one in the state. I can still drink for free at Clarkie's because of that shot."

She stood up. "You are hero because of game?" She frowned and hung her loofah on the faucet.

"Right. Just a game. I didn't rescue anyone from a goddamn burning building. Just a lousy fucking basketball game." It pissed me off because she was right. The crowning achievement of my life was nothing. Just a game.

"I know games are important," she said. She didn't say that to make me feel better. That wasn't in her makeup. She was simply stating a fact as she understood it. "Before I make it to America I was on Soviet girls tennis team."

Daina was from Jurmala on the Baltic Sea. It's supposed to be a great vacation spot, at least if you're a Latvian. She wasn't one of the stars on the team, more of a sparring partner for the team's ranked players.

"We were playing a tournament in Helsinki. My roommate Pasha had an attack of the uh, appendix."

"Appendicitis?"

"Yes, that's it. I called the team manager and the hotel doctor rushed to the room. It was very confused situation and while everyone was running about, I disappeared."

She just walked out of the lobby into the night. She walked away from her hotel, her country, her family, her whole damn Latvian life. A year later she had her Green Card and was driving a cab in Skokie.

We'd finished our shower with shower-sex and as Daina was sitting naked on the bed smoking a filterless Camel, an ashtray propped carelessly between her legs, I asked, "So how did you get to America? I didn't think the U.S. government routinely gave Green Cards to runaway teenage tennis players?"

She took a deep drag, blew the smoke towards the tarnished chandelier, and then stubbed her cigarette out. An ash dropped in her tangled blonde pussy hairs. I could feel my hard-on returning. She flicked the ash away and stared at me. No smile. Her look made me shiver. I went limp.

"I did vut I had to. How not important. I made it out. That's all that matters, Darvin."

I never asked her again. I learned that when she put my name at the end of her speech it meant our discussion was over.

Billy took a long draw on his cigar and filled the truck cabin with the fruity Cuban smoke. "That wife of yours is something else. She's never gotten over me, has she?"

"Something like that."

He leaned over and studied his face in the rearview. "It's a curse. These damn women keep falling in love with me. Maybe it's my hair." Billy still had a full head of hair, but the red was now a rusty gray.

"Or your money."

His brow furrowed as though that possibility had never occurred to him. "You think?"

"You keep marrying those women you're going to die broke." Billy was paying alimony to two ex-wives. No children though.

"Dying broke is the plan. I ain't taking it with me." He started laughing and that sent him into a coughing jag and he had to drop his cigar into his chewing tobacco spit cup. I didn't love his cigar smoke, but it was way less disgusting than his Redman habit.

"You ought to have that cough looked at. Or at least stop smoking that damn cigar."

"It ain't nothing. Just clearing the lungs." He gunned his new Acura MDX and passed my neighbor Ed Mackey, who was driving his twenty-year-old pick-up his usual thirty miles per hour. Billy gave him the finger and Ed returned the salute, smiling. "Your fucking neighbor is the craziest Black man I've ever met and I've met plenty. Dude is scary-crazy, you know that, right?"

Ed Mackey returned from Viet Nam in 1972 convinced the world was going to hell. He had spent the last thirty years preparing for the journey. "He's a little eccentric," I said.

"No." Billy shook his head. "Not having a telephone or TV or making your own clothes — that's eccentric. You ever been inside his place? He's got a fucking arsenal: automatic weapons, shotguns, grenade launchers. With real grenades! He's got fucking live-ass grenades." Billy started coughing again and I thought he was going to drive off the road. "Of course if the shit does hit the fan, maybe he'll let you in his bomb shelter. But I like Daina's chances better."

I laughed. "Me too. Ed's sort of sweet on Daina." The Acura tires squealed as Billy took the curve too fast. "You can slow down now."

Billy cackled. "I love this ride. Three hundred goddamn horses, a GPS system that tells you everything but when to take a shit. And feel these seats. That's not some kind of cheap-ass Corinthian leather, pal."

"I'll bet the gas doesn't cost much either."

"Roger that, pardner."

Billy hadn't owned a car in ten years. This car was a "loaner" from SunCal. The company sold ten million cases of motor oil a year through AutoPro and they were always eager to show their appreciation. Along with the car, they furnished Billy with a SunCal credit card. It was in Billy's name, but in the ten years I'd been taking care of the bills, they'd never sent Billy a statement for his gas or maintenance.

"Well Dar, great match. You brought your A game today. Lucky for us that stud, Blainey missed his last putt, though, huh?"

"We must be living right. Imagine a former PGA touring pro three-putting the last two holes. Acted as if he didn't want to win."

"Fuck you. They played us straight up. We were just too good for them. Ah shit!" He hit the brakes but we skidded past Rourke Road. "God damn it. Why don't you clear away some of those trees? I always miss your fucking road."

"Maybe you should put your sign back up."

As we turned into my driveway, Billy pulled out a manila file folder from the console between the seats. "I almost forgot about this," he said, handing me the folder. "This is that new company I set up, 'Worldwide Condo Storage.' I made you Treasurer this time."

Billy was always setting up companies for his real estate deals. He usually made me Secretary. He needed someone who could provide a signature without bringing in a bunch of lawyers. "Condo storage?"

"I told you all about it last week. I got a partner whose buying up those private storage properties and then we're gonna make them into storage condos. Instead of leasing a space to store all your junk you get to own the property where you're storing your junk. It will be a fucking gold mine."

"Who's the partner?"

"Trust me, you don't want to know him. He's very private."

"Do I get paid more for being Treasurer?" I usually got five hundred bucks for being a signature on Billy's deals.

"You cheap son-of-a-bitch, Burr." He twisted in his seat and pulled out a wad of bills from his pants pocket and stuffed them in the console cup holder. "Here's the grand I won from Collins today. That's double your regular payment cause I feel sorry for Daina having to put up with a tightwad like you. Buy her something nice and sign the goddamn papers."

Astra was back out in the driveway, in her gray sweats, shooting baskets.

"Hey, your girl has the same sweet stroke you had," Billy said as he parked halfway up the driveway. "Is Mudge going to start her, or is that too bold a move for the fat slob? Someone ought to tell that guy it's not illegal to score."

Marty Mudge had been the girls' basketball coach since Title IX had forced the school board to create a girls team back in '74. He graduated a few years before Billy and me, but never made it beyond the JV team. He'd been running the same 1950s weave offense for thirty years. His teams were not only bad, they were boring.

Billy jumped out of his car to greet Astra. "Hey, darlin', that's a great looking shot." He held up his hand for a high-five.

Astra smiled and swished a twenty foot set shot. She liked Billy. She could be acting like a typical moody pain-in-the-ass teenager, and Billy would drop by and tell her some stupid joke that would make her laugh. She skipped over and slapped his hand. "Thanks, Billy."

I knew I should probably at least read the documents Billy had shoved on me, but I never understood all that legal bullshit. I trusted Billy. He could be a pain-in-the-ass and a sleaze, but he always looked out for me. I signed my name by the three red arrow flags, grabbed the cash from the cupholder and left the folder on the front seat.

"Getting ready for practice, hon?" I asked.

She turned to me and her smile changed to a frown. Not the pissed frown, though. This was the worry frown. Her Daina-look. "Coach Mudge has been hospitalized with chest pains and they're saying he can't coach us this year. There's a meeting at the school tonight to let us know what the plan is. Boo Boo said they might have to cancel the season if they can't find a coach." Boo Boo Redmond had been the team's point guard the last two seasons.

Sweet kid, worst point guard I'd ever seen. It was painful to watch her try to bring the ball up the court.

"Cancel the season?" Billy said, sputtering. "No way. We'll find you a coach. Hey, Dar. You can coach them. I can see it now, 'Darwin Burr, legendary high school basketball hero, leads Claxton girls to their first victory in ten years. The legend returns.'"

I glared at Billy, letting him know I didn't need him meddling in family matters. It was pointless. Subtlety didn't work on Billy. It usually required a verbal two-by-four to the head to get his attention. "Don't you have to get to your poker game?" I asked him.

"I'm serious. You'd be a great coach."

I sighed. "You have to be a school employee."

Billy frowned. "Says who?" He turned to Astra. "You take your old man to that meeting. I'll make some calls. Remind some folks of their civic duty. "

"What are you going to do, Billy?" Astra asked. She had lost her worried look. She had an overabundance of Billy-confidence.

"Play a few cards," he said, winking at her. "Pull a few strings," he added, because for Billy one metaphor was never enough. "They ain't canceling the season." And with that he jumped in his car and drove off, Acura tires burning rubber on the asphalt.

"Dad?" Astra studied me, trying to determine whether I was pissed off at Billy or just mystified — mystified being my default position when Billy got a hair up his ass about something.

I shrugged. "No telling what Billy's going to do, but I wouldn't bet against him."

**Chapter 2**
*(Saturday, October 22, 2005)*

The high school's new guidance counselor, Fariba Pahlavi, was tied to one of the strings Billy pulled. Or maybe she was one of the cards he played. Whatever her connection, when Astra and I walked into the gym, Fariba — tiny, dark and serious — was standing at center court next to big Charlie Wainwright, the do-as-little-as-possible athletic director for Claxton High.

Fariba could have passed for a teenager, but I found out later she was thirty-four. I didn't know her, but I knew immediately who she was. Everyone in town had known who she was since the day she arrived last year to replace Duane Laurence who had gone missing. Candy Gotham, who Duane had been guidance counseling, had also vanished. Most folks figured they had run off together, but some had their doubts. At least Billy did.

"Duby Laurence couldn't find his ass with both hands. He ain't smart enough to shack up with some teenager and not get caught. I'll betcha her old man turned Duby into pig food." Billy made that declaration the day they discovered the pair were missing. Candy's father had the biggest hog farm in the county and I suspect Billy had been watching *Deadwood* when he came up with that notion. The bad guys were always being fed to the hogs in that show.

In the 70s, when I was in school, there might have been some parental reservations about having an Iranian Muslim woman as the high school guidance counselor. Back then there were no racial issues because everyone was white. And religious diversity, of which the people of Claxton were very proud, amounted to the peaceful coexistence of three Baptist churches, two branches of Methodism, and a breakaway Presbyterian church.

But today over twenty percent of the population was Black or Hispanic, most of whom had escaped from Chicago and settled on the east side of Claxton. In addition to the original churches, the east side had added a Southern Baptist congregation and a Catholic church where the services were in Spanish, while on the west side there was now a small reform synagogue and a smaller radical Episcopal church with a lady preacher. Given all those changes, bringing in Fariba was not such a big deal. Especially when most of the parents believed she was replacing a sleazy pedophile. Fariba was warmly accepted by the teachers and students and all the fine folks from the PTA from the day she stepped off the Greyhound from Chicago.

The AD, Charlie Wainwright was husky (or fat if you listened to Daina). He had a thick thatch of white hair that was never quite combed and he wore a baggy dress shirt that would have made a great pup tent. I thought he looked a lot like Tip O'Neil, but he sounded more like Barney Fife.

A section of the bleachers had been pulled out for the meeting. The girls who were trying out — there were about twenty of them — were seated in the front of the bleachers. The players who were on the team last year sat in the first row and the newbies were in the second and third rows. The parents were scattered behind them. Astra was the only girl who wasn't accompanied by both parents.

Daina seldom made it to the after-school functions like parent teacher conferences or school plays or basketball games. She had to work most evenings — as that was the only time she could meet with some of her clients. She used the dining room as her office, and today when I walked in to tell her about the Mudge development the dining room table was covered with her client case files. Even though she was clearly not in a mood to be interrupted, I went through the ritual of asking her if she wanted to come with us to the team meeting.

"Why?" she asked, her eyes narrowed with suspicion like I was one of her junkie clients trying to con her.

I shrugged. "I don't know. To show Astra we support her?"

Daina scoffed. "She knows that. Haven't you spent hours working on her longshot?"

"Jumpshot." I should have just let it go. I hadn't changed her mind on anything, ever. But of course, I didn't. "They're threatening to shut down the program."

"Who is threatening? How do you know this?"

I didn't have an answer and she stared at me like I was some gossipy teenager. I huffed, angry at myself. "Forget I asked. I'll let you know what happens." I wheeled around and stomped out of the dining room, using as much body language as I could, to let her know I was pissed. She didn't notice, but even if she had it wouldn't have made any difference. Empathy was never Daina's thing.

As Astra left me to sit with the other girls, Wainwright hailed me from center court. "Darwin. Come here."

He could have walked over to talk to me, but that would have taken too much effort. Big Charlie was big on energy conservation. I walked out to center court and I have to confess it brought back memories. Hadn't been on my old high school court in thirty years. "What's up, Charlie?" I asked, even though I didn't really want to know. Teachers. Coaches. Daina. Whenever those folks called for me my scrotum tightened up — a primeval reflex to protect me from the possible kick in the balls.

"You know Fariba, right?" he said, turning to smile at the young woman, like he was the emcee of one of those old quiz shows.

She smiled at me sympathetically. She had a good guidance counselor smile. "It's a pleasure to meet you, Mr. Burr. I'm Fariba Pahlavi." Fariba had a clipped, cultured voice where every syllable seems to get its own space. She sounded sort of British. People who spoke like Fariba always made me feel like they were about fifty IQ points smarter than me. Usually they weren't, but in Fariba's case, that was probably an underestimation.

"Call me Darwin." We shook hands. She had a firm grip.

Wainwright cleared his throat and checked his watch. "Okay, Dar. I'm going to say a few words outlining the game plan and then introduce Fariba and you."

He could tell that I had no idea what the fuck he was talking about. I didn't have to say anything.

"Goddammit! Billy didn't talk to you yet?" he said.

I was pretty sure I heard Fariba sigh. It was the kind of reaction you develop after a short time dealing with Billy and his schemes.

Wainwright ran his hand through his mane of hair. Then he smiled gamely. "No biggie. Here's the deal. Fariba is going to be the acting head coach. And Billy, bless his heart, is going to make you available at no cost to the school to be her unpaid assistant. Needless to say, Fariba didn't have much chance to play basketball back there in Baghdad. Am I right, honey?"

Fariba looked at Wainwright as though she was trying to figure out if he was telling a joke, or just was a joke. She decided, correctly, on option B. "I grew up in Tehran, in Iran, not Baghdad, in Iraq. But you are correct, Mr. Wainwright. I did not play basketball. Field hockey was my sport."

Confusing Iran and Iraq didn't faze him. "Well there you go. You and Darwin are going to make a great team. A helluva a team. Let's get this party started."

## Chapter 3
*(Saturday, October 22, 2005)*

I wasn't really pissed at Billy for coming up with this cockamamie scheme. It could work and I have to admit the idea of getting back in the game, even as a coach for a team that hadn't won a game in two seasons, had me stoked.

But not showing up or even bothering to give me a heads up, that was too typical of how Billy operated. And even then he managed to get credit for his generosity in making me available for an activity, most of which was not going to take place during the work day. Basketball practice started at 4, and even on the days when corporate was in town and we had to look extra busy, I never worked past 4:30. So Billy was covering just a few hours of work time a month and it wasn't even coming out of his own pocket. Billy had a knack for that kind of deal.

I glanced at Fariba as Wainwright started explaining to the parents what the plan was. I wondered what her deal was with Billy. The guy who had been my goofy sidekick had grown up to be the Godfather. Generous as hell, but there were always strings attached. Fariba just didn't appear to be the kind of person who would owe Billy.

Wainwright kept his talk short. He wasn't one of those teachers who fell in love with the sound of his own voice. And he didn't like working overtime.

"All right, you didn't all come out to hear me blather. Please welcome your new interim head coach, Ms. Pahlavi." He pivoted toward Fariba and clapped loudly. He kept it up until he was joined with somewhat less enthusiasm by the girls and their parents.

Wainwright addressed the audience from center court. He liked to keep his distance. Fariba acknowledged Wainwright with a smile and a slight nod as she walked toward the bleachers, close enough so she could make eye contact with the girls and their parents. "Thank you, Mr. Wainwright. I'm honored and grateful for this opportunity to fill in for Coach Mudge while he convalesces. I know we all wish him an expeditious and complete recovery." Fariba might not have known squat about basketball, but she was the first person I'd met in real life that could string words together into complete sentences that made sense. No "ums" or "ahs" or "you knows." Her comments were also refreshingly free of the usual coaching clichés about giving 110 percent or seeking guidance from the man upstairs.

She paused in her remarks and scanned the room, making brief eye contact with everyone. "As Mr. Wainwright correctly observed, I am not an expert on basketball. That is, a generous understatement. But I am willing to work hard and learn as much as I can about the game and I sincerely appreciate Mr. Burr's willingness to assist me in that endeavor. I need not waste your time tonight so I beg your indulgence. We will begin tryouts Monday at 4 p.m. By that time I hope to have had an opportunity to meet with Mr. Burr so we can establish a plan for going forward. I thank each of you for your attention and support." She turned to me and smiled. "Do you have anything you wish to add at this time, Mr. Burr?"

It felt as though everyone were staring at me. Hadn't had that feeling in a long time and I'm certain I was blushing. I grinned like a schoolboy and said, "Darwin. Just call me Darwin."

"Very well." She scanned the bleachers where the parents were seated. "Does anyone have a question?"

On those television dramas like *Friday Night Lights,* this is the point where some prickly mom or a blowhard dad would say something obnoxious like, "What's your plan for beating Claypool?" But that didn't happen. We were the beneficiaries of not just lowered expectations, more like zero expectations. You can't fall off the floor, and the girls team had been down for so long that there wasn't anywhere to go but up. At least that's what I thought.

It didn't matter to those parents that Fariba was Iranian. Or Muslim. Or a woman. It didn't bother them in the least that she knew nothing about basketball. They were just happy that there was going to be a team. Pleased that their girls would have a chance to play. I thought that was neat.

And Fariba. She had been totally cool. I was impressed. I imagined, that like Daina, she'd faced tougher situations adjusting to a whole new country, language and customs. I thought it would be fun to work with her. And on that score at least, I was right.

## Chapter 4
*(Sunday, October 23, 2005)*

Fariba and I made plans to meet the next morning at Walter's Pancake House on Prairie Street. I suggested we get there early before the sunrise church services were over. Those Baptists liked their pancakes. So did the Methodists.

I had just pulled into the parking lot behind the restaurant when Billy called me. "Where you at Dar? I'm hungry." Billy's MDX was parked three feet from the door to the kitchen in a spot marked, "No Parking."

"You're illegally parked."

"Walter don't mind. Get your ass in here. I want to order."

"What are you doing here?"

"Helping you get acquainted with Fariba."

My relationship with Billy and with Daina had evolved — or maybe a better word is mutated — in similar fashion. It used to be they'd do something to piss me off and I'd tell them not to do that anymore. But at some point in the last ten years I gave up. I could play out the conversations in my head and I knew it would end with them doing whatever they wanted despite anything I said. So I stopped trying to change Billy. Or Daina. I just went with the flow. It was easier that way.

"See you inside, Billy," I said, but he'd already hung up.

Billy was seated in the booth in the back, just off the kitchen. He was animated — Billy was always animated — using his hands almost as much as his mouth. With guys he was always chest-poking or sleeve-tugging or neck-squeezing; with women he had learned to be a little more restrained. He was clearly in story-telling mode, leaning forward in the booth with his hands moving around as though he were conducting an orchestra. He could be entertaining. My problem was I'd heard most of his stories a hundred times. Fariba's back was to me as I approached the booth, but I could tell by the way she leaned forward and nodded her head that he had her attention.

He saw me coming and paused his monologue. "...and here's the man now. Darwin, tell her how the game ended."

Fariba turned and smiled at me. She appeared even younger than she had looked at the gym. She was wearing tight-fitting Levi's and a black sweatshirt. Even when she dressed casual she seemed more sophisticated than all the folks in the restaurant who had just come from church. "Mr. Burr." She caught herself. "Sorry. Darwin. Billy has been telling me about your championship season. What a thrill that must have been."

Billy had man-spread so that there wasn't any room on his side of the booth. I wanted to talk to Fariba, not Billy, and it's a lot easier to talk when you are sitting across from someone, but I had no choice. I slid into the booth next to Fariba. Billy had been silent for almost twenty seconds. That was about his limit. "I was telling Fariba about the championship game," he said.

I twisted in the booth so I could semi-look at Fariba. "I hope he's giving you the short version. Sometimes when Billy tells that story, it takes longer than the actual game."

She giggled. "Oh no. He's telling a very fast-paced narrative about how you singlehandedly kept your team in the game."

"Tell her how the game ended, Dar," Billy said, reaching across the table to tap my forearm.

I didn't mind telling the story. I just didn't appreciate all the hype. I knew that however I described those final seconds, my version wasn't going to be acceptable to Billy. I decided to save us all some time. "Billy stole the ball, passed it to me and I made the shot and we won the game. State Champions. It was cool."

Billy's face twisted up like I'd just farted in church. "You are so lame, Burr. You could make the end of the world sound boring." He turned to Fariba and told his version of "The Shot." Screaming, insane fans. Hot cheerleaders. The smell of twenty thousand sweaty fans, the choreography of players on the court. My last-second shot and the look on the face of Mr. All American, Leroy Williams, who had never lost a high school game. I could tell by the look in Fariba's eyes that she was there. She could feel it, hear it, taste it. Billy Rourke was a master storyteller.

And here's the thing about Billy. He was a blowhard, but he wasn't a braggart. He would brag on me all the time. Too much. But half the time when he told stories about our athletic exploits you wouldn't have even known he was there. He didn't make a big deal of the fact that if he hadn't stolen the ball with ten seconds to go, there wouldn't have been any shot.

"…and the crowd went wild. They picked up Darwin and carried him around the court. He was the Prince. It was the greatest high school championship ever. And it was all Darwin. That's why I'm so excited he's going to help you. You guys are going to make a great team."

First Charlie Wainwright, now Billy. Everyone was convinced that Fariba and I were going to make a great team. I wondered if Fariba thought so.

Walter Maroney pushed through the swinging doors of the kitchen. With his signature white tee-shirt and jeans and a silver-gray crewcut, he looked more like a Marine drill sergeant than the owner of a pancake restaurant. Walter was lean and grizzled like a dog's chew toy and I doubt he weighed more than a buck forty. He was a distance runner — ran a sub three hour marathon in his prime and most every morning when I drove to work I'd see him out running on the County Highway. His restaurant was always packed, but it wasn't because of Walt's winning personality. It was my experience that those long distance runners lived in their own world. I always got the impression Billy annoyed him so I was surprised when he spotted us and a big grin lit up his face. He grabbed a menu from a waitress and headed toward our table.

Billy spotted him. "Hey, Walter, waiting on us yourself? I guess we rate, eh Fariba?" Billy winked, pleased that his rep had warranted special attention from Walter, who, like I said, wasn't the friendliest guy in the world.

But I don't think Walter even noticed Billy sitting at the table. Or me. "Fariba, have you checked the new menu? I'm going to make you famous."

I could tell by the way Fariba smiled at Walter that they were friends. "What did you do, Walter?" She scanned the menu and Walter stood over her, his foot tapping like an anxious schoolboy.

Billy beat her to the punch. "Holy shit. The Fariba Slam! A stack of pancakes, three egg omelet, hash browns, large orange juice and a side of bacon." He leaned over the booth and pointed to the section where the restaurant specials included such entrées as, 'The Marathon Stack' and 'Roadrunner crepes.' "Didn't know you were a regular here, Fariba."

She blushed, and grinned at Walter. "Oh my. You've immortalized my workout meal. I'm so, so honored, Walter. Thank you."

"Are you a runner too, Fariba?" I asked.

"She's a triathlete" Walter said, beaming like a proud parent. World class. She did that Ironman race in Hawaii last fall, finished in under twelve hours. She joins my run group three times a week and then goes off and bikes or swims."

"No shit. Twelve hours?" Billy said. He was surprised. I could tell he didn't like it that Walter knew more about Fariba than he did. "Must be a damn long race."

"You could say that," Walter said. "They swim over two miles in the surf, then they jump on their bikes for a 112-mile bike ride. And then…" he paused dramatically, "…and then, after all that, they run a marathon."

I was vaguely aware of the Ironman, but had never actually met someone who competed. It sounded crazy. "You should have told Wainwright," I said. "Maybe his introduction wouldn't have been so lame."

There was a clatter of dishes breaking in the kitchen. Walter winced and glanced over his shoulder toward the kitchen. "Sounds like I'm needed. You folks enjoy your breakfast."

31

"Hey Walter, how about a special price on the Fariba?" Billy shouted as Walter disappeared into the kitchen. He acted like he hadn't heard Billy, but I think he did.

Dolores, our regular waitress, hustled back to take our order. Billy and Fariba ordered the Fariba Slam, I ordered a waffle. I was trying to stay under 220, which was still twenty pounds heavier than when I played ball.

"Are you still training?" I asked.

Fariba nodded. "Always. It keeps me sane. Today I biked. Over to Claypool and back."

"This morning?" Billy asked. "That's over forty miles. You ride in the dark?"

"I do. I have a light that provides adequate illumination. I love the early morning rides. So quiet. No trucks to contend with. It gave me time to think about our basketball team. I don't know much about the game, but I think I can help with the girls' conditioning."

While Billy wolfed down his breakfast like someone might steal it from him, Fariba and I went to work on our coaching plan. She pulled out a spiral notebook and pen, prepared to take notes.

"I have a question. I thought about asking this at the team meeting, but decided it might not be appropriate. Why aren't any of our Black students trying out for the team?"

Another one of those questions I should have had an answer for, but didn't. But for better or worse, usually worse, Billy always had an answer. "Because they didn't want to play for Mudge. Christ, his offense was so boring he put people to sleep. He would have banned the jumpshot if they'd let him."

Fariba looked at me to see if Billy could possibly be right. I shook my head. "It's a good question. The boys team had three Black starters last year, so I don't think it's exactly a racial boycott."

"Maybe Mr. Wainright could make an announcement encouraging more participation?" Fariba said.

Billy scoffed. "Don't hold your breath. For Charlie, girl sports are a waste of time and money. He would have been fine with having the season tanked when Mudge went down."

"I see. Very well. I will make some inquiries on my own." She flipped open her notebook. "Let's begin. What's the first step, ?"

"We need to develop a real offense. Billy's right. Mudge ran that damn weave for the last twenty years. We should get some whiteboards so we can diagram plays for the girls."

"Should I ask Mr. Wainwright?" Fariba said as she made a note on her pad.

Billy stuffed a forkful of hash browns in his mouth. "Nah. Just go to Ryan Sporting Goods," he said as he doused his stack of pancakes with maple syrup. "Jack Ryan will take care of you. Have him put it on my tab. Wainwright won't spend a nickel on girls' sports."

Fariba frowned. But not about the continued dis toward women sports. "That's very generous, Billy. Are you sure?" She thought Billy was actually going to pay for the whiteboards. Billy had tabs all over town, but I had never seen him pay one.

"Absolutely," he said. He wiped his chin with his napkin, tossed it onto his plate and slipped out of the booth. "You kids are hitting on all cylinders. I'm going to run over to Dillon and catch the late mass with Father Murphy. I'll light a candle for the team."

I confess I was glad to see Billy leave. I slipped over to his side of the booth.

"Billy is a devout Christian?" Fariba asked.

I shrugged. Billy was a devout dealmaker. "He goes to church." With Billy I was pretty sure that St. Anne's was just another connection in his network.

By our third cup of coffee we had put together what I thought was a practical coaching plan. With Fariba's guidance, we would focus on conditioning. If our girls had superior stamina, we'd be able to dial up the defense. Defense doesn't take great athletic skill, it just requires some understanding of the fundamentals and a big heap of "want to." We'd stress defense and develop a simple offense that kept the ball moving so that the other team would have to work on defense. Wear them down. If we held our own for three quarters, with superior conditioning, we'd own the fourth quarter.

It was a reasonable plan. But as Mike Tyson used to say, "Everyone has a plan until you punch them in the face."

## Chapter 5
*(Monday, October 24, 2005)*

Twenty-one girls showed up for practice on Monday afternoon. Fariba invited several Black girls who had counseling sessions with her, to try out for the basketball team. "Not one of them was interested," she said as we all filed out of the gym for a three-mile warm-up jog. "I got the impression they considered girls basketball to be a "white-girls only" sport. I don't know why."

Against my better judgment I joined them on the run. I never saw the attraction of running if I didn't have a ball in my hands. It seemed like a great way to spoil a beautiful Fall day.

And it was a beautiful day. The Maple trees had all their autumn colors on display and the cool air smelled fresh and clean. The sun was warm on my face, but without the burn-feeling you get in the summer. It almost felt good to run.

I may have lacked ambition, as Daina said, but I was feeling content, comfortable with my life. I had a decent job, a daughter who I loved more than life itself, and a good wife. Daina was a pain-in-the-ass, but in a good way. And she was actually pleased I was coaching. I could tell even though she didn't say so.

I am grateful I didn't know what was coming. I shuffled along at the back of the pack, winded, but savoring the moment and trying not to embarrass myself or Astra. Fariba glided effortlessly from girl to girl, giving them tips on running form and introducing herself to girls she hadn't met. When we got back to the gym, she wasn't even breathing hard. Neither was Astra.

I started the practice with an exercise where the players raced baseline to foul line and back and then baseline to half court and back and then baseline to baseline and back. It's called the Suicide drill. It sounds bad, but it's a lot worse than it sounds. Fariba gained a lot of respect from the girls (and from me) by joining the girls in the workout.

After six rounds, everyone but Fariba was wobbling, their legs rubbery. I only gave them two minutes between sets. Just enough time to grab a quick drink and try to catch their breath. No one chattered during the breaks — they were all too busy sucking up water and oxygen. The gym was a sweatbox with poor ventilation and after the fifth round two girls puked, which didn't help the air quality.

In the first three rounds, Astra finished in the middle of the pack, but by the last two rounds she was ahead of everyone. Our summer workouts had paid off.

For the last fifteen minutes of practice I rolled out the rack of basketballs and demonstrated the fundamentals of an effective jumpshot. How to balance the ball in the fingertips. How to coil and elevate, engaging calf muscles, not just quads, and how to snap the hand forward giving the ball a proper backspin as you keep your eyes glued on the front of the rim. "Don't look at the ball," I said as I lined up a shot, staring hard at the basket. "Stay focused on the rim." The ball swished through the net, which always makes the demonstration more impressive.

Most kids with a little training can master the basics of shooting and it's not too difficult to shoot a decent percentage when you're rested and no one is bothering you. But in a game situation when you're winded and a defender is harassing you and there is so much crowd noise it's hard to concentrate — the basket starts shrinking. That first day of practice, Astra was the only player who still could shoot effectively after the drills.

The Suicides took their toll. Five girls didn't return for Tuesday's practice. I added the Slide drill, which combined footwork with conditioning and made Suicides look easy. In the Slide drill, players established a defensive posture — knees bent, hands up — as though they were defending against someone bringing the ball up the court. The player gives ground, zigzagging, first to the left and then back to the right. They travel the full length of the court and then sprint back.

I had Fariba demonstrate. She had great footwork and off-the-charts cardio fitness. She never seemed to be out of breath. It was almost disgusting. The girls were red-faced and wobbly-legged after thirty minutes. We followed that with twenty minutes of shooting drills and the percentage of made baskets was still scary low. If our shooting didn't improve it was going to be difficult to win any games.

After practice, Fariba and I waited in the gym, while the girls showered. "What do you think of our team so far?" Fariba asked.

She must have been reading my mind. "None of our seniors have ever experienced winning. That worries me. You lose every game and that's what you expect. It can be tough to overcome. We might have a better chance with the younger kids."

"You mean like Astra?"

"Astra should definitely start. And I'm not saying that because she's my kid. Right now she's the only one who can consistently shoot under game conditions. Thanks to you, all the team's going to be in much better condition. And because of that I think we'll have more than adequate defense. But at the end of the day, we have to score."

Fariba picked up one of the basketballs from the rack. "Can you show me how to shoot?" She bounced the ball over to the basket and flung it toward the rim with both hands. It caromed off the backboard missing the rim entirely. "Aah." She chased the ball down and looked back at me quizzically.

"Not like that. Come over here." I stood at the double door entrance to the gym. "EAGLES" was stenciled in foot high letters above the door. Fariba hustled over with her basketball. "I want you to aim for just above the G. An easy toss."

She stood in front of the door and rested the ball in both hands.

"No. Remember what I told the girls." I took hold of her right hand and cocked her wrist back like she was going to balance a tray on her upturned palm. "Cradle the ball here and use your left hand for support." I stood in front of Fariba and demonstrated.

She watched me intently and then reached for the ball. "Let me try," she said.

"Okay. Square your feet and flex your knees. Now line up your right elbow with your bellybutton."

She looked at me and grinned. "Really?"

"You need to be properly aligned."

"Like this?" She was wearing one of her sleeveless triathlon tops. With her flat stomach and toned arms, it looked great on her. She pulled it up so her navel was uncovered. "See. Right in line."

"Yeah, that's very good alignment. Now use your left hand to steady the ball."

She brought her left hand up to the side of the ball.

"No. Now you've lost the alignment. Your hand needs to be under the ball, not to the side." I pushed her left elbow down so it was almost in line with her right elbow.

Fariba balanced the ball and flexed her knees getting comfortable. "I have a question. What do the girls with large breasts do? It seems that they would make alignment challenging."

"You're right — boobs can get in the way. Luckily you don't have that problem."

Fariba snort-laughed and dropped the ball. "Don't make me laugh when I'm trying to shoot." She settled back into position and flicked the ball toward the G.

It only took her a few tosses to get the rhythm and timing down. She had great hand-eye coordination. "Okay. That's looking good. Let's try one from the foul line."

She clapped her hands like a school girl and dribbled the ball out to the line.

"Don't stare at the ball while you dribble. Keep your eyes up." She raised her head and bounced the ball off her foot.

"Shit!" she said. "Oops, sorry. I mean, shucks."

"I know what you mean." I ran the ball down in the corner. I picked it up and pivoted toward the basket, flinging the ball toward the rim. I knew the instant I released it, that it was a sweet shot.

"Hah! Nothing but net," I said, extremely pleased with myself as the ball ripped through the net.

Fariba cheered. "Great shot! . That was a set shot, right?"

I laughed. "No one has taken a set shot since 1958. That was a jumpshot by a guy who is too fat to jump anymore."

"You are not fat," she said, brow furrowed. "Perhaps just a little too well-fed."

"You're slightly more diplomatic than my wife." I picked up the ball and passed it to her as she stood on the foul line. "Try a free throw. No jumping. Just bounce the ball three times and then coil, elevate and release."

"How long have you been married?" she asked.

"I don't know. Twenty, thirty years. Something like that. Shoot the ball."

She bounced the ball three times, sank into a deep squat and then exploded upwards. The ball flew over the top of the backboard.

"A little less explosion. But that was good rotation on the ball."

She tilted her head and stared at me like I was some painting hanging in a gallery. "You must have been married very young. Was it an arranged marriage?" She smiled coyly.

It almost sounded as if she were flirting with me, but I knew better. Guys my age are always wanting to believe that girls like Fariba are interested, but the truth is that we are either invisible to them, or they see us as so old that we're considered harmless. That was me in spades. "Focus, Fariba. Put the ball in the basket."

Her next shot was two feet short of the rim. I tossed the ball back to her and she started to ask me another question, but I gave her my serious face and she shut up. This time the ball smashed against the backboard and dropped in. I bounced the ball back to her. "Good, but try not to break the backboard."

She pressed her lips tight, concentrating extra hard, took a deep breath, and with a smooth easy motion sank a perfect free throw.

"Good shot. You're a natural."

She beamed. "You're a good instructor. I'm going to stop on that positive note. You'll teach me some more tomorrow, right?" she said.

"You bet. We'll work on your dribbling. No more bouncing those balls off your feet. Dribbling is just a special kind of dancing." I did some fancy dribbling from one hand to the other and through my legs as I dribbled the ball over to the ball rack. Pure schoolboy showoff stuff.

"I love to dance. I'll bet you're a good dancer."

"You'd lose that bet. Billy's the dancer." I placed the basketball back in the ball rack and wheeled it over to the equipment corral.

Fariba frowned. She didn't like my answer. "He's not a good dancer."

I decided that was not a discussion I wanted to have. For some reason the picture of Fariba dancing with Billy bothered me.

Fariba followed me over to the equipment corral. "Do you think our workouts are too hard?"

I shook my head. "We need to cut the team down to twelve. Easier if they cut themselves instead of us having to making the call. But I really wish we could keep some of the sophomores who would have been on the jayvees if we still had the team."

"Why can we only have twelve players? Is it a rule?"

It was like one of those simple Daina questions. Something I should have had an answer for but didn't. "I don't know why. Maybe because we only have twelve uniforms?"

"That's a silly reason. Billy could get us more uniforms or we could keep four extras and not suit them up for the game. They would still be a part of the team."

I shrugged. "I guess we could handle sixteen. Of course if Billy supplies the uniforms he'll want "Sponsored by Billy Rourke" plastered on the back."

# Chapter 6
*(Wednesday, October 26, 2005)*

The day my world turned upside down started off like every other day at the DC. I'd been at the office since six a.m. because it was Wednesday and most of the long-haul carriers arrived as soon as it was light so they could drop their load and make it back home by Friday. The driver from Orange Freight had been a pain-in-the-ass as usual, wanting to unload immediately even though he was the seventh rig in line.

After listening to him bitch for fifteen minutes, I got back to my office a few minutes before nine. Billy hadn't shown up yet and I was about to call to remind him we had a lunch scheduled with Federal Mogul when Kelly Craven, our receptionist called.

"Mr. Burr, Mr. Poindexter and Miss Washington are here to see you."

"Mr. Burr?"

She said it so naturally it took me a second to realize something had to be wrong. For her to call me "Mr. Burr" someone must have had a gun pointed at her head. Kelly dealt with truck drivers all day long. Most of them she referred to as "that driver." After a few years, if they stopped trying to hit on her, she might identify them by their last name, but she never called me or anyone else Mister. Or Miss.

I had not met Harry Poindexter, Jr. but his memos on all the great management opportunities in the AutoPro family had been coming to my house for eighteen months. He was the number two guy in Human Resources. Billy hadn't said anything to me about a visit from corporate. And that wasn't like Billy. When it came to corporate honchos Billy could suck up better than anyone. He always made sure their every need was met. Or had me make sure.

"I assume you have no fucking clue why they are here? Where the hell is Billy?"

"I'll tell them you are on your way," Kelly said, in an unnaturally almost unrecognizably demure voice.

"Put them in the conference room and get them some coffee, while I call Billy." Our "conference room" was the holding tank for the drivers. It had a card table, a few ancient folding chairs and a pile of dog-eared issues of *Truck & Driver*. Not the best place for HR bigshots, but I didn't want to put them in Billy's office and I was starting to have a bad vibe about this visit.

"They don't want coffee," Kelly said. There was a clear edge to her voice now. "You need to come out here, right now."

My mind was spinning, but I was not getting any traction. I hung up the phone and walked down the hall to Kelly's desk. Kelly was a nicely packaged early-forties brunette. She usually wore tight jeans and a tube top, which the drivers all appreciated. She had a funky snake tattoo that curled around her neck — the regrettable result, she confessed, of mixing tequila and vodka one night.

I could usually count on killing ten to fifteen minutes every morning bullshitting with Kelly about almost anything. She was a great source of advice on how to deal with a moody teenager as she had a twenty-three year old daughter whom she had raised with no help from her ex. But I could tell by the look in her eyes that this was a no-bullshit moment. As she nodded her head toward the conference room, she seemed to be holding her breath. If I didn't know better, I would say she was scared.

I walked into the conference room. A smug-looking man in a corporate blue suit with gold cufflinks and a starched white shirt was standing next to a stylish tall black woman with shoulder-length straight black hair wearing a well-tailored beige suit that contrasted nicely with her milk chocolate complexion and did its best to conceal a nice pair of breasts. They had cleared the ashtrays from the card table and were standing, almost at attention, waiting. For me.

"Hello, Darwin." The man stepped forward and extended a well-manicured hand. "Harry Poindexter. This is Stephanie Washington. Stephanie is our assistant general counsel." Washington had an "I-am-a-serious-bad-ass," look on her face. She appeared to be about thirty, but might have been older. It was hard to tell because her face was unlined. I figured she hadn't worn it out cracking a lot of smiles. She nodded sourly at me and clearly felt no need to shake my hand. Just as well as Poindexter was one of those guys for whom handshaking was some kind of bullshit macho ritual.

He finally let go of my hand and invited me to sit down at the card table. That was typical HR behavior. Come into a place and act like you own it. Poindexter and Washington perched on the edges of the folding chairs on their side of the table. I didn't blame them. No telling whose ass had been on those seats earlier in the day.

Poindexter tugged on the knot of his tie and cleared his throat, as though he were preparing to say something important. And, as it turned out, he was. "Darwin, we're here to see Billy Rourke. Do you know where he is?"

"No," I said. Poindexter waited, expecting me to elaborate, but I'd watched too many episodes of *Law & Order* to fall into that trap. Nothing good was going to come of this visit. My only goal was to get it over with without making matters worse. There had always been a Teflon aspect to Billy. He had crossed more lines than I could ever keep up with, but he was always, in his own reckless way, very careful when it came to corporate. Nobody from HR had ever paid us a surprise visit before. Something had to have gone seriously off the tracks and I had a bad feeling about it all.

Poindexter gave me a disappointed smile. "You're his number two man. You should know where he is at all times."

Under normal circumstances I would have laughed at that notion because I usually preferred not knowing where Billy was. But Poindexter was Sunday church serious so I played it straight. "I'm sorry, Harry. I don't know where he is."

I offered my most sincere look, but Ms. Washington wasn't buying it. She tapped Poindexter on the sleeve of his suit, like one of those tag team professional wrestling matches. "Mr. Burr, I don't think you appreciate the serious nature of our visit. The FBI wants to interview Mr. Rourke. We were planning to deliver him to the Peoria office this morning. Since he's unavailable and no one seems to know where he is…" she turned to Poindexter and continued, "I think we should bring them Mr. Burr. Don't you agree, Harry?"

Holy shit. What had Billy done now? And why did they think I was involved? I had to take a breath and replay in my head what she had just said. The FBI wanted to talk to Billy. That was really bad. But if they couldn't have Billy, then The Federal fucking Bureau of Investigation wanted me. Darwin Burr was wanted by the FBI. That was a hundred times worse than bad. When I got stopped by a small town cop for speeding a couple years ago I was so nervous it took me five minutes to find my car registration. There was no way I could talk to a real FBI agent.

When Washington made her suggestion that they take me to the FBI, Harry Poindexter's face had tightened as though he had a bad case of indigestion. He didn't get to be the number two guy in the department by sticking his neck out. He followed the book and chain of command was an inviolable principle to him.

I decided to play the Wally card. "Of course I'm going to cooperate with the FBI," I said, addressing my comments to Poindexter. "But I don't work for either of you. Since Rourke's not available, my orders have to come from Weidman." Wally Weidman was the director of operations. He was a dinosaur. Or maybe a Neanderthal. Hated lawyers. Weidman was a regular golfing buddy of Billy's. At Cog Hill last summer I remember him telling us, after his fifth or sixth scotch, that he couldn't stand any of the corporate schmucks, but he really hated the HR schmucks. Weidman was not someone who kept his opinions secret.

Poindexter's lips were pressed so tight I could practically see the outline of his teeth. He cleared his throat again and turned toward the lawyer. "I don't think we need to bring Wally into this right now."

Again, I had to replay what he had just said. They were planning to take Billy (and me) to the FBI and they hadn't told his boss — the third ranking executive in the whole company? This whole deal had just gotten ten times more serious.

Washington stared sullenly at Poindexter. I stood up and gave Harry my most sincere I-just-work-here look. "I can't talk to an outside organization without Billy or Wally's authorization." I didn't need to add that that would be a violation of AutoPro policy. I made a show of looking at my watch. "This is our busiest day of the week. I've got a hundred trucks queued out there and twenty more arriving every hour." That was a slight exaggeration, but those seemed like nice round numbers that would get their attention. "If I don't get outside there will be a clusterfuck like you've never seen. Which means those trucks won't get unloaded, the stores won't get their merchandise and the Customer. Won't. Be. Satisfied."

Not satisfying the customer was the worst possible offense at AutoPro. In the corporate culture of AutoPro you could fuck your employees (literally or figuratively), chisel the suppliers and cheat the government, but you had better keep the customer happy. The customer was King. Or Queen. It didn't matter how big of an asshole a customer might be, they were always right. The customer even trumped the FBI.

Poindexter tugged on the knot on his tie, like it was starting to choke him. He stood up and cleared his throat again. "We'll wait for Mr. Rourke to show up. Please have him call me as soon as he arrives. And it goes without saying that this is a matter of upmost confidentiality. Do not discuss our meeting with anyone."

Stephanie Washington snapped her briefcase shut and pushed back from the table. She had lost this round and was not happy about it. I didn't want to cross her — she was clearly not someone who lost graciously — but I didn't know how to avoid it. No way was I going to see the FBI until I talked to Billy. Whatever he had done — and this time it must be huge — it wasn't going away.

## Chapter 7
*(Wednesday & Thursday — October 26-27, 2005)*

After Poindexter and Washington drove off in Washington's black Lexus, I waited five minutes and then phoned Billy's cell. The call went straight to voicemail. In *Law and Order* the Feds were always getting wiretaps on the bad guys. I didn't know how that would work with a cellphone but I wasn't going to take any chances. I didn't leave a message and I resisted the impulse to call him again. I knew that sooner or later he would have to contact me. But I had a gut feeling Billy wasn't coming back anytime soon. I hoped he had a plan because I sure didn't.

That evening, I had just finished watching the White Sox sweep the Astros to win the World Series when I got a text from a "No Caller ID" number :

> WAY TO GO SOX!!!!
> Bobby Jenks is the MAN!
> I'm off to VG for a few days.
> Weidman knows. Everything is cool.
> Give my love to Daina.
> Be careful with Fariba. Ciao.

There was no phone number ID so I couldn't reply. VG was Virgin Gorda — the remotest of all the islands in the Caribbean. Lousy cell service, no direct flights, even electricity was spotty. Billy had a house there — up in the hills. He had shown me pictures. Great view, lots of wild chickens and a local lady and her two kids who lived on the lower level and took care of all his needs.

I called Billy's cell number but this time I got one of those recordings telling me I had reached a number that was no longer in service. That son-of-a-bitch and his last minute vacations. Weidman knows what? And telling me to be careful with Fariba — what was

46

that supposed to mean? Did he know the goddamn FBI was on his ass? Did he care? I was staring at the phone wishing I could reach through it and grab Billy by the throat when Daina walked into the TV room with an armful of case files, headed for the dining room, which she used as her home office.

"What's wrong?" she asked, glancing at me and then at the television where a Chicago news gal was trying to give a report from a raucous south side bar celebrating the White Sox victory.

I know some guys tell their wives everything. They let them know how their day went, how they're feeling, what's bothering them. They share. It's a good thing I'm sure. I'm not one of those guys. And to be honest, Daina's not one of those wives who wants to know everything. Does that make us a good team, too?

There was no way I was going to tell her about the visit from HR. She'd be upset that Billy was fucking up my "career," and she'd be annoyed I hadn't taken the opportunity to pitch Harry Poindexter Jr. on my management potential.

I grabbed the remote and turned off the television. "Nothing. Just some office bullshit I can deal with tomorrow."

She shrugged and walked past the television into the dining room. "Remember my car is in shop. I need ride to work." She dropped her files on the dining room table and sat down, ready to work.

I hadn't remembered, but there was no need to share that either. "You bet. What time you want to leave?"

She looked up, annoyed, like we'd already discussed it, which we probably had. "Seven. I have to check on client."

Now it was my turn to be annoyed. Her client calls could take an hour. Longer, if there were problems and there were always problems. "Are you kidding me?"

She gave me the icy blue stare so I could be certain she wasn't kidding. Not that she ever kidded any more. "It's quick drop-in. Will take few minutes."

Daina's client was Bedelia Wallace, a seventeen year old with a six week old baby girl. She lived with her grandmother in a rundown brick bungalow on Fulton Street on the east side of Claxton. The houses in that neighborhood were all built after the second world war to meet the housing needs of the returning GIs. They were one bedroom starter homes, thrown up in a hurry. The materials and workmanship were shoddy and sixty years later, many had been razed or abandoned and the rest had peeling paint, sagging roofs and patchy yards of weeds and unmowed grass.

While Daina went inside to check on Bedelia and her baby, I waited outside at the curb where I could keep an eye on my ride — an AutoPro pickup Billy let me use as my personal vehicle. It was a ten year old Chevy Silverado with five hundred thousand miles on it, but nothing was safe in the neighborhoods where Daina made her calls. I was still pissed she couldn't postpone the call until she had her car back. I know that sounds inconsiderate, but consideration is a two-way street and there hadn't been much traffic on her side of the road lately.

I had parked at the curb because in the driveway, a tall Black girl in sweatpants and a gray hoodie, was methodically launching three-point-range jumpshots from one side of the driveway to the other. She made seven in a row before she missed. The ball rolled my way and I scooped it up.

"You've got a great shot." I bounced the ball back to her. "My name's Darwin." I don't normally introduce myself to random teenage girls, but I did this time. I don't know why, but I'm glad I did.

"Darwin? Like the evolution dude?" She casually dribbled the ball from one hand to the other as she sized me up. She had high cheek bones and her eyes were wide, not in a frightened way, more like she was trying to take everything in. Her hair was pulled back into a stubby ponytail.

"That's right. What's your name?"

She turned away from me and took another shot. It rimmed out. "Toni. With an I. Like Toni Morrison," she said as she hustled after the ball. It was as if she couldn't stand around talking when she had a basketball in her hands. I knew that feeling.

I didn't know who Toni Morrison was, but I didn't tell her that. "Can I take a shot, Toni?"

She zipped the ball over to me like she meant business. I bounced it on the driveway a couple times and then fired a jumper from twenty feet. It was a good shot, but it hit the rim and bounced out. "Stiff rim," I muttered more to myself than Toni. I retrieved the ball and fired another shot from the corner. I gave it a little more arc and this time it swished.

"Not bad," she said dribbling in place and eyeing me. "You want to play HORSE. Five dollars."

"Five dollars? You trying to hustle me?"

"If you're scared I'll spot you a letter."

I shook my head. "No, I'll play you straight up. Let's make it a buck. Keep the game friendly."

Her mouth twisted downward. " Ain't hardly worth breaking a sweat for a buck." She shrugged. "Whatever. Take your shot." She bounced the ball to me.

I dribbled to the elbow and shot a fifteen footer. With a bored look, she matched it. I followed with a couple of eighteen footers from the corners, both of which she made without wasting her precious sweat.

"You keep taking those pussy shots, we're going to be here all day. Show me something, Darwin."

I grinned, dribbled hard toward the basket and took off. In high school I could dunk easily, and even when I played in the Elks League ten years ago I could still throw it down. But apparently those days were gone. I hit the back of the rim with my dunk attempt and the ball boomeranged, landing halfway back up the driveway.

Toni whooped as she chased the ball down. "Didn't you see that movie about white men and their jumping ability?"

She pumped in a thirty footer from the top of the key and I missed my shot for an H. She followed with two more long distance bombs that I also missed. She tried one from the corner and it rimmed out.

"Okay. You got HOR, I got nothing. You should have taken the spot."

"Talk's cheap, Toni. Try this." I drove the key again but veered wide and windmilled up a ten foot hook shot with my left hand.

"Damn, that's a funky old man shot. Looks like something from 'Hoosiers,' she said.

"Don't forget to use your left hand."

She missed everything and I came back and repeated the shot from the right side. Her shot caught the rim, but rolled out. I took another one from the top of the key with my left hand and she whiffed again.

"You better learn to shoot with that other hand," I said. I took mercy on her and pumped in a twenty foot jumpshot which she made. Next I rolled toward the basket like I was going to take a right handed layup but at the last moment I reached under the basket and flipped it up on the other side with my left hand.

"Cool shot. For an old guy, you got some game." Toni took the ball and made the shot easily. She had great body control and ball handling skill. I launched my next shot from three point land but missed. She scooped up the ball, dribbled toward the basket, and did a quick turnaround jumpshot from the top of the key. My shot rimmed out and she followed with a bomb from just in front of my truck. My matching shot wasn't even close. She won HOR to HORSE.

"Nice game, Toni." I pulled a five from my wallet.

"Thanks. I ain't got change."

"It's okay, you earned it. Who do you play for?" The private prep schools were always recruiting ringers like Toni.

"I don't play for anyone. I go to Claxton High. Second year."

"Are you kidding? I'm helping coach the girls team there. Why don't you come out and practice with us. We could use someone who can shoot like you."

She shook her head. "That's a white girls team."

"It doesn't have to be. Give us a chance."

She shrugged. "I can't. Grandma wants me home at night."

"Is Bedelia your sister?"

She shook her head. "Cousin."

"Do you know Miss Pahlavi? The Guidance counselor?"

"The Arab chick?"

"She's Iranian. If your grandmother changes her mind and you want to play, let Miss Pahlavi know. She's the coach I'm working with."

Toni frowned. "She play ball?"

"She's learning."

Toni nodded toward the house. "Is the nurse your lady?" she asked.

Daina had stepped out of the house and was heading toward the car. Her five minute call had taken a half hour, but I wasn't going to say anything.

"Yeah. That's my wife. I gotta go now. Talk to your grandmother. We'd love to have you on the team."

"Who was that girl?" Daina asked as I backed the car out of the driveway.

"Toni. With an I. Bedelia's cousin."

Daina's lip jutted out and her brow furrowed as she flipped through her case file. "I think they're half-sisters. But Monique is taking care of both of them. As best she can."

"The girl has a lot of basketball talent. She beat me at HORSE. We could really use her on the team. But she says her grandma wants her home at night."

Daina sighed. "Monique has hands full with two teenage girls and baby. She doesn't want more babies."

"She'd be safer playing basketball at the high school than hustling ballplayers in this neighborhood." We were stopped at the corner of Fulton and Saltonstall. On the east side of Fulton there was a tired bodega with two homeless people in dirty sleeping bags camped out under the awning, and on the west side a burned out

Church's Fried Chicken with a large Star of David painted on the plywood that covered the windows.

"Do they have Jewish gangs here?" I asked.

Daina shook her head. "That's symbol for Gangster Disciples. East Claxton Gangsters is like minor league team." She surveyed the landscape dispassionately. If you didn't know Daina, you might think she didn't care. She had a tough exterior. Claxton was too close to Chicago. It was a small town with big city problems. Daina had to deal with junkies and hustlers and teenage moms and gangbangers and judges and cops and social workers and self-righteous bureaucrats. They were all part of a system that didn't quite work. Daina did her job better than most. And she didn't give into heartbreak or despair or rage like many of her colleagues.

But the job took its toll. The frisky, fun-loving girl who drove the boys crazy and who loved me more than all of them, had vanished long ago. I missed that girl, but I understood. Nothing lasts.

Daina sighed. "I'll talk to Monique. Persuade her to let girl play. She has the good longshot, yes?"

A slight smile creased her face. Daina had actually told a joke. "Yeah. She's got a longshot to die for."

I was so pleased with my recruiting coup I didn't think about Billy or Poindexter or Ms. Washington or the FBI until I had dropped Daina off at Social Services and was headed out to AutoPro. I was praying I wouldn't have to deal with any of them today, but those prayers never seemed to get answered.

# Chapter 8
*(Thursday, October 27, 2005)*

I was still thinking about Toni when I walked into my office. With her and Astra I was convinced we would transform the winless Claxton Eagles into a conference powerhouse. Maybe even go to the state championship. Okay, I was getting ahead of myself, but that's how pumped up I was over her potential. I was so distracted by my daydream fantasy I had almost forgotten about the Billy Rourke disaster looming on the horizon.

Kelly Craven brought me back to reality before I had settled into my chair. She stormed into my office with that same deer-in-the-headlights-look she had yesterday. Seeing Kelly scared creeped me out more than the hardball tactics of Assistant General Counsel Washington. She was clutching two brown accordion folders. The kind that had a flap and an elastic wraparound cord to seal them. We stored our bills of lading and other freight documentation in those folders. The auditors wanted us to keep freight paperwork for ten years — so we had an entire storeroom of filing cabinets filled with those accordion folders.

Kelly dropped the two folders down on my desk, like they were too hot to handle. "You need to do something with these," she said.

All the freight folders had white labels with the month and year marked on them with felt pen. The folder I picked up didn't have a date. Instead it was marked "PC." "PC?" I asked.

"Petty cash," Kelly said. "Billy kept it in my desk. I don't want it there when those HR schmucks come back. I don't need those kinds of problems."

I tried not to smile. Billy always liked to have 'walking around money,' so he could take care of special situations where using company money wouldn't look right. Just last month he gave Frankie Conroy, who drove for FEDEX, a couple hundred dollars to pay a speeding ticket and fifty dollars so that Sleepy Martin could buy something special for his wife who caught him over at Clarkie's after work being a little too friendly with Wendy Barnes, one of our inventory clerks. Money well spent, and even a tight-ass like Poindexter wasn't likely to have a hardon over that violation of company policy.

I opened the folder and dumped the contents on my desk. There were about twenty rubber-banded stacks of cash. Small bills, fives and tens and a few ones. Probably a couple grand, tops.

"I'll take care of this. Don't worry." I picked up the other folder. Clear carton-sealing tape had been wrapped around it several times. It was labeled, "NPC."

"NPC?"

"Not Petty Cash." She shrugged. "I just marked it like that so I wouldn't confuse them. But I don't know what's in it. Billy kept it in my desk, but I never touched it. Every once in a while he'd take it away and when he brought it back it had new tape."

I grabbed a letter opener and started to slice through the tape.

Kelly backed away from my desk, like I was opening a letter bomb. "Okay, I'm going back to my desk. I don't need to know what's in there."

"Stay here, Kelly. This isn't a big deal."

Kelly stamped her foot like Astra used to do when she was two years old. "Let me restate that. I don't WANT to know what's in there."

"Sit," I said, trying to sound boss-like. "Stop being such a pussy." I sliced open the folder and dumped the contents on the desk.

"Holy shit," Kelly said. She dropped back into the chair. "Holy, holy shit."

The desk was covered with stacks of hundred dollar bills. A holy shitload of stacks. Like Billy had robbed a bank or an armored car. No haphazard rubber band stacks. These were professionally wrapped and each one was marked "$5,000."

Her surprise seemed genuine. "You didn't know what was in there?"

"It was Billy's business. I didn't want to know. I was hoping it was dirty pictures. What are we going to do?"

"Why don't you go out to Receiving and grab me a cup of coffee. By the time you get back everything will be cool. This meeting never happened."

For the first time in two days Kelly had her attitude back. "Okay, but don't think this coffee fetching is going to become a regular thing."

"Understood. Black, no sugar."

She gave me her patented scowl, but as she got to the door she turned around and smiled. "Thanks, boss."

"No problem."

Of course it was a huge problem. But sharing it with Kelly wasn't going to make it any smaller. Better that she didn't know what I was going to do.

I stashed the petty cash folder into my briefcase and stepped into the hallway. There was no one in sight. I hustled over to the store room with the NPC folder. There were five banks of filing cabinets containing all the shipping documents from 1995 to 2005. I went to the file cabinet marked "1999" and in the middle of the middle drawer marked "JUNE-99" I filed Billy's quarter million dollar stash.

If the auditors yanked all our files, it would be months before they ever discovered the cash. Of course even then I realized we didn't have months.

The hits kept coming. I had just finished returning all the missed calls from the day before when Kelly walked back into my office and stood in front of my desk, looking like her dog died.

"We have to stop meeting like this, babe. People will talk." I gave her the Darwin charm smile but it didn't take.

"Wally Weidman has resigned. Effective immediately." She handed me the HR bulletin. It was another Poindexter memo, full of Human Resources bullshit thanking Wally for his years of dedicated service. Blah blah fucking blah. It said everything except what was important. Why? Weidman was 58, he was in his prime earning years in a cushy job that he could phone in. He would never quit. He had to have been pushed out. But why? It had to be something to do with why the Feds wanted to talk to Billy. And maybe something to do with Billy's stash.

"Fuck," I said.

"There's more. It gets worse." Kelly handed me another memo.

She was right. Another HR notice. This one from the big bopper, Randall Judd, the head of Human Resources. 'Effective immediately, and until such time as a replacement is appointed, the position of Vice President of Operations will be filled by Harry Poindexter, Jr.' 'Double fuck. Shoot me now, Kelly. Put me out of my misery. Poindexter? Shit."

"I wonder if he plays golf," Kelly said, almost smiling.

I had been so proud of my gamesmanship yesterday. I didn't know I was playing checkers and Harry Poindexter, Jr. was playing chess. My dumb ass comment that I didn't work for him was about to be shoved up my ass.

Checkmate.

## Chapter 9

Thirteen girls showed up for practice. I had hoped Toni would show, but I wasn't surprised she didn't. We cut back on the Suicide drills and the Slides because we were going to finally have the girls scrimmage. Three on three games to eleven, with the winner staying on. It would be fun and a taste of competition, while allowing the girls to put into practice the drills we'd been working on.

Fariba stood by me with her clipboard as the team started their layup drill. I peered over her shoulder. She had given each of the girl's nicknames. "What's all that?" I asked.

She snugged the clipboard to her chest, embarrassed. "This will sound awful, but I have trouble telling some of the girls apart. Especially when they're all dressed the same."

"You mean all white girls look alike to you?"

"No. They all look different, but I forget what makes them different. So I give them names that will help me remember."

"Is it working?"

Fariba pursed her lips. "I believe so. Test me."

"All right. What's the name of the little freckled blonde who just blew her layup?"

"That's Norma Stanton. I remember her as Norma Rockwell because she's so wholesome looking. And her father is a popular pediatrician. A storybook family."

I resisted the urge to tell Fariba that Norma's mother was a country club alcoholic and their family was more Peyton Place than Norman Rockwell. I didn't want to puncture her sweet fantasy. "How about the girl who just pulled a Fariba?"

She scrunched up her face. "What?"

"The gal who just dribbled the ball off her foot." I pointed to Boo Boo Redmond who was captain of the cheerleaders and a far better cheerleader than point guard. Her father, Frank Jr., had been the second generation president of the First National Bank of Claxton, and was dumped when Wells Fargo bought the bank five years ago. But thanks to Billy Rourke, Frank Jr. landed on his feet. More than just landed, actually.

He became a stockbroker for Charles Schwab and six months after he started Billy convinced AutoPro to let Redmond manage the DC employees' 401k assets. A fifty million dollar chunk of business that netted Frank Jr. a half million dollars a year in commissions. A classic example of how Billy built his empire.

"A Fariba!" Fariba said with a faux scowl. "You will eat those words, Mr. Burr. I have been practicing my ball bouncing. That girl's name is Boo Boo Redmond, who I call Bunny Boo Boo."

"Well I call it dribbling, not ball bouncing. Boo Boo already has a nickname. Why add Bunny?"

Fariba looked around as if we were being monitored and then leaned in closer to me and whispered, "She has a bunny tattoo."

I watched Boo Boo as she drove in for a layup. No visible tattoo. "I don't—"

"I'm not telling you where."

"Good. I don't want to know." Nothing good would come from that knowledge. I was starting to realize there were many additional challenges to coaching the girls team that I hadn't anticipated. "Okay. Pick one more girl to play with Norma and Boo Boo. Someone less twig-like to bang the boards."

Fariba studied her clipboard and then scanned the girls in their shoot-around. "How about Sandy Smiles?"

"You mean Sandy Galvin? Great nickname. And a good choice." Sandy Galvin always had a smile. She was a sturdy five seven — taller than most of the girls. Her parents owned the Radio Shack on Main and Sandy and her two brothers helped out there after school. Basketball was one way she could get out of that duty for a few months.

"Who shall their opponent be?" Fariba asked. "Those girls all started last year, did they not?"

"Yep. They're all seniors. Let's match them up against some of the youngsters. Astra…" I glanced sideways at Fariba. "Do you have a nickname for her?" I asked.

"Darwin's daughter."

"Very catchy. Let's go with Astra and the Chiappones. Mary Jo and Dede."

Fariba nodded. "Mary Jo Shy Pony and Dede Diva."

Mary Jo was a Junior and Dede was a Sophomore. Irish twins, born eleven months apart. Their father, Joey, worked at the Veteran's Hospital as a maintenance supervisor. Their mother, the former Jenny Johnson, was a prom queen who I took to the Junior Prom thirty years ago. After graduation she got a job at the high school in the administration office where my mother worked. Mom didn't like her, but she didn't like anybody.

Dede, the youngest daughter, took after her mother and had a sense of entitlement that comes with being a pretty teenage blonde girl. Maybe Daina would have had that too if she hadn't spent her teenage years just trying to survive. "I understand the Diva label for Dede, but what do you mean by Shy Pony?"

Fariba smiled. "It reminds me how to pronounce Chiappone. You think the younger girls are going to win, don't you?"

"It's not even going to be close." It wasn't. Dede Chiappone's sense of entitlement was bolstered by extreme competitiveness. She had no intention of losing. The first time the seniors put the ball in play Norma Stanton juked past Mary Jo and had what looked like an easy layup but Dede, who was guarding Boo Boo, jumped in front of Norma and the two girls crashed to the court.

Norma lay face down on the court whimpering as Dede quickly jumped to her feet and retrieved the ball. "There's no crying in basketball, Norma," she said with perfect mean girl inflection.

On the next play, Mary Jo passed to Norma and as Norma drove to the basket all three of the senior girls converged on her. She smoothly whipped a pass to Astra in the corner for an easy twelve foot jumpshot. The Newbies beat the Veterans 11-1.

Fariba assembled another team: Jane "Tinker Bell" Moore (five foot nothing and a pixie haircut), Carol "Macaroni" Macri (friendly brunette with short wavy hair whose family grocery story had become a 7-11 when Safeway and Jewel moved into the new mall just off I80), and Linda Blair "Witch" (tall with raven dark long hair;) They did better than the first team but went down 11 to 5.

Next up was Gretchen "Farrah" Frantel (dark brown hair in a Farrah Fawcett style; parents were both shrinks at the Veteran's hospital;), Tracy "Soapbox" Hoekelman (she was always speaking out on some cause such as gay rights or abortion;) and Marcia "Mumbles" Buck (dirty blonde hair, always looked and sounded like she'd just woke up;) Marcia's father, Leslie, was the lead minister of Trinity Lutheran and she was doing her best to be the stereotypical rebellious preacher's kid.

The winners had been playing hard for over thirty minutes. Dede and Mary Jo were running on fumes. Astra wasn't fresh, but she still had something left in the tank. Gretchen and Tracy took advantage of the Chiappone sisters' fatigue, getting by them for easy layups. Astra kept them in the game with her outside shooting. With the score tied 6 to 6, Astra grabbed a rebound, but Marcia ripped it out of her hands knocking Astra to the floor. The other girls all ran over to see if she was okay, while Marcia turned and put the ball in the basket.

"That's a foul!" Dede yelled at me, hands on her hips.

"Play on. If you don't hear a whistle you keep playing. Good rebound, Marcia." Marcia Mumbles was a scrapper. But I was proud of Astra. She bounced right back up. No whining. And she scored the next five points to finish them off.

It sounds like I'm bragging, and I guess I am, but she was a natural.

After practice, Fariba was anxious to demonstrate her dribbling skills. "I bought a basketball from Ryan Sporting Goods. The Michael Jordan model."

"That's a good playground ball. How much it cost you?"

She grinned nervously. "I don't know. I charged it to Billy. I wasn't going to, but Mr. Ryan insisted. He said Billy would be angry if I paid for it."

Jack Ryan was one of the men in Billy's high stakes poker game at the Claxton Country Club. "Maybe you can get Jack to sell Billy one of those portable basketball hoops that all the kids have now."

"I don't think my landlord would appreciate that. But there's a park across the street with a basketball court so on the weekends after my run I will practice my shooting there. Today I practiced dribbling on my morning run."

"You dribbled and ran?" This woman was crazy.

"It slowed me up quite a bit, but I got so I could do it without looking at the ball. That is the idea, right?"

"Did you switch hands?" I asked. Her face fell.

"No," she said, staring down at her shoes. "I only used my right hand." She picked up a ball and started dribbling with her left hand. She bounced it a few times. "Look, Darwin…shit!" As she took her eyes off the ball she hit the toe of her foot and the ball rolled right to Charlie Wainwright, who had just walked into the gym. Charlie, like a golfer scooping a missed putt, let the ball roll over his foot and with a pooch kick grabbed it, so he didn't have to bend over. Like I said, Charlie was big on energy conservation.

"Just the folks I'm looking for. How's the team looking, Fariba?" He bounced the ball back to her.

"Very well, Mr. Wainwright. We are making excellent progress. We had our first scrimmage today and—"

"Wonderful." He pulled an envelope from his rumpled sports coat. "Darwin, your boss has come through as I expected he would." He walked past Fariba and handed me the envelope.

I stared at Wainwright. "You've seen Billy?"

"Nah. That man's a ghost. Always on the move. He sent those to me with a note to give them to you and Fariba. Two tickets to the Bobby Knight high school coaches clinic up in Evanston."

"You want us to go a coaching clinic? When?"

"Weekend after Thanksgiving. No games scheduled that weekend. This is a great opportunity. I don't know how Billy pulls these things off. That thing has been sold out for months. He even comped you rooms at the Orrington. Stayed there with the Missus, a few years back. Mighty fine place."

"Thanksgiving weekend?"

"You can bring your wife along. She can go Christmas shopping on the Gold Coast while you and Fariba do the clinic thing."

I tried to imagine Daina's reaction to that idea. She hated shopping. And Chicago. At least the Gold Coast part. She'd be more likely to skip Michigan Avenue and check out Cabrini Green. "That's not going to happen, Charlie." I was still trying to get my head around Billy reaching out through Wainwright. What was wrong with him? "This is sort of short notice." I looked at Fariba. This would disrupt her triathlon training. I was certain she wouldn't want that to happen.

"Thank you, Mr. Wainwright. I would be delighted to attend. Mr. Knight is an exceptional coach, is he not?"

Most of the time when I talked to Fariba she sounded like everyone else. But when someone of authority was on the scene (even though it was hard to think of Charlie Wainwright as being an authority figure) she would ramp up her Iranian-British accent and use prissy phrasings like 'delighted to attend' and 'exceptional is he not.' I could almost imagine her daintily sipping her tea with her pinkie pointed just so.

Of course in that sense she was just like Wainwright, who grew up in a posh suburb of St. Louis, but tried to sound like a good old boy. "Hell yes, he's well-known," Wainwright said with his fake bellow voice. "Great coach. Just don't get on his bad side, right Darwin?"

A coaching clinic in Evanston? Billy was up to something. I put the envelope in my pocket. "If you hear from Billy tell him to call me. He's been a little scarce at work lately."

Wainright made his fake bellow again. "I hear you. That man has more irons in the fire than the village blacksmith. Yes sir, he's something else." He clasped me on the back, smiled at Fariba, and heavy-footed it to the exit.

Fariba raised her eyebrows and smiled. "Road trip!"

## Chapter 10
*(Monday, October 31, 2005)*

I decided not to tell Daina about the coaching workshop. It was still a few weeks away and with new developments coming at me every day, the weekend after Thanksgiving was too far away to worry about. We finished the week without any more Billy surprises. We had one more week until our first game and despite all the turmoil at work I found myself spending more time thinking about the team than about my missing best friend and all his baggage.

Monday was Halloween. It has never been my favorite holiday. Don't care for candy or costumes. Fittingly, Poindexter and Washington were waiting for me Monday morning when I arrived at work. "They're in Billy's office," Kelly said. "Sleepy's napping in the conference room. He's extra ripe this morning. I didn't figure they would want to share space with him." As I approached Billy's office she added, "They're wearing their Halloween costumes."

Our offices were on the mezzanine level of the DC. Billy's office had a large window that overlooked the warehouse floor. He could have kept an eye on activity in the warehouse if he had been so inclined, but he wasn't. Until today, any time I had been in his office the louvered blinds had been closed. But Poindexter, or maybe it was Washington, had opened them and the two of them were standing in front of the window looking down on the forklift drivers stacking pallets of motor oil.

Poindexter and Washington weren't wearing costumes, but they were dressed differently. Poindexter had gone corporate casual: khakis, a red AutoPro polo shirt, and polished cordovan loafers. He was like a knight without his armor. Uncomfortable. His fake smile tight, less confident.

"Darwin, good to see you. Sorry for this unannounced visit." He glanced out the window again. "Look at that gal on the forklift,

Stephanie. She drives like you." Poindexter actually winked at me and stage whispered, "Stephanie takes no prisoners on the Interstate."

Stephanie Washington had opted for the corporate-hottie look. She wore a navy blue corporate mini-skirt, expensive-looking cream colored silk blouse and lethal stilettos. But today, instead of daggers, she smiled at me like we were old friends. "Hello, Darwin," she said as she extended her hand. Presumably to shake, not to kiss.

Poindexter picked up his briefcase. "We need to discuss some things with you." He glanced around Billy's spacious office. In the corner, Billy had a coffee table and a black leather sofa that I never saw him use, although he claimed he had banged Kelly on it after the company Christmas party two years ago. Told me her snake tattoo slithered down her belly all the way to the homeland. I didn't want to believe that (about the sex not the tattoo), but Billy didn't usually lie about women.

Poindexter pulled up a chair and positioned it opposite the sofa. He plopped his briefcase on the coffee table. Stephanie followed him and perched on the edge of the sofa, as though she had suspicions as to how Billy had used it. Her skirt was tight and short and as she settled into position, I couldn't help but notice that she had really nice legs.

Billy didn't have meetings and he didn't encourage visitors. The only other chair in the office was his '50s vintage office chair. Sweat-stained, shiny cracked leather, and about as mobile as a tank. I had no intention of sitting in it. "Right here, Darwin," Stephanie said, patting the spot next to her on the sofa.

I sidestepped in between the coffee table and the sofa. There wasn't much room and it was hard to maneuver. I dropped down hard on the saggy sofa cushion, which caused Stephanie Washington to topple over on to me.

"Whoa!" she cried.

I instinctively put up my hands to catch her and grabbed a handful of her breast. Her bra was really thin. "Sorry," I said, as she regained her balance.

She giggled as she adjusted her blouse and looked down at her boobs, probably checking to see if I had left any smudges on them.

Poindexter cleared his throat. "Well now, this has been a hectic few days, to say the least. You no doubt have read about Wally Weidman's unexpected retirement." He paused and frowned as though good old Wally had died.

"Congratulations on your new position," I said.

He waved me off. "Just temporary. While we search for the best candidate."

I knew I should say something like, "I'll help you anyway I can." Normally I can lie and suck up as well as anyone. Well, not as well as Billy, but good enough to get by. But all this friendliness had me extra suspicious. If I had grabbed Stephanie's boob at that earlier visit she probably would have had me arrested. So I didn't say anything. Just nodded and waited for them to reveal their true mission.

"We can't find Rourke. Weidman insists he's on a vacation in the Caribbean, one of those hard-to-reach islands. Said he approved the vacation and that Mr. Rourke will be back in three weeks. Do you know anything about that?"

I shook my head and tried to look extra sincere. "Billy was always off to the islands, but not usually for three weeks." If they didn't know about his place in Virgin Gorda they weren't going to learn about it from me.

Poindexter nodded, like he wasn't expecting me to give him any useful information. "The company is going to accept Weidman's assertion, even though we believe it's a lie. We plan to terminate Mr. Rourke and we would have done the same with Mr. Weidman, but letting him retire is less messy. But for the moment we are all going to pretend that Rourke is on some beach working on his tan. Is that okay with you, Darwin?"

Billy had really dug himself a big hole this time. I didn't want to fall in it with him, but I wasn't going to help them bury my friend either. "Not my call. I just work here."

Stephanie Washington turned toward me. "I have investigated this mess with Rourke and we don't believe you are a part of Mr. Rourke's criminal activities. But you are an enabler. You've run the DC so well, that Mr. Rourke has been free to develop his empire. Now we want you to enable me."

"What?"

Poindexter did another godawful throat clearing. "Stephanie is temporarily taking over as DC Manager while we wait for Rourke to resurface so we can fire him. And, of course, deliver him to the FBI."

Stephanie put her hand on my forearm. Gently. Like she was my friend. "I know nothing about running a DC. I'm only down here so I can fully investigate Rourke's enterprise. I'm counting on you to keep the DC running smoothly."

I wished I'd listened to Daina and applied for one of those boring management opportunities. I took a deep breath and tried to smile. "I can do that. No problem."

Stephanie's smile tightened. "I'm not asking you to turn on your friend, but if you hear from him, we need to know. Okay?"

It was pretty clear they didn't trust me any more than I trusted them. I glanced at my watch. "I need to get out to the yard before those drivers start making up their own rules." I stood up and Poindexter followed me to the door. Stephanie stood up too, but she walked over to Billy's desk and sat down. She was taking over.

# Chapter 11
*(Friday, November 4, 2005)*

The Claxton Eagles opened their season at home on Friday evening against the Claypool Rockets. Last year Claypool slaughtered us. We lost both games by over thirty points. I met Fariba at the gym two hours before tipoff to prep her for her first game.

We sat in the empty gym on the first row of the bleachers where the team would sit during the game. "I'll be back here," I said, pointing to the row behind the players' bench. "I'll give you suggestions and answer any of your questions, but you're going to be the one making the calls."

Fariba started to protest, but then she stopped and thought about what I said. "Okay, " she said, nodding. "That makes sense." She rubbed her hands together. "This is exciting. Do you think there will be a large crowd?"

"There will be a good-sized crowd, but not on our side. Claypool has built a following. They'll be coming in by the busload. On our side of the court, there will be a lot of empty seats. That's what happens when you lose forty in a row."

"We will have to change that, Mr. Burr. Won't we?"

"Yes we will, Miss Pahlavi. Okay. First decision. Who is your starting five?"

Her jaw dropped. "You want me to make the selections? I thought—"

"You know these girls as well as I do. Better, actually," I said, remembering her comment about Boo Boo Redmond's hidden tattoo.

Her bottom lip rolled out as she studied her clipboard. "Well, Astra has the best shot so she should start at shooting guard." She stared at me anxiously to see if I agreed.

I wrote Astra's name on the whiteboard. "Who else? You need four more starters."

The tip of her tongue peaked out from between her lips as she considered the options. "Dede Chiappone, is the best passer and dribbler so she should bring the ball up."

"They're both sophomores. You've got a young backcourt. But I agree with your choices." I wrote Dede's name below Astra's.

"For rebounding, Sandy Galvin, and for the other slots in the forecourt, Gretchen Frantel and…." She chewed on her lip as she mulled her final selection. "Marcia Mumbles. I mean Buck."

"Why Marcia?" The girl was athletic, but morose, almost surly. The preacher's kid had attitude in abundance. But I wasn't sure if it was good attitude or bad.

"It's a hunch. I think she will flourish with added responsibility and maybe live up to an assignment she hasn't really earned yet." She paused as though she were considering the right words. "Also, she can be nasty. She scares some of the girls."

I smiled. "You're right. Nasty can be good."

The girls started trickling into the gym. I remembered that nervous, excited feeling getting ready for that first game of the season — like the first day of school only a hundred times better. The seniors, Boo Boo Redmond, Norma Stanton and Carol Macri arrived together. They'd all been starters for the last two years and now they'd be on the bench. But if we followed our game plan of running hard everyone would get playing time. Fariba seemed to have earned the respect of all the players. And I think they were in awe of her athletic prowess. Her ability to work twice as hard as anyone else and make it look effortless.

I stayed on the bench while Fariba went back to the locker room to announce the starting lineup and go over their game plan. When they ran out of the locker room and started their layup drill I asked her how it went.

"Excellent," she said. I could tell she was happy. She didn't have much of a poker face. "There were a few gasps when I announced that Marcia was starting, and she was surprised, but I think pleased.

They're excited." She sat down next to me and squeezed my hand. "This is much fun. Thank you, Darwin."

"Fun's the idea. Winning would be nice too."

Fariba and I watched the teams go through their warm-up drills. I don't usually put much stock in how the other team looks during the pre-game, but I couldn't help but notice that the Claypool Rockets shot lights out. They were deadly from all over the court. Two of the players shot nothing but three point bombs and they seldom missed.

"They appear to be very accurate," Fariba said.

"Yep. So what do we do?" I asked.

She smiled smugly like one of those annoying kids who always knows the answer to the teacher's question. "Shooting is confidence. We make them less confident."

"I feel like that Zen Master in the Karate Kid. The sparrow is ready to fly on her own."

Fariba looked at me, puzzled. "Sparrow?"

"You had to see the movie." The electronic scoreboard horn bleated. The pre-game warmups were over and the players hustled back to their benches. The girls all huddled around Fariba.

"All right ladies, this is why we did all of those tortuous drills. They are excellent shots, but you will make them far less excellent. Stay in their face. Don't let them go where they want to go. Make them uncomfortable. Tire them out. Don't let them have any easy shots. Do you understand? No. Easy. Shots."

No yelling. She spoke clearly and calmly and confidently. It was a hell of a speech. The girls were fired up and ready to rock. I thought about what a great story it would make: Underdog Claxton, with its forty-five game losing streak, guided by an inexperienced rookie coach triumphs over league powerhouse Claypool.

It didn't happen. But we didn't get blown out either.

The girls showed them in the first minute that this was a different team than last year. Claypool won the tip and then made a lazy, cross-court pass that Astra intercepted and took in for an easy layup. On their next possession Claypool's point guard got around Dede on a drive but was wiped out by Marcia as she went up for her layup. An NBA-style hard foul which sent the girl crashing to the court. It knocked the wind out of her and after that the Claypool sharpshooters stayed out of the paint and relied on their long range shooting.

They had impressive shooting skills and jumped out to an early lead. But Marcia's intimidation and our team's relentless defense wore them down. They had a ten point lead at the half and we cut it to 6 by the end of the third quarter. But midway through the 4th quarter Marcia fouled out and Claypool got a few easy buckets inside to hold us off. Astra scored sixteen and made half of her shots. No one else was in double figures on our team and no one shot over thirty percent.

We lost by ten, but Claypool knew they had been in a game.

Fariba was in the locker room, giving the girls a postgame talk while I waited with the other parents in the nearly empty gym. Frank Redmond came up to me, grinning broadly.

"Best game these girls have played in three years. Nice work, Darwin."

"Fariba did a great job getting them ready. The girls played hard."

"Have you heard from our friend lately?" Redmond asked.

Our friend was Billy. He had become the man whose name could not be spoken. "He's on vacation," I said. "In the islands."

Redmond frowned and shook his head, consternated. "He called me to ask about a loan on his 401k but then he went and sold the AutoPro stock in his 401k and reinvested in some storage company."

Condo storage? I remembered those papers Billy had me sign for Worldwide Condo Storage. The company with the mysterious partner. "Don't know anything about that, Frank. Billy's got a lot of irons in the fire. You can get a loan on your 401k?"

"Absolutely. Fifty percent of the vested balance, but a max of fifty k. He wanted a couple hundred grand. I told him he can't do that and next thing I know he's sold his AutoPro stock and invested in some unlisted private company. I need documentation that shows he's not a controlling owner. You can't invest 401k assets in a company you control." His brow furrowed, trying to decide whether talking with me was going to do any good. "Ah hell, this ain't your concern, Coach. Great game. If you see that knucklehead though, tell him to give me a call." He spotted Reverend Buck, Marcia's dad in another clump of parents. "Hey, Leslie, your gal's a real tomcat. Thought Lutherans were supposed to be non-violent."

As Redmond rambled off, I felt a tap on my shoulder. It was Toni.

"Hey, Toni! You came to our game?" I was surprised and pleased. And hopeful.

"Don't you have anyone on that team who can shoot?"

"Not like you."

"Ain't no one in this whitebread school can outshoot me. Number 7 wasn't bad though. She your kid?"

"Astra. How could you tell?" Astra didn't look like me. She had lucked out and got her mother's looks.

"She got the same funky stroke." She shrugged. "She needs to shoot more because the rest of that team…" she shook her head, "…bricklayers." She looked uncomfortable, as though she needed to be bouncing a basketball to hold a conversation. "Anyway, my grandma says it's okay for me to play. I think your nurse lady twisted her arm."

"My wife can be persuasive. That's great news, Toni. Monday. Right here. Practice at 4. Be ready to run."

She smirked. "I grew up in Cabrini-Green. I know how to run."

I was pumped. And even though he was totally responsible for the shitstorm of the last month, I wished I could call Billy and tell him about Toni and how well Fariba and Astra and the rest of the team had performed. He would have understood how someone like Toni could make a huge difference in the team. And he would have been motor-mouth excited about Fariba's performance. But he wouldn't have taken credit, even though if he hadn't got Fariba involved there probably wouldn't have been a team. I still wanted to know how he was connected to Fariba, but I figured the only way I was going to find out was to ask her, because my friend Billy wasn't coming home.

Not now. Maybe not ever.

## Chapter 12
*(Saturday, November 5, 2005)*

It was Saturday morning. Thanksgiving was less than three weeks away. And even though the temperature was in the low forties, if Billy hadn't disappeared on me, we would have been playing golf at the Claxton Country Club. The course had been closed since the end of October, but they always let Billy on. He teed it up until snow covered the greens. I wasn't a big fan of those November golf matches, but the last few years in return for my accompanying him, Billy helped me take my patio awning down.

The awning was attached above the sliding glass doors that opened on to our patio from the family room. When I was young and strong, I could take it down without help. It was a simple job — remove the cotter pins on each side that secured the horizontal supports and let the awning hang flat against the windows. I would climb up on the step ladder and loosen the wing nuts that held the awning. I'd work one end and then other, back and forth with the ladder until the awning was held by the two fasteners in the middle. I'd release the last two nuts and slowly lower the tarp to the ground.

Four years ago, on a chilly October morning, the awning slipped out of my grip and when I twisted to grab it, the step ladder tipped over and I crashed to the deck. Somehow I managed to escape with just a badly sprained wrist. After that episode I recruited Billy to help me. He was even less of a handyman than me, but all he had to do was steady the awning as I lowered it to the ground. It took us less than fifteen minutes.

I had postponed the awning chore hoping Billy would return, but I couldn't put it off any longer. I needed it down before the snows started. I dragged the step ladder out to the patio and was giving myself a pep talk, when the memory of my failed attempt to stuff the ball at Toni's popped into my head. I was kidding myself. I was no longer capable of doing this job solo. I needed help.

Through the sliding doors I could see Astra in the family room watching MTV. She would be more help than Billy, but a moody teenager on a Saturday morning was not an appealing choice. Daina was a better bet. She was in the dining room writing a paper for school. I entered the TV room through the sliding patio doors. Astra was sprawled in front of the television, whispering into her phone. She stopped talking and waited until I cleared the room. That was fine with me. Everyone has their secrets.

I slipped in to the dining room. Daina looked up from her laptop with a perplexed expression, as if she didn't recognize me. "Did your mother ever talk to you about her immigrant experience?" she asked.

"Her experience? She was a war bride. She married my father in London and came to Claxton to live. Why?" It must have been tough for my mom to go from a place like London, to a hick town like Claxton. Unhappiness was my mother's natural state. But maybe part of it was she was lonely.

"I'm writing paper for sociology class on immigrant experience. Your mother is my research subject."

"Sort of a challenge, her being dead for the last twenty years."

Daina shrugged. "I have good imagination."

"Why don't you write about your own immigrant experience. I'd love to read about that." Daina never talked about how she made it to America. She walked out of that hotel room in Helsinki in January 1980 and in February 1981 she was living in Skokie, driving a cab. What ever happened to her in those thirteen months, she never talked about.

She gave me the Daina-dagger look. "I'm writing about your mother. Do you have any letters?"

I scoffed. "There was no reason for her to write. I never left home and neither did she. Mom got married in a hurry and regretted it for the rest of her unhappy life."

"Was your father unhappy too?"

I shrugged. Daina asked more questions than the company shrink. "I don't know. Some people just can't figure out how to make themselves happy. No matter how much they have. My dad was the opposite. I look back at his life — almost killed in the war, stuck with an unhappy, never-satisfied wife, working for assholes in a dead-end job — he had every reason to be unhappy. But he wasn't. He made the best of his situation."

"Was he faithful?"

Most people would probably not say my father was faithful, since he had a girlfriend for the last twenty or so years of his life. But I define the term more generously. Despite all the shit Mom would dump on him, he was dependable. And loyal. Just not monogamous. I thought I could make a great case for his faithfulness, but I didn't see any upside to trying to explain my viewpoint to Daina. "Faithful? Sure."

Daina bit down on her lower lip and stared at me with what I would say was a small measure of Latvian skepticism. "Why? Your mother sounds like cunt."

Daina was never one to mince words. I suppose a better son would have defended his mother, but I had other priorities. "Can you give me a hand with the awning?"

She frowned and looked into the TV room. "Okay. Astra can help too. Make a quick job of it." She stood up. "Astra get off phone. We need to help your father."

Astra teenager-sighed but hung up her phone and followed us out to the patio. I released the support arms so the awning hung straight down, covering the sliding glass doors. I explained to Daina and Astra that I just wanted them to stand on each end and hold the awning as I released it. Daina didn't approve of my plan. "You are tallest and strongest. You should be on ground. Let Astra be on ladder. She's not clumsy like you."

"I don't want her up on the ladder. And I'm not clumsy."

Astra sighed melodramatically. "Oh god, can we just get this done?" She plunked the ladder down at the left edge of the awning and scampered up like it was a staircase. No denying she was more agile, but I still took exception to the clumsy label. Cautious, not clumsy.

Astra quickly unhitched the left and right side and then set the ladder down in the middle of the awning where she could unhook the middle fasteners. She twisted open the last one and pulled the awning off the hook. "Okay, it's clear."

Astra released her grip on the awning, but as she started to descend, a gust of wind blasted through the trees and caught the awning like a sail. Daina lost her grip and the awning whipped away from the house and knocked over the stepladder. Astra screamed as she flopped backward off the top of the ladder like a high diver attempting a backflip.

When I replay the incident in my mind, it's still hard to believe it happened the way I remember. When the awning was wrenched from her grip, Daina was knocked to the ground. With some instinct that must have been imprinted on her brain during thousands of hours of tennis drills, she bounced back up and lunged like a tennis player reaching for a rocket serve.

She dove toward Astra who screamed as she fell backwards head first toward the concrete deck. Daina managed to twist her body so she was on her back when Astra collided with her. The two of them lay on the deck, both of them on their backs like a two-man bobsled team. Astra started to cry, but Daina was still, her eyes closed and her arms wrapped tight around her daughter.

Fractured skull. Broken neck. Those were almost for certain Astra's fate, if not for her mother's impossible rescue. I dragged the fucking awning out of the way and rushed to them. Astra was just scared. There wasn't a scratch on her.

"Daina? Can you hear me?" I knelt over her, my heart pounding.

"Mom, I can't breathe."

Daina released her death-grip on Astra and opened her eyes. In all our years together I'd never seen fear in her eyes before. "She's not hurt, Daina. You saved her life."

Astra and I crowded over Daina, both of us still in shock trying to figure out how she had done what she'd done.

Daina's frightened look vanished so quickly I will never be certain I actually witnessed it. She frowned and sat up, rubbing the back of her head. "Are we done now? I need to write paper." She slowly got to her feet and brushed off her jeans. "Next year get Billy to help you."

## Chapter 13
*(Monday, November 7, 2005)*

Kelly called me on my way into work. That was never a good sign. "That bitch has been here since five," she said. Her voice echoed like she was on her cellphone.

"And good morning to you, too," I said. "I'm guessing you're referring to our new boss?"

"She's going through all of Billy's expense reports. This is bad . Very fucking bad."

"Where are you calling from? It sounds like you're underwater."

"I'm in the ladies room. Trying to throw up so I can go home."

"No hurling. I'll be there in ten minutes."

I had been hoping for a Stephanie-free morning to go over stuff with Kelly. Stephanie was commuting from Chicago, sixty miles on the interstate and ninety minutes at rush hour. The crazy woman must have left her house at four.

I parked in the back end of the parking lot and walked slowly across the lot. I wasn't anxious to start my day having to deal with Stephanie Washington. At least Poindexter hadn't returned. The roach coach was parked at the front of the lot. There was no line, so I stopped and ordered a breakfast burrito (chorizo and eggs with peppers) and a large coffee.

"Hey, Mr. Burr, have you heard from Billeee?" Felipe asked me as he started to wrap the burrito in foil paper.

"Don't wrap it. I'm going to eat it here."

Felipe smiled and handed me the burrito on a paper plate along with a fistful of napkins to sop up the grease. Felipe's burritos were greasy in the best possible way. He drew a large cup of coffee from the a tank. It was so hot it smelled as if it were melting the Styrofoam. "The new lady jefe,' she don't like my coffee so much." The word on Billy and his replacement had leaked out. I wasn't surprised.

"She tell you she didn't like it?"

"No, but she dumped it in the trashcan over there. Only took one sip."

"Well, your coffee sucks. But it's hot."

"Gracias."

I stuffed the rest of the burrito in my mouth and tried to wash it down with a gulp of coffee. A bad idea. The coffee scorched my tongue and I probably would have dumped it out too, but didn't want to hurt Felipe's feelings. "This is fucking hot. Maybe you want to turn the burner down a notch?"

He shrugged. "Only have two settings: on and off. Nobody wants cold coffee." He reached under the counter and pulled out a fat envelope. "I pay you or the lady?"

I tried to remain as ignorant as possible of Billy's shadier deals. But it was hard not to be aware that Billy was shaking down, or in his words, "charging rent," to the roach coach operators. He was always leaving the envelopes in his truck. He split up the business so each shift had its own coach. He collected a hundred dollars every week from the first and second shift vendors and fifty dollars from the night shift.

Taking that envelope might look bad, but if I didn't take it, Felipe might have given it to Stephanie, and that would have been seriously bad. In the end I guess it didn't matter.

"I'll take it, Felipe. Thanks." I stuffed the envelope in my pocket and grabbed a handful of napkins to wrap around the cup so I could carry it.

There were only a couple of trucks unloading — a gleaming forty footer from Pennzoil and an eighties vintage box truck from Spartan Engines. Remanufactured engines were DC items, meaning each DC manager got to select the vendor instead of the buyers at corporate. They were another gold mine for Billy. Spartan wined and dined Billy in Vegas last month and he anointed them as the DC's engine supplier.

I couldn't kill any time on the loading dock — everything was moving smoothly. I walked into the warehouse and checked with our warehouse manager, Paul Meron. He was an AutoPro lifer. A sandy-haired crew-cut ex-marine with a perpetual two-day growth of beard. If there had been an Olympic event in forklift driving he would have won several gold medals. Paul still raced his stock car most Friday nights in the summer at the Grundy County Speedway.

"Gotta show you something," he said, waving his arm at me as he jumped down from his forklift. "Follow me." He led me down the main aisle of the warehouse, which was sort of like walking down the interstate at rush hour, except everyone was driving forklifts and actually knew how to drive. He looked back over his shoulder at me as I quick-stepped it to catch up to him. "Have you heard from Rourke?" he asked. It was a snarl, but snarling was Paul's default tone of voice, so I couldn't be sure he was upset.

"Nothing. Vacation. He's not checking in."

"Bullshit." That was definitely an upset snarl. "I heard they fired his ass. Replaced him with that lady lawyer. How you two getting along?"

Obviously no secrets in the warehouse. Kelly had never been known to keep a tight lip. "What do you have to show me, Paul?"

"What do I do with this?" In the back of the warehouse there was a three foot long, narrow white box with **SPARTAN CRANKSHAFT** printed on the side.

"Put it with all the other crankshafts."

He shook his head. "This is a performance crankshaft. Special ordered for Rourke."

I sighed. "What the hell does he need that for?"

Meron shrugged. "It's gotta be for his nephew. Tim Dolan races over at Sycamore." He toed the box. "These fuckers set you back a grand, easy. I wish I had an uncle like that."

"Is it on the manifest?" I asked, even though I knew the answer.

He smirked. "Those Spartan guys aren't great with their paperwork."

That was the kind of vendor Billy preferred. "Can you just stick it on the shelf with the rest of the shafts. No bar code." Without a bar code the product would be invisible.

"That'll work until yearend inventory."

For the yearend close we had to do an actual physical count of the inventory. "Maybe Billy will be back by then," I said.

Meron looked around for a place to spit. "I wouldn't bet on it."

With the breakfast burrito, the stop at the loading dock and the visit with Meron, I had put off having to face Kelly and the new boss lady for almost an hour. As I climbed the stairs to the office mezzanine, I could hear what sounded like Kelly laughing with another woman. I was relieved and a little surprise at her quick recovery. When I walked into the bullpen I was more than a little surprised. Sitting on the edge of Kelly's desk, giggling like a schoolgirl was Stephanie Washington. As soon as she saw me, she stopped laughing and slipped off the desk.

"Good morning, Darwin," Stephanie said, smiling and looking like women look when they're sharing some juicy gossip. I didn't want to know. Even if they were laughing at me, which was probably the case, it was better than any of the other scenarios I expected to find.

"Morning, ladies." There were a pile of snapshots on Kelly's desk. She gave me a Charlie Brown grin as she shoved them back in her drawer.

"Kelly was just showing me what a good time you had at the last Christmas party. Great pictures of you doing your Ray Charles imitation. It's offensive on so many levels." She laughed again. "Does your body look that stiff because you were dancing?"

It had been a drunken game of charades. And it wasn't at the Christmas party. And it wasn't Ray Charles. I had an urge to tell the ladies that it was too bad we didn't have pictures of Kelly and Billy on his black leather couch after the real Christmas party. I was asshole enough to do that, but not stupid enough. "Not Ray Charles. Little Stevie Wonder. The other blind Negro singer," I said.

"Ah, that explains the mop on your head," Stephanie said.

"Negro, Darwin?" Kelly said. She pretended to be mortified even though I've heard her be a whole lot less politically correct.

"I didn't think we were supposed to say colored anymore," I said.

"Well I'm looking forward to this year's party," Stephanie said. "I do a great Madonna impression."

"Yeah, I can totally see that." I could probably learn to dig Stephanie if I could forget that her mission was to destroy my best friend — and me, if I got in her way.

I had barely sat down at my desk when Kelly hustled into my office with a FEDEX envelope. She was back to serious again. "For you," she said. "From Billy." It had been shipped from Evanston. No sender identified.

"How do you know?" I asked as I pulled the zipper tap to open it.

"I know."

It wasn't a very good answer, but I didn't push her. She was right. In the envelope were the Articles of Incorporation for Worldwide Condo Storage, a corporate resolution creating a special category of preferred stock that required my signature, and a fifty thousand dollar cashier's check made out to Frank Redmond. "Why is he sending Redmond fifty thousand dollars? And where's the money coming from?"

Kelly shrugged. "No idea, but Frank Redmond wants to meet you after basketball practice tonight," she said. She handed me a pink phone slip. "He called this morning while I was bonding with my dear friend Stephanie."

"What was that all about?"

"Trying to distract her. She'll have gone through all of Billy's expense reports before the end of the day."

"She's fast, huh?"

"No. That's the problem. It doesn't take any time at all to go through Billy's reports. He doesn't spend any money. It looks really bad."

She was right on both counts. Someone always paid for Billy. "So you figured to distract her with your party pictures. How many photo albums you got?"

She wrinkled her nose. "My videos are much better. But I'm not showing her those."

I sighed. I wasn't much of a multi-tasker. And there wasn't anything I could do about Stephanie Washington and her relentless pursuit of truth or justice or whatever it was she was pursuing. Frank Redmond must have known I was getting that check. I had the feeling Frank knew a lot more about Billy than I did.

## Chapter 14
*(Monday, November 7, 2005)*

When I arrived for practice, Toni was looking at the trophy case outside the gym that celebrated our championship season. The state championship trophy was tarnished but still pretty damn impressive. There was a plaque next to it that had been donated by the Boosters Club with all our names engraved on it, and the scores of all 23 games in that perfect season, including the state championship over Darien Central. There was a team photo and plenty of action shots, mostly of me.

"Hey Toni, you ready to practice?"

She grinned at me and then pointed at the photo. "That you, Darwin?"

I shrugged with false modesty. I was glad she discovered the trophy case. I wanted her to see what a big deal a state championship could be. And maybe I also wanted to impress her. She was a ballplayer and her opinion mattered to me. I wanted her to know that once upon a time I was a pretty fair ballplayer too.

"Man you were one skinny dude," she said, oblivious to all the championship accolades on display. "Cool sideburns, but how come you guys are all wearing hot pants?"

I should have known Toni wouldn't be easily impressed. 1973 was ancient history for these kids. "Styles change. You'll learn soon enough. Someday your children will ask you why you always wore that hoody."

She frowned and I regretted those words immediately. "I ain't having no babies. And I ain't got fancy clothes like all the whitebread."

She picked up her duffel bag and flung it over her shoulder. For a moment I was afraid she was going to take off. Fortunately, Fariba arrived before I could do any more damage.

She walked up to Toni and extended her hand. "Hello, Toni. So nice to see you again. Darwin tells me you're going to join us. I'm very pleased."

Toni lost her attitude with Fariba. She shook Fariba's hand self-consciously and stared down at her shoes. "Hello, Miss Pahlavi."

"The other girls are in the locker room already. Come with me and I'll introduce you."

Toni followed Fariba into the locker room. When they emerged ten minutes later, Toni was talking with Marcia and Astra like they were old friends.

"How did it go?" I asked Fariba as the girls started their warmup drills.

She tilted her head as though she wasn't sure. "I think most of the girls are a little scared of her, actually."

"Toni can be a little intimidating."

"I think she's just shy and her angry face is her mask she wears for protection."

"Is she getting on with Marcia and Astra okay?"

Fariba nodded and then rolled an errant basketball back to Boo Boo. "Keep your eyes up while you dribble, Boo Boo. Don't look at the ball. Trust gravity."

"Trust gravity. That's a good one. I should write that down." Fariba had continued her running and dribbling workouts and had become a skilled ballhandler. She was committed to helping Boo Boo overcome her inept dribbling skills. It seemed as though every day I was finding something more to admire about Fariba. Not just how she had taken to the coaching challenge, but in her everyday living she was just a very genuine person. She cared.

"Marcia and Astra admired Toni's navel ring," she said.

"What's Toni doing with a Navy ring?"

Fariba giggled. "A bellybutton ring. I should say rings. They were quite impressive. She offered to do the piercing for the girls."

"Yeah. That's not happening."

"You are being a fuddy-duddy. Tattoos and body piercings are commonplace now."

"Really? You got any?"

She smiled cryptically and then blew her whistle to get practice started.

Toni was everything I expected and more. We scrimmaged five on five and I had her play with the second team. She destroyed the starting group. The few shots she missed, she got her own rebound and scored, and when the starters began to double team her, she had an uncanny ability to find the open player. Suddenly, girls who couldn't shoot to save their lives were making buckets. And on defense, with her long arms and quick feet, she stole the ball time after time.

I always had the feeling when I watched Magic Johnson or Larry Bird, that they could have scored every time they touched the ball. But they passed more than they shot. They were great because they made everyone better. Toni had that quality. I couldn't wait to unleash her on our next opponent.

We finished scrimmaging and sent the girls off to the showers at quarter to six. I really wanted to hang around and talk with Fariba, but I had agreed to meet Redmond at Walter's Pancake House at six and that was at least a twenty minute drive.

"Toni is a marvelous player. She's going to really help us, isn't she?" Fariba was as excited about her as I was. "Whose starting position should she take? Marcia's?"

I shook my head. "Astra, I think."

"Astra? But she was our best all round player last game. Shouldn't they play together?"

"They will. They're just not starting together. " I looked at my watch. With traffic I was going to be twenty minutes late if I didn't take off right now. Last thing I needed was for Redmond to bolt on me. "I've got some more Billy business to take care of. I'm meeting Frank Redmond over at Walter's."

Fariba knew Billy had gone missing. She smiled when I told her I was meeting with Redmond, almost if she expected that. "I hope you're not having pancakes for dinner."

"Just coffee. It's going to be a short meeting." At least I hoped it would be.

"Well I'm anxious to hear your thinking on the starting five," she said and then added almost too casually, "And I'd love to know what is up with our friend Billy. He's a mystery man, isn't he? Maybe we could get together after your meeting. Grab a burger and a beer at Clarkie's?"

I'll admit I loved that idea. "Are you famous there too?" I asked her, smiling.

"I wouldn't say famous. They haven't named a burger after me. Or hung my picture over the bar."

She gave me that grin that stirred memories of when girls used to flirt with me. But I knew better. Clarkie's was the closest thing Claxton had to a sports bar. Multiple widescreen TVs and lots of sports memorabilia — mostly Cubs, Bears, Black Hawks and of course Bulls.

Wayne Clark, the original owner of Clarkie's, had the photo of my winning shot in the state championship game framed and hung over the bar. For all the years he owned the bar, my money was no good there. But Wayne sold in '93, the year the Bulls won their sixth NBA championship. The new owners replaced my "shot" with the slightly more famous (and impressive) shot of Michael Jordan nailing a jumper over Craig Ehlo to win the Bulls first division series. They also decided my free drink privilege was not a tradition they needed to sustain. That pissed off Billy and he refused to give them any of his business, which was probably a good thing for the bar as Billy was never much of a paying customer. I didn't blame them. Nothing lasts. And there was no shame in being replaced by Michael.

"I should be able to make it by seven thirty. Is that too late for you?" I asked.

"That would be ideal. I will look forward to it, Darwin. Now shoo." She pushed me toward the door. "Don't keep Mr. Boo Boo waiting."

## Chapter 15
*(Monday, November 7, 2005)*

Frank Redmond wasn't waiting for me. He'd already ordered and was halfway through his three-egg cheese and bacon omelet by the time I arrived at 6:15. The restaurant was less than half full. Mostly senior citizens finishing their early supper. Frank was in the booth in the back and there was no one else seated in his section.

He seemed lost in thought and didn't notice me until I slid into the booth across from him. "Oh hey, Darwin," he said. He reached across the table to shake my hand. He glanced down at his omelet and seemed surprised that he had almost finished it. "I guess I was hungry." He half-smiled. "Do you want to order?"

"I'm just having coffee." I turned over the white porcelain coffee mug and magically, Walter appeared with a coffee pot.

"Your gals almost won the other night," he said as he filled my mug. "Tell Fariba we miss her."

"She's not running with you anymore?"

Frank shook his head. "Not since she started the coaching thing. Too busy I guess. You know what you want, Dar?"

"I'm good with just the coffee." I could have sworn Fariba had told me she was still running with Walter's group. I couldn't seem to keep anything straight anymore. I blamed Billy for that. He had really fucked things up.

Redmond finished his omelet and had started on the side stack of pancakes that came with every omelet. "You okay, Frank?" His face was damp with sweat and he had that gray look, as though he had just puked his guts. He was eating robotically, like he needed something to do, but he wasn't enjoying his meal.

"You bring the check?" he asked. He was trying to whisper, even though there was no one else in our section to overhear him, even with his gravelly voice.

I pulled the envelope out of my jacket and handed it to him. He quickly stuffed it in the chest pocket of his sports coat. "Fifty k?"

"Yep," I said. I was determined not to ask him what he and Billy had cooked up. Whatever it was, it wasn't agreeing with him. Frank was a professional smiler. Always quick with the backslap and latest joke. He and Billy made a good pair. Today he was definitely off his game.

He opened his briefcase and pulled out a bulky manila envelope. "Take this," he said. "Don't open it here."

"Jesus Christ, Frank. What the fuck is going on? You're acting like a bag man for the mob." Probably a bad choice of words. Redmond almost choked on his last forkful of pancake.

He wiped his mouth with his napkin and leaned forward across the booth. "Listen to me, Darwin. In the envelope is Billy's anniversary gift for Kelly."

"She's not married."

Redmond shrugged. "Fine. It's her birthday gift. Just make sure she gets it. There's also five grand for you. Cash. It's your director's fee for Worldwide Condo." You got those corporate documents, right?"

Birthday gift? Five grand in cash? Billy was never that generous. "I didn't bring those papers, Frank."

"Just mail them to me. Kelly can notarize your signature."

It was obvious Kelly knew a whole lot more than she was letting on. There were a dozen more questions I wanted to ask Redmond, but I knew I wouldn't get an honest answer. "Are we done here, Frank?" I asked.

"One last thing." He paused to stifle a burb. "You see that son-of-a-bitch Rourke, you tell him I'm done. No more of his fucking deals."

Parking for Clarkie's used to be in the dirt field next to the bar. Now the field was paved, striped, and well-lit. I'm sure it was more secure than the old lot, but I didn't want to take any chances. I slipped the cash envelope in the front pocket of my jeans. Kelly's "gift" was a three inch square insulated envelope. It was sealed securely, not that I wanted to open it anyway. I stuffed it in the other pocket.

Clarkie's had changed inside too. It used to be a comfortable dive, with mismatched tables and chairs, sawdust on the floor and a jukebox that played nothing but country tunes. There was complimentary popcorn and peanuts (always generously salted) which was the only food Clarkie's offered, not counting Wayne Clark's homemade beef jerky that was kept in a jar by the cash register. I never saw anyone actually try the jerky.

The new owners had classed up the joint, turning it into a fern bar, minus the hanging plants. The old mahogany bar was still in the front, but now along the perimeter of the barroom there was a cushioned bench with matching tables and chairs lined up opposite the built-in seating.

Instead of the tacky lighting provided by Budweiser and Coors, each table had a Tiffany style lamp providing soft, forgiving illumination. There were huge flat-screen TVs over the bar and on every wall, but no jukebox. And now they offered bar food — burgers, nachos and wings. I had a lot of good times at the old Clarkie's, but no complaints about the changes. Softer lighting, less noise and a good selection of junk food were all solid improvements in my book.

The other big change of course was that in the old days when I walked into Clarkie's everyone knew who I was. Tonight was Monday Night Football and there was a decent crowd — not as many as in the old days when football on Monday was a big deal — but the place was over half-filled. Even so, no one but Fariba recognized me. She was in the back corner and she waved shyly as I stepped into the barroom. "Darwin. Over here." She had a way of smiling that made me feel good in spite of myself. As though I were special, even though I was certain she bestowed that same sweet smile on the busboy who filled her water glass. Busboys were also a new addition to Clarkie's.

The group at the next table had borrowed the two chairs from her table. I started to grab one from another table, but Fariba patted the spot next to her on the cushioned bench, "You can sit here. Give you a better view of the game."

I slipped in next to her, careful not to repeat the copping-a-feel incident I'd had with Stephanie. Fariba had changed out of her teacher-clothes into snug-fitting designer jeans, knee-high leather boots and a powder blue cashmere sweater. She was the sexiest girl in the place and now I was especially thankful for that dim lighting. Fariba was out of my league, but with the gauzy lamplight my age and looks deficiencies weren't so obvious. Sitting thigh-to-thigh with her in the corner of Clarkie's Bar made me feel young again.

"Been here long?" I asked.

"Long enough to study the food being served. I recommend the cheeseburgers. This is a new sweater and the nachos look dangerously messy."

"Sweater looks soft."

"Feel it." She took my hand and rested it on her forearm."

"Nice," I said. I could feel my face warming like I was some high school kid on a first date.

The barmaid hustled over to our table. Thankfully, there had been no attempt to refine the waitstaff. Pam didn't tell us her name. She let us figure it out from the nametag pinned over her boob. She also didn't offer any advice on the menu or ask us if we had dined with them before. She just waited impatiently for our order. I looked at Fariba. "Cheeseburger?"

"Yes," she said frowning at the menu. "With tater tots and a pitcher of Bud. Regular, not light." A girl who liked burgers, real beer and tater tots. Fariba was just about perfect.

Pam nodded at me. "You drinking anything?" Only the hint of a smile revealed she might be kidding.

"Bring two glasses. We'll share," I said.

"My mother sent it to me," Fariba said.

I looked at her, puzzled.

"The sweater. It's cashmere. Did you know Iran makes the finest cashmere in the world?"

"I did not. Is your mother still in Iran?" Billy told me Fariba had left Iran with her mother.

"She returned last year." Her smile faded. "She never fit in here. My mother missed Tehran — her friends with the university, the food, all her sisters. I think she felt I didn't need her anymore." Fariba shrugged. "But I did."

She bit her lower lip, but her smile returned as Pam set the pitcher on the table between us. She grabbed it and expertly filled both our glasses.

"Looks like you've poured a few pitchers in your day."

"Hydration is very important for triathletes. Now tell me your reasons for not starting Astra."

I took a swallow of beer and set the mug back on the table. I shifted on the seat so I could look at Fariba while I talked. My shoe rubbed against her boot.

"In Iran, if a boy steps on your foot, it means he wants to ask you out. If the girl doesn't move her foot away, it means she will say yes."

She hadn't moved her foot. "Really?" I asked.

"No," she said, and did her snort laugh. "I enjoy making up stories about Iranian culture. People in this country are very gullible. Now what about Astra?"

I leaned over the table and grabbed the napkin dispenser. Then I took our spoons and the salt and pepper shaker and arranged them on the table. Fariba stared at me, fascinated. "Are you diagramming a play? This is just like Hoosiers."

I smiled at her with what I'm pretty sure was my best shit-eating grin. Fariba frowned and then punched me in the shoulder. "You asshole. You're messing with me."

"Yep. Iranian people are very gullible too." I moved the implements back to their positions. "Here's the deal. For us to win, we have to out-defense everyone. Even with Toni we don't have enough firepower to win a shootout. That means one hundred percent effort from every gal. They need to go as hard as they can for as long as they can and then we'll replace them. We need to have a rotation of nine or ten to keep all the legs fresh. Effectively two teams and that means we need two floor leaders. Astra has to lead the team when Toni comes out. But if the game is on the line at the end, they'll both be playing and that will give us more options. The other team can't just focus on Toni."

The New England Patriots were playing the Indianapolis Colts on Monday Night Football. It was a lousy game, but I didn't care. Fariba was remarkably easy to talk to. She seemed interested in everything. She had a magical way of getting people to talk about themselves. It must have been part of her guidance counselor training. I'd ask her about what it was like growing up in Tehran and before I knew what had happened she had steered the conversation so I was blathering on about our championship season.

By halftime we'd killed two pitchers and started on a third. With the Colts up by twenty points only the Peyton Manning fans and the serious Patriots-haters remained. At the end of the third quarter, Fariba — with her voracious triathlete appetite — ordered the Supreme Nachos (her hunger overcoming her fear of a cashmere disaster). Pam brought them almost immediately and I realized we were the only folks left in the joint, other than the three drunks at the bar.

I kept trying to get Fariba to talk about herself and she kept changing the subject. Until I asked her about her father.

She took a deep, cleansing breath and sank back into her seat. "My father was a professor at Iran University of Science and Technology. He was a classmate and close friend of Mahmoud Ahmadinejad."

She said that as if I should know him, and the name did sound familiar. But my face must have revealed my cluelessness.

"He's the new president of Iran," she said. Her brow furrowed, probably in amazement at my ignorance.

Then I remembered. "The guy who gave the speech at the U.N.? He denied the holocaust?"

"Actually it was Columbia University, but that's the man. He and my father were in school together when Khomeini's so-called students took over the U.S. Embassy. Ahmadinejad joined the group, my father stayed in school, became a professor. He was an Engineer. He wasn't political like his friend."

"Did he stay in Iran?"

Fariba swallowed hard. "He was naïve. He thought he could just be a teacher and leave the politics to people like Ahmadinejad. That's not possible. To those zealots, if you're not part of the Revolution then you're an apostate. An enemy. I was only nine when a delegation of Khomeini's followers showed up during our family dinner. They were oh so polite and they asked my father to come with them. I didn't understand why my mother was so upset. They didn't seem any different from the students who used to visit him."

Fariba smiled sadly and stared off in the distance. "My father was a gentle man. Kind and loving. And brave. He did not show fear. As they were taking him away he kissed me on the forehead and told me not to worry. I never saw him again."

There was nothing I could say to that. I put my arm around her and she rested her head on my shoulder.

The football game ended. The Colts won by three touchdowns and even the drunks at the bar were cashing out. "Quitting time," Pam said as she handed me the bill. We'd consumed forty dollars of beer, burgers and nachos.

I only had thirty dollars in my wallet. I pulled out the cash envelope Redmond had handed me. I tried to unobtrusively open it, but Fariba noticed immediately.

"From Billy?" she asked, like she'd seen that kind of envelope before.

"He left it with Redmond. My director's fee. For some new storage company he started."

Fariba frowned. "Billy is playing with fire."

Why did it seem as though everyone knew more about my friend than me? "That's all Billy ever plays with." I unsealed the envelope.

It was full of 100s, 50s and 20s. It definitely was in the five grand neighborhood. I pulled out three twenties and stuffed the envelope back in the front pocket of my jeans.

While Fariba was in the ladies room I walked over to the cash register and handed the three twenties to Pam. She gave me a weary smile of appreciation as she tucked the bills into her apron. "Thanks, Darwin," she said.

I must have looked surprised.

"I was on the Junior High pompom squad when we won the state title. I had such a crush on you. Pissed me off that they took down your picture here."

I shrugged. "It's okay. Hard to compete with Michael Jordan," I said, looking up at the photo that now hung over the bar.

Pam glanced at Fariba, who had returned to our table and was putting on her coat. "You be careful."

"Of course," I said, trying to act as cool as I imagined she had remembered me. I wondered about her warning, though. Careful about what?

As I walked Fariba to her car she asked, "Did you know our waitress?"

"She was a schoolgirl fan from my glory days. Surprised she remembered me. That was thirty years ago."

Fariba had a bemused almost-smile on her face. "I'm not."

It had started to snow and the soft puffy flakes had turned to slippery, icy slush on the asphalt parking surface. I stepped carefully, trying my best not to look drunk. I took hold of Fariba's arm, foolishly thinking an elite triathlete would need the support of a middle-aged ex-jock.

Despite my best efforts, as we reached Fariba's Corolla, I slipped on the ice and dragged Fariba down with me. I lay there in the parking lot, wet snowflakes melting on my face with Fariba on top of me like a cashmere blanket. I was mortified, but Fariba laughed so hard, it made me laugh too. I might have appeared drunk, but it was Fariba's friendship, not the beer, that made me lightheaded and clumsy.

"What does it mean in Iran when a boy trips a girl?" I asked her.

She cupped my face in her hands and kissed me. On the lips. I think she meant it to be one of those friendly cheek kisses that just happened to be on the mouth, but some baser instinct of mine took over and suddenly we were kissing for real, like lovers. And then she pulled back and smiled at me. "It means it's time to go home."

## Chapter 16
*(Tuesday, November 8, 2005)*

I kept telling myself it was just a kiss, but my head wasn't listening. It had been a ridiculously long day and I desperately wanted to go to sleep, but I couldn't take my brain out of gear. I used to have the same problem after a big game. I'd lie in bed, tossing and turning and replay the game over and over, dwelling on all the things I could have done better — drive the lane instead of settling for a jumpshot; fighting through the pick instead of going under the screen; concentrating more on that one missed free throw that rimmed out.

With Daina sleeping soundly next to me, I stared up at the moonlight shadows on our vaulted ceiling and ran through all the events of my day. I had set a Darwin Burr personal record for stupidity. This day needed a half-dozen mulligans.

I shouldn't have taken that bribe rent from Felipe. I shouldn't have told Meron to lose Billy's steel crankshaft. I should have made Kelly tell me what she knows about Billy and Redmond and this whole Worldwide Condo mess.I shouldn't have told Stephanie Washington that lame joke about Ray Charles. The woman was out to destroy Billy and me. What I was doing giving her more ammunition?

I shouldn't have let Frank Redmond get away without giving me a real explanation as to what was going on with Billy and Worldwide Condo Storage.

But those were just standard-issue Darwin screw-ups.

It was the evening with Fariba that kept me up all night. Like watching game films where the coach runs the plays over and over again, I replayed my night at Clarkie's.

Why did I blather on and on about my stupid championship season? And when I finally stopped talking long enough for Fariba to share the pain of losing her father, why was my response so lame? So totally inadequate? And then after all that, to fall on my ass in the middle of the parking lot like a drunken fool and drag Fariba down with me was beyond embarrassing. But all of that paled in comparison to my ultimate stupidity.

The Kiss.

I couldn't get that scene out of my head. I wished it had never happened, and yet I desperately wanted to kiss her again. She had obviously intended it as a friendly, slightly drunken, gesture of affection, and I had taken the whole thing to DEFCON 4. I'd made a fool of myself. I'd become one of those creepy old guys who falls for a young chick who doesn't even know he's alive.

More exhausted than when I went to bed, I got up at dawn and took a shower, trying to clear my head. As the hot water pelted my back I tried to come up with a plan to fix things with Fariba, but I kept imagining her in the shower with me, her dark arms wrapped around my neck, her body pressed tight against me.

Jesus. This obsession had to stop. I needed to apologize to Fariba. Right now. Nip this adolescent infatuation of mine before I made things even worse. I had enough problems with Billy and Stephanie Washington and Poindexter and Wally Weidman and big Frank Redmond and now, even Kelly. I didn't need to be making more trouble for myself. And I damn sure didn't want to become the high school's sequel to the Duby Laurence scandal.

Daina, naked, except for a towel draped over her shoulder, walked in while I was toweling off in the steam-filled bathroom. "Did you leave me any hot water?" she asked as she hung her towel on the peg next to the shower.

Daina still had a great body. She had resisted aging far better than me. That famous Latvian determination, I guess. "I thought you liked cold showers," I said.

She smirked and tugged on my cock, which was still semi-hard from my Fariba fantasy, as she stepped into the shower. "You shouldn't whack off so long. You'll get blisters."

Great. Busted just for sex-dreaming. "Thanks. I'll be careful." I was going to add something more witty, but she had already turned on the water and tuned me out. She was in Dainaworld.

I badly needed coffee, but didn't want to take the time to make it. I could stop at Walter's on the way to work and grab a coffee to go, so I wouldn't have to suffer through Felipe's Roach Coach coffee. As I walked into the kitchen, Astra was at the kitchen table, typing on her laptop.

"You're up early," I said. I grabbed the orange juice from the fridge and poured myself a glass.

"I have a history paper due before Thanksgiving. I want to finish this first draft so I can give it to Miss Pahlavi."

"Fariba? I thought she was a guidance counselor."

"It's about the Iranian Revolution. You know, when they deposed the Shah. Took over the U.S. Embassy. Miss Pahlavi is Iranian. She said she would let me interview her about what happened."

"Uh, she must have been pretty young when all that went down."

"She was eight. She said she has a lot of memories from that time and would be happy to help."

"That's very nice of her."

"I like her, Dad. I think she's a good coach and a really nice person. And she is a way way better guidance counselor than that perv, Mr. Laurence."

I almost coughed up my orange juice as I grabbed my car keys from the counter. I needed to square things with Fariba before they started hanging that perv label on me.

"Hey, Dad?"

"Yeah?"

"Really cool that you got Toni to come out for the team. She's awesome. Can't wait until our next game."

"We have to thank your mom for that. Daina did some arm-twisting to convince Toni's grandma to let her play."

Astra smiled. "Mom's good at that. You and Mom make a great team."

Just what I needed to hear.

It wasn't quite 6:30 as I pulled on to Hoover Road. Fariba said she worked out from five to six each morning so if I called now I should be able to catch her before she left for school. I needed to apologize before I lost my nerve.

I was about to dial her number when I saw that she had texted me at 5 a.m.

> Had fun last night.
> Too much beer. Headache.
> See you at practice.

I was ridiculously, teenage-boy happy to read her text. She wasn't pissed at me or freaked out or creeped out. Or, if she was, she was being very nice about it.

We could pretend the whole thing never happened.

And I would do my best to make sure it never happened again.

## Chapter 17
*(Tuesday, November 8, 2005)*

I stopped at Walter's on the way to work. Fariba's text had given me a boost, but I knew it wouldn't last. After a night of very little sleep, I needed coffee. There was a line for Walter's coffee, but I knew it wouldn't take long. Walter was a coffee purist. He offered one roast, in one size (large), for two dollars cash, tax included, and no charge cards accepted for coffee orders. He was the anti-Starbucks.

I pulled out my wallet and nodded at the waitress.

"Room for cream?" she asked.

I shook my head no.

Walter's wife had convinced him to offer cream despite his insistence it would ruin his coffee. He walked out of the kitchen as I was about to pay. "I got this," he said, waving off the counter girl. "Fariba ran with us this morning. She was singing your praises." Clearly I wasn't the only old guy charmed by her. I'd stopped for coffee at Walter's hundreds of times and the most I ever rated was a chin nod if he were in an exceptionally expansive mood. The Fariba seal-of-approval had certainly elevated me in Walter's eyes.

"She's very good with the girls," I said. "They like her and respect her."

Walter nodded enthusiastically. "Such a regular person. It's amazing given her background."

It obviously showed on my face that I had no idea what he was referring to, because Walter leaned in closer to me and literally talked out of the side of his mouth like he was some gumshoe in a B movie. "Your buddy Rourke told me Fariba's father was a university informant for the Shah's Secret Police and when the Shah left the country and the Ayatollahs took over…" He made a throat-cutting gesture with his finger. "….it was bad news for his supporters. But her Uncle — her father's brother — escaped with billions. Billions, Darwin. And here she is teaching at our rinky-dink high school. Go figure, huh?"

"Billy told you all this? When?"

Walter bit down on his lip like he was constipated. "Uh, let's see. Hey! It was right after you all were in here a few weeks ago. That was a Sunday, right? He came back just before closing to buy a coffee to go. Told me he had to drive to Chicago and needed a caffeine boost. Then he started coughing and couldn't stop. I got him a glass of water and sat down with him at that table over there.

"Not sure, but he might have been drinking. He had more attitude than normal. Damnedest thing. He seemed to resent my naming a menu item after Fariba. Told me I didn't know anything about her. He said he got her that job at the high school. And then he told me about her father being an informant and her uncle escaping with all that money." Walter shook his head. "I know he's your friend, but I have to say, the man's an asshole."

I shrugged and tried not to look like I had just been kicked in the balls. "Billy is definitely an acquired taste. Did he say why he was going to Chicago?"

Walter shrugged. "No. He just wanted to talk about Fariba."

I secured the plastic lid on my cup. "Thanks for the coffee, Walter." I headed for the parking lot wishing I'd settled for Felipe's Roach Coach coffee instead of Walter's special brew.

It was only a ten minute drive from Walter's to the DC. I hoped to get there before Stephanie so I'd have some quiet time to enjoy my coffee and digest all the unsettling news Walter had dumped on me. But Stephanie was standing in the doorway to Billy's office — check that, her office — when I walked into the bullpen. "Good morning, Darwin. Do you have a minute?"

She walked back into her office without waiting for me to answer. But of course, she wasn't really asking.

I had an important decision to make. If I followed her into her office, she would expect that kind of immediate response every time she asked for something. Bosses, like children and puppies have to be trained.

"I'll be there in a minute," I said as I waltzed past her open door. "Need to hang up my jacket." I was past her office too quickly to notice her reaction, but I know she wasn't happy. It wasn't much of an act of defiance, but the best I could do. I walked on down the hall to my office, wondering whether evil or good Stephanie had shown up today. I actually preferred evil Stephanie, because I would never let my guard down with her. That other version was a lot nicer, but more dangerous.

I hung my jacket on the wall hook by the door. It was my AutoPro warm-up jacket — a gaudy red, white and blue number with stars on the sleeves — a gift from Billy after we won the AutoPro-sponsored league basketball championship back in 1995. I hadn't worn it in years, but with Stephanie in the office I planned to find more reasons to be out in the warehouse and the jacket was perfect for walking around in an unheated warehouse on a cold November morning.

It brought back good memories of Billy. He used to be a happy-go-lucky guy, thrilled to death that the bosses gave him this dream job. It was fun working with him back then. He might have cut a few corners, but nothing major. Somewhere along the way, Billy went off the tracks. I hated to admit that, but I knew it was true. I missed the old Billy.

I took a sip of Walter's coffee and thought about his revelations on Fariba and her father and Billy. Did any of it really matter? I guessed someone could be both a police informant and a loving father. Fariba hadn't necessarily lied about her father. Maybe she just chose to remember the good things about him. I didn't know what to think about the billionaire uncle, but I had to believe he was somehow tied in to Billy's interest.

Kelly popped into my office, looking frazzled again. "She wants to see you. Now."

"Good morning, Kelly. You're looking exceptionally hot today." I tossed the unfinished cup in the trashcan and gave Kelly my heartiest fake smile as I strolled down the hall.

"Fuck you, Darwin," she whispered.

"Absolutely."

Stephanie was sitting on the corner of Billy's desk. That seemed to be her thing. It made it sort of difficult not to look at her legs. She was wearing another version of her corporate lawyer skirt and blouse. But a longer skirt this time, so less legs to avoid looking at, and less lethal-looking heels. "Do you have anything critical scheduled for this morning?"

I had the feeling that anything short of open heart surgery would not pass her test of criticality. Probably not even that. "No. Nothing Kelly can't handle."

Stephanie's smile seemed almost genuine. "You have obviously never had to work in the corporate office. You're always supposed to make people think you're indispensable."

"My notions of indispensability vanished a long time ago. I'll be easy to replace." It was true. My special talent had been managing Billy. If he was gone, AutoPro could plug in any number of guys to do my job. Most of them would actually know something about auto parts.

Stephanie slipped down from the corner of the desk where she was perched. "I want you to accompany me to DeKalb."

"Which one of the stores?" AutoPro had opened a cluster of three stores there about ten years ago.

"No store visits. I want to go to the Kishwaukee Country Club. Didn't you and Billy used to belong there?"

We hadn't played at Kishwaukee in years. Billy had moved up the country club food chain and only played at the exclusive Chicago area clubs like Medinah or Cog Hill. But in the early, fun years, Kishwaukee, only ten miles from Billy's house had been our home course. It might have been the last course Billy actually paid for golf. I had no idea why Stephanie would want to go there, but it couldn't be good.

# Chapter 18
*(Tuesday, November 8, 2005)*

"Do you mind if I drive?" Stephanie asked as we walked down the back stairway to the employee parking lot.

"I was hoping you'd volunteer. I want to see if that Lexus is as good as everyone says." Stephanie was driving a new 430 Lexus. It was supposed to be the top of the line. Before SunCal upgraded Billy to his Acura MDX, they used to loan him the 330 model Lexus, and I wondered how they compared. I almost mentioned that to her, but I caught myself in time. Bringing up Billy and loaner cars would not take the conversation in a good direction.

Even with her heels, I had to hustle to keep up with Stephanie as she clip-clopped across the parking lot, which fortunately had been plowed. Stephanie didn't have to worry about slipping. She glanced back over her shoulder at me. "I think it's an awesome machine, but I've never owned a car so I'm probably not the best judge. But look. Isn't this cool?" She grabbed the handle of the driver's door and the doors unlocked. "I don't have to take the key out of my purse."

I had to agree that was a nice touch. As I opened my door I noticed a car seat strapped in the back. "You have a kid?" I hadn't associated Stephanie with anything so domestic as an actual family.

"Two boys. Devante's eighteen and Hakeem's two and a half."

"Good names. Easy to remember, too."

She set her purse on the floor and pressed a button to start the ignition. "No key to turn. Just need to have it someplace in the car." She slowly backed out of her parking spot, checking her mirror several times to make sure she didn't put a scratch in her shiny new car. "We just made up Devante's name, but my husband named Hakeem after his friend Hakeem Olajuwon." She stopped at the exit to the AutoPro parking lot and checked for traffic coming from either direction, then carefully eased the Lexus on to Harter Road.

"*The* Hakeem Olajuwon? Your husband play ball?" I asked.

Stephanie laughed. "No. Tremaine's a professor of anthropology at the University of Chicago. He met Olajuwon when he was on a dig in Nigeria ten years ago. Tre didn't even know Olajuwon was in the NBA. He can be clueless that way, but he's a sweetheart. He bought us this car for our fifteenth wedding anniversary."

Married fifteen years? Eighteen year old kid? It didn't seem possible. "How old are you?" I asked.

Stephanie grinned. "You definitely failed political correctness class. Didn't your mamma teach you it was impolite to ask a lady her age?"

"I'm just trying to do the math. You can't be more than twenty-eight." Actually I thought she was around thirty-two, but I didn't need my mother to tell me that when it came to a woman's age or weight, it was never a bad strategy to guess low.

"I'm thirty-four," she said. I could tell she wasn't displeased I had suggested a lower number. "Pregnant at sixteen, married at eighteen. Undergrad at Marquette, law school at U of C, four years at Schiff Hardin, three years with the U.S. Attorney and now this new gig with AutoPro."

"You can't seem to hold a job," I said, trying not to smile. The woman had Daina-like ambition.

"Very funny."

"Why does a U.S. Attorney take a job with a company like AutoPro?"

She frowned and I could tell she was trying to decide whether to tell me the truth or just give me her interview answer. "I lost faith in the criminal justice system."

"Oh. Why?"

"My son Devante has been in Cook County Jail for nine months awaiting trial for an alleged home invasion." She held the steering wheeling at two and four, like someone who had just passed her driver's test. "They claim he's part of a street gang, but he was just in the wrong place at the wrong time."

"No bail?"

"It's a crackdown on gangs. Devante's collateral damage." Her voice cracked and her chin was waffled.

"Damn. I'm sorry. That's tough."

The light changed and we continued west on Harter, past the "Leaving Claxton / Drive Safe" sign, the Caterpillar distributor, Ladecky's Body Shop and the Highway Department office where my father had worked for thirty years.

The Birds Nest Motel at the top of the first hill outside of Claxton was boarded up.

"Damn. I didn't know that place closed," I said.

Stephanie gave me a sideways glance. "Were you a regular customer?"

"Back in my day, the high school graduating class always rented two or three of their cabins for the graduation party. Instead of a bunch of drunken kids looking for trouble we were all contained. Parents loved it."

"Too bad it closed. Maybe they couldn't compete with that new Holiday Inn Express that just opened off the interstate."

I shook my head. "That Holiday Inn caters to different customers. It's on the east side — more urban over there."

"Urban? Is that your code word for Black?" Stephanie asked.

That wasn't what I meant but there was an element of truth to what she said. The section of Claxton east of the Rock Island line, the side closest to Chicago, was where most of the Black and Latino families fleeing the city had settled. The west side was still small town rural. "No," I said, wondering if she could possibly be joking, but guessing she wasn't. "It's not a code word. Where would you or Poindexter or Weidman or any of the other AutoPro suits stay if they ever had to spend a night in Claxton? The Birds Nest was for truckers and traveling salesmen and occasional one night stands. The Holiday Inn with its mints on the pillow and a mini-fitness center is for all you city folks on expense accounts."

"Fair enough."

I was pressed back into my seat as Stephanie smoothly accelerated.

Isn't this beautiful?" she said. We were racing past a plowed-under cornfield and a pasture where a few disinterested cows grazed.

"The cows or the cornstalks?"

"The open road. There's so much traffic in Chicago, I never get to enjoy my new toy."

Going through town and starting and stopping, Stephanie drove like someone who had just taken a course in Drivers Ed. But once she got out on the highway, she drove like a teenager, way too fast for her skill level. I gripped the armrest and pushed down on my imaginary brake. We made the twenty minute trip to the Kishwaukee Country Club in less than fifteen minutes.

I was surprised the clubhouse was still opened. When Billy and I used to play there back in the early 90s, the restaurant closed in mid-October. But now, two weeks from Thanksgiving, they had a dozen breakfast customers scattered around the dining room.

Stephanie marched over to an unoccupied table that overlooked the putting green. She ordered us coffee. Race-car Stephanie had been left in the Lexus and I was back to dealing with the all-business version. I reminded myself to think before I spoke. I silently rehearsed my mantra: *This woman is not your friend. This woman is not your friend. This woman—*

"Cream or sugar?" Stephanie was holding up the bowl of sugar and fake cream packets.

"No thanks." I sipped the coffee, which was nowhere near as good as Walter's.

Stephanie pulled out a sheaf of papers from her briefcase. "I want to go through this stuff before Granger arrives."

"Stu Granger?" Granger was one of the store managers when we opened the DeKalb stores. He was now the Midwest Area Marketing Manager.

"Yes," Stephanie said, not looking up from the papers she was scanning. Her lack of elaboration gave me a bad feeling.

She pushed a legal document across the table. "Kishwa Realty. Know anything about it?"

"Doesn't ring a bell." I ignored the documents. I knew they were just a prop. Whatever I had to do with Kishwa Realty, she'd tell me soon enough.

"Really?" She grabbed the file back and turned to the last page. "Is that your signature?"

It was some kind of corporate resolution. Billy had signed as President and someone named George Sinjaradze had signed as Treasurer. My name and signature as Secretary was at the bottom of the page. "Looks like it," I said. The resolution was dated March 12, 1993.

"Don't remember anything about it?" She tried to sound incredulous.

I gave her my most earnest look. The one I hoped would convey that I wanted to help but was just too dumb to be much use. "That was twelve years ago. I have trouble remembering what I had for breakfast."

She pulled a stack of similar-looking files from her briefcase. She opened the top one. "Crestview Realty? Sound familiar?"

I shook my head no. She asked me some variation of that question for each file in the stack and each time I told her I couldn't recall anything, which was the truth. Billy had done dozens of deals where I was just the convenient signature for him. He paid me five hundred for signing my name. I didn't read the stuff and I didn't ask questions.

After she completed that exercise, and that's all it was, Cross-examination Stephanie took a break so that Good-cop Stephanie could have a crack at me.

"Darwin." She leaned across the table and tried to hypnotize me with her soulful brown eyes. "I'm not the enemy here. I know you don't trust me, but I can help you. How can I make you see that?"

I shrugged. "I trust you, Stephanie." She would have to do better than that. I could see no upside to cooperating.

She was about to try another tact when she spotted Stu Granger at the receptionist's podium. She stood up and waved. "Mr. Granger! Over here."

Stu used to be part of Billy's foursome when we played here. I hadn't seen him in over ten years. He'd put on about twenty pounds and lost most of his hair.

Stephanie shook his hand. "So nice to finally meet you, Stu. You know Darwin?"

"You bet. How you doing, Dar? How you stay so slim? Still playing ball?" He didn't wait for an answer. To Stephanie he said, "Has Dar told you how he won the high school state championship? Great story."

Stephanie smiled. "I've heard of his fame, but Mr. Burr does not seem to enjoy talking about himself."

Granger grinned. "That's old Dar for you. Billy tells that story way better."

"And unfortunately, I have not had the opportunity to visit with Billy, which is why we are all here."

Granger nodded, putting on his all-business face. He could act like the good old boy anytime it was required, but he was a serious, ambitious manager, intent on rising in the management ranks of AutoPro. He had to know that saying the wrong thing to Stephanie Washington could seriously damage his career prospects.

"You were appointed store manager of…," Stephanie flipped through her notes, "Store 1123, on Sycamore Road in April, 1993. Is that correct?"

Granger thought for a moment. Or acted as if he were thinking and said, "That sounds right. I was assistant store manager in Elgin when Wally gave me the promotion. I remember it was just before Easter."

"Was that Wally Weidman?"

"Correct. He had the job I have now. Midwest Area Manager. They were opening a bunch of stores in DeKalb and I got the nod. Pretty big move for me. But hell, I was just a wet-behind-the-ears twenty-four year old. Billy Rourke was Weidman's man. He called all the shots. Right, Darwin?"

I modified my mantra. *This man is not your friend. This man is not your friend.*

"So Weidman gives you the news in April. And you started right away? Where did you live?"

Granger smiled. "I got lucky. Rourke drove me around the whole county looking at places, but nothing was available right away. But then, at the end of the day, he shows me this spec house right on the golf course. The builder was desperate for a buyer. It was perfect. And AutoPro helped with the financing."

Stephanie pretended to act surprised. "Helped with the financing? That's a very generous benefit to offer a store manager, isn't it?"

Granger hesitated, sensing a possible trap. "Uh, I guess so. I think it was a new program Weidman started. I might have been the first to use the financing. It became real popular."

Stephanie arched her eyebrows. "I can imagine. Do you remember who the builder was?"

"Quality local builder. Just died last year. George Sinjarzy?

"Do you mean…" and Stephanie went back to her notes again. I realized that was her lawyer trick to build drama. "…George Sinjaradze?" She glanced in my direction but I didn't react.

"Yes. That's the name. Excellent Polish homebuilder."

"Actually he's Georgian. The country, not the state." She flipped through her notes some more. "Correct me if I'm wrong, Stu, but I believe that the other two store managers who relocated here, along with two of the assistant store managers, also bought houses from Mr. Sinjaradze."

"Yes, ma'am. That's right. We called the stretch of holes from 15 to 17, AutoPro Corridor. Me, Reggie Fry, Paul Hoban, Bill McCarthy and Jimbo Walsh could all walk out our backdoors right on to the fairway. Billy Rourke came through big time for all of us. Those were good times, eh Darwin?"

*This man is not your friend.*

Granger's story must have satisfied Stephanie, so on the drive home, she relaxed and attempted small talk. "Kelly told me you're a local legend. She also said I should persuade you to tell the story of the state championship game."

I scrunched up my face. I seriously doubted that Kelly had told her that. "Definitely not a legend. That was a long time ago. Only a few us old farts who can even remember the game."

"Oh, I think you're wrong. I played basketball at Marquette. The men's team won the NCAA Championship back in 1977 and everyone talks about it like it was yesterday."

"Of course. That was the team coached by Al McGuire. It was his last season. Dead four years later. I think Al did it right. Had his greatest achievement at the end of his life instead of at the beginning." That came out more wistful-sounding than I intended. I did a quick change of direction. "I didn't know you played ball."

Her face lit up. "It paid for my education. I was second string, but it was a great experience. Now tell me about the game."

She acted as though she were really interested. I wished I had Billy's gift. I could kill the rest of the drive just telling that story. "State High School Championship. 1975. Darien Central had won 89 straight games. No one thought Claxton had a chance, but we hung tough and beat them with my shot at the buzzer. It was all downhill after that," I said. It was supposed to be obvious that I was kidding, but Stephanie didn't take it that way. Her eyebrows crinkled.

"I'm just joking, Stephanie. It hasn't been all downhill."

"That's the worst description of an epic basketball game I've ever heard."

I shrugged. "Billy's the storyteller."

She shook her head, exasperated, but in a good natured way, not pissed off. "I wonder if I'll get a chance to meet the famous Mr. Rourke. Do you think I'd like him?"

I thought she must be kidding but it was hard to tell with Stephanie. "Well, he's a good dancer."

She sniffed. "If we do meet, I doubt it will be on the dance floor."

She slowed down, finally, as we approached the sign welcoming us to Claxton, population 12,456. The sign hadn't been updated in ten years and that number didn't reflect the migration from Chicago in the last decade. It was as though the Chamber of Commerce wanted to pretend Claxton was still the bucolic small town they remembered from their youth.

"Are you enjoying your stint as the girls' basketball coach?" Stephanie asked.

I wasn't expecting that question. It disarmed me and I forgot my mantra and started blabbering about my coaching experience. I rambled on about how Fariba was developing into a real coach, how proud I was of Astra and how I discovered Toni and what a difference she was going to make in our next game.

"When is your next game? I would love to see your team play."

I kicked myself for talking too much. "Uh, this Friday. It's an evening game though. Not convenient for you Chicago commuters."

She bit down on her lip, weighing pros and cons. "I might just stay over. Try out that new Holiday Inn built for people like me."

We were stopped at the traffic light at the Highway Department intersection. "You should see how different you look when you start talking about coaching. Like someone who actually cares about something. Someone who wants to make a difference not just be Billy Rourke's…" she stopped as if she'd said too much.

"Billy's what?" I asked.

She sighed and, with what appeared to be honest-to-goodness sincerity, said, "Do you understand the importance of Stu's story?"

I was pretty sure I did, but I wasn't going to do her work for her. "Not really."

She sighed. Her perception of my IQ was probably down to low double digits by now. "Kishwa Realty owned by George Sinjaradze and Billy Rourke bought real estate dirt cheap on a dying golf course and built spec homes. A ridiculously risky proposition. Except, of course, Billy knew — because Wally Weidman told him — where AutoPro was going to add stores; and Weidman promoted managers who would need housing and would be captive candidates for those so-called spec homes. Those ambitious young managers were offered a deal they couldn't refuse, an unexpected and probably undeserved promotion, a brand new house ready for them and their families to move into with special financing provided by AutoPro.

"Jesus, what a sweet deal that was. Rourke and Sinjaradze cleared a half million on that project and Weidman got a hundred thousand dollar kickback. I'm sorry. I mean "commission," from Sinjaradze. And what did the faithful secretary of Kishwa Realty receive?"

I shrugged. She was starting to annoy me with her *Law & Order* theatrics. "Mr. Darwin Burr earned five hundred dollars. Nice going, Darwin." She shook her head mournfully, as if she couldn't believe anyone could be that stupid. "How do you feel about that?"

It was easy for me to play dumb because I had no clue what Billy had been up to. I was surprised and not surprised to hear how Weidman was involved. "I guess they made a lot of money."

She pulled into the parking lot and I could tell she was revved because she didn't slow down to a crawl as she had when she was starting out on our road trip. "Damn, Darwin. That's nothing. It's a small sample. An example. Billy and Weidman were just getting started. They made dozens of those deals in the Midwest and when Weidman got to be ops manager, they went nationwide. We're talking millions of dollars.

"I know you're a lot smarter than you're pretending to be. I also know you're going to be the fall guy for these crooks if you don't step up. You have to choose a side. You're not a crook, Darwin. But you have a bad friend and you need to cut him loose. Billy Rourke is going down. Don't let him take you with him."

**Chapter 19**
*(Tuesday, November 8, 2005)*

I expected meeting Fariba at basketball practice would be awkward because of the incident from the night before. But it wasn't, thanks to Stephanie. She was trying to scare me with her warnings about Billy bringing me down and she was doing a great job. Up until now, when I headed for my coaching time with Fariba I stopped worrying about Billy and the mess at AutoPro. But tonight on the drive over all I could think about was what would happen to me if Stephanie was right. What if I was being set up? With that weighing on me, I didn't think about last night's encounter with Fariba. When I met her outside the locker room, I was still too distracted to be nervous. And Fariba noticed immediately.

"Are you okay?" she asked.

I wouldn't be a good candidate for therapy. I don't think talking about my problems helps. Never really considered it with Daina. Compared to what she went through, any problem I had was trivial. Living with Daina, I had become accustomed to not taking my problems too seriously. But Fariba had such a sincere innocence I couldn't just blow her off.

"The lawyer who's investigating Billy says he's going down and if I don't help them I could go down with him."

Fariba shook her head sadly. "Billy." She sighed. "So they want you to be an informant against your friend?"

I hadn't thought of it in those words, but that's exactly what they wanted.

The girls were trickling out of the locker room and starting to go through their drills. Astra dribbled over to us. "Hey, Dad, Toni's coming over after practice to study. Can you give her a ride home, later?"

"Sure." I was pleased that Astra and Toni were hitting it off. I remembered all the times I had hung out over at Billy's house to escape my mother's dark moods. Astra and Toni could be good for each other.

"Mom will be out doing her house calls. Maybe we could order pizza? And some Coke?" Astra grinned hopefully.

"Don't push your luck, girl." Daina didn't allow soda in the house and she wasn't a big pizza fan either. "Okay on the pizza."

"Cool. Miss Pahlavi is coming over on Thursday, but she doesn't need a ride." Astra grinned impishly and dribbled back on to the court.

I looked at Fariba.

"Astra wants to interview me for the paper she's writing about the overthrow of the Shah. Do you think Daina will mind?"

"No." I laughed even though the situation wasn't really funny. "Maybe she'll want to interview you, too. She's writing a paper on the immigrant experience."

Fariba put her hand on my forearm. "We should talk about your problems with Billy. It's a terrible thing what they are asking. I'll help you any way I can."

I'd love to have her help, but there really was nothing she could do. "I appreciate that. But let's not forget our priorities. We've got a basketball game to get ready for."

Fariba laughed and walked out to center court and blew her whistle. "All right ladies, gather round. Three more days to get ready for Dillon Central. They beat us soundly twice last year. That's not going happen on Friday. Right?"

The girls whooped it up. "No way! Bring 'em on! We're going to kill Dill!"

Fariba scanned the group looking each player in the eyes. "Today we scrimmage. Five on five. Game conditions."

More cheering. Playing the game was always more popular than the drills.

"Did you hear me say 'game conditions'?" Fariba asked. "How do we do that? By first having a rigorous workout so we're playing the game under game conditions."

A collective groan from the team. They knew what was coming. For the next thirty minutes Fariba ran them ragged with wind sprints, suicides and the slide drill. When they were exhausted we took a break and I explained how we would have a starting team led by Toni and a second team led by Astra. The goal would be for the first team to play as hard as they could for three, four, five minutes and then be replaced by Astra's team. Most teams utilized seven or at most eight players and the starting five played most of the time. We would use ten, or eleven or twelve players. By the fourth quarter, if not before, the other team would be worn down and we would still be fresh.

The scrimmage went almost exactly as I expected. Astra and Toni battled each other up and down the court. Astra really made her work, but she was no match for Toni and her team won easily, all three games. But I was confident that playing against each other was going to make both of them much better players. No one who guarded them on Friday night would be half as tough.

As we walked through the parking lot to my truck, Astra yelled, "Shotgun!"

"No way," Toni said. "We kicked your butt three games to nothing. You squeeze your skinny ass in that backseat."

Astra laughed and settled herself in the Silverado's narrow clubseat. "We almost had you in that last game," Astra said.

"How you going to win with a point guard who can't dribble, pass or shoot? You need to promote that chick back to the cheer squad." Boo Boo had been harassed all over the court by De De. Despite Fariba's best efforts her ball-handling skills were still abysmal.

"What do you want on the pizza?" I asked. "And what are you studying?"

"Pepperoni, no anchovies," said Toni.

Astra leaned forward, "We're writing a book report on *The Bluest Eye,* by Toni Morrison."

"Toni with an I," I said.

"How'd—" Even in the dark I could see Astra's jaw-dropping surprise. Kids don't think their parents know anything.

I titled my head toward Toni. "The other Toni told me."

"It's about racism," Astra said.

"Don't forget the incest," Toni said and they both laughed. "That's why it's banned from most schools."

I took Toni home at nine. Daina hadn't yet returned from her house calls. As I drove down Fulton past the boarded up Church's Fried Chicken, I noticed that someone had spray painted a large V over the gang graffiti we spotted the other day. Toni saw it too and gasped. "Damn that Ray. Shit!" She pounded the dash with her fist and then slumped back in her seat and held her face in her hands.

"Who's Ray?"

"Bedelia's useless boyfriend. He's with the Vice Lords and that V is his work. The Vice Lords trying to take some of GD's action. It's going to bring a whole lot of trouble. For everyone."

I'd read about all the gang violence in Chicago. Hard to believe that could happen in the little town where I grew up.

"Gang war?" I asked.

She exhaled slowly. "Cabrini was a war zone when anyone challenged the Gangsters." She shook her head. "Damn," she said softly.

## Chapter 20
*(Wednesday, November 9, 2005)*

I had expected another full court press from Stephanie on Billy and what might happen to me if I didn't cooperate, but something came up and she had to stay in Chicago until Friday. Kelly gave me that news the moment I walked into the office. I couldn't help but respect Stephanie — she had a job to do and she was damn good at it — but it was a relief to know we would have two days without her. That gave me an opportunity for a "Come to Jesus" talk with Kelly. She knew more than she was telling me.

"I've got some docs that need to be notarized," I said after she gave me the news about Stephanie.

"Sure thing, Jefe. I'll get my stamp." She set her coffee down on my desk and walked out to the bullpen to grab her Notary Public valise.

I pulled out the Worldwide Condo Corporate documents. Last night I tried to read the Articles of Incorporation and the preferred stock resolution, hoping to find something I could sink my teeth into, but all the sentences started out clear enough, but then got all mucked up with clauses and parenthetical asides and by the time I finished a paragraph the whole thing might as well have been written in French for all that I understood.

I signed both documents and pushed them across the desk to Kelly.

"I need your driver's license," she said.

"Really? Why? To prove my identity?"

"It's required. I have to fill in your license number after I stamp the document."

I handed her my license. "Glad you're so conscientious. We wouldn't any corner cutting on one of Billy's projects."

She wrinkled up her nose. "Your sarcasm is duly noted."

I slipped the papers back into the envelope. "I need for you to mail those to Redmond."

Kelly started to stand up.

"Wait. I have a couple more things to discuss."

"Is one of them Fariba?" she asked as she settled back into her chair. She had a funny expression, which I guessed was her attempt to leer.

"No," I said, refusing to take the bait.

She pouted. "You're no fun at all."

"So I've been told."

She wasn't going to be deterred by my reticence. "How was Monday Night Football? Weren't those Patriots awesome?"

"They lost by twenty points."

"Oh. Well, I heard you weren't watching the game anyway. You and that Arab chick were too busy making snow angels in the parking lot."

"Actually she's Persian, not Arab." Small town life definitely had its drawbacks.

Kelly turned palms up in surrender. "You're cool. I'll give you that."

"Aren't you going to tell me to be careful?"

"I don't figure a woman with a snake tattoo around her neck should be telling anyone to be careful. You didn't get a tattoo did you?"

"No. I don't like needles," I pulled Billy's gift envelope out of my pocket. "Isn't your birthday in April?"

Her brow furrowed with suspicion. "Yes. Why?"

I dropped the package on the desk. "Happy Birthday, from Billy."

She frowned but didn't make a movement to pick it up. "What is this?"

"From Billy via Redmond."

She grabbed the envelope and stuffed it in her front jeans pocket without even looking at it.

"Aren't you going to open it?"

She shrugged her shoulders, as if she got mysterious envelopes from Billy every day. For all I knew, maybe she did. "No," she said. She drummed her fingers on the desk. "I have inventory reports I need to file."

"Well, I won't keep you. I know how much you love to file." She stood up and then in my best Colombo imitation, I added, "Just one more thing."

She gave me her don't-fuck-with-me look, which worked great on annoying truckers, but not so great on me. I'd seen it before. "Who lives at 1717 Ridge Road, apartment 508 in Evanston, Illinois?"

Her jaw literally dropped. "What?"

"Not much of a poker player are you, Kelly? Who lives there?"

"How would I know?" she asked, stunned, like a boxer given a standing eight count.

"Is Billy staying there?"

Her face got all wrinkled as if that were a disgusting suggestion. "Jesus, Darwin. Why would you say that?"

"Maybe because that FEDEX package you were so confident was from Billy was shipped from that address?"

She shook her head. "It was shipped from a FEDEX store. There was no address on the package."

I smiled. I knew I had the winning hand. "That was a favor from someone at FEDEX. They picked that package up from 1717."

"Who told you that?"

"Frankie."

"Frankie Conroy?"

"Wasn't he one of your petty cash beneficiaries? What was it? Two hundred dollars for a speeding ticket? He must have really been hauling ass. I persuaded him to do the right thing. So he told me. He picked up the package and had the paperwork show as though it came from the store."

Kelly sat there staring at me defiantly, like a girl caught red-handed, but still trying to deny that it's her hand in the cookie jar.

"I was thinking I'd drive up and knock on the door at 508, see who answers. Or maybe you could save me the trouble."

"Screw you. When did you become Dick Fucking Tracy?"

'I guess when your friend Stephanie told me I might be spending my golden years at Dixon Correctional."

Kelly sat back in her chair and exhaled slowly. "My mother lives there."

I wasn't expecting that. "Holy shit," I whispered. I had been thinking more along the lines of it being a fuck-condo that Billy had set up for one of his lady friends. Not for Kelly's mother.

"Heather? The fitness trainer?" I knew Kelly's mom lived in Evanston and had become a personal trainer after she got divorced.

"I only have one mother. My father was a son-of-a-bitch through the whole divorce process and Mom didn't have any place to live. Billy owned that condo and he's let her live there for the last three years. No strings attached. He has stayed there a few times — in the spare bedroom. He can be a really decent guy when he wants to. He even pays the condo fees."

"Is he there now?"

She shook her head. "But he had someone drop off those documents and check and ask Mom to send them to you. She doesn't know where he is either."

Fuck. There was never anything simple with Billy. "So what's in the envelope?"

"Diamonds. About forty grand worth, I think. I'm supposed to bring them to my Mom and she'll get them to Billy."

"What's he need diamonds for?"

"He says they're better than travelers checks. They really are accepted everywhere."

"So Billy takes fifty thousand dollars from his account, sends it to Redmond and gets back forty thousand dollars in diamonds. Sounds like money laundering. No wonder Redmond is so antsy."

Kelly fluttered her lips. "Antsy hardly describes that guy. I think Billy made a big mistake trusting him."

Sleepy Martin stuck his head in my office. "Can you sign my voucher, Kelly?"

Under normal circumstances, Kelly would have ripped him a new one for interrupting her when she was talking with me, but today was not normal. She actually smiled at him as she jumped up from the chair in front of my desk. "Sure thing, Sleepy." She turned to me. "Gotta get back to work, Dar. We can talk later if you want."

"Oh I want. For sure. I want to know everything."

I said that and I sounded like I meant it. But to be honest I didn't know what I wanted. Maybe a time machine.

## Chapter 21
*(Thursday, November 10, 2005)*

On Thursday, after I'd handled all the issues Kelly wasn't able to resolve while I was on my daytrip to Kishwaukee with Stephanie, I asked Kelly if she would go to lunch with me so we could talk with some privacy.

"Privacy? In Claxton? You're kidding, right?"

"I made reservations at Francesca's On the River in St. Charles."

Kelly smiled a sad-looking smile. "That was Billy's favorite restaurant. Pricy."

I shrugged. "It seemed like an appropriate place for us to talk about him. We'll use his petty cash stash. I think Billy would have appreciated the irony."

"You keep talking about him in the past tense."

"I know. So do you. Let's stop doing that."

The lunch crowd had thinned out by the time we arrived at one. We got a secluded booth in the back and ordered an antipasto and a carafe of house Chianti.

"Isn't drinking on the job a violation of AutoPro policy?" Kelly asked as she filled her glass.

"Don't tell your friend Stephanie. Although she probably has enough violations of company policy to keep her busy for a while."

"Did she really threaten to send you to prison?"

"She said Billy's going down and I shouldn't let him take me down too."

Kelly frowned, but held her tongue while the waiter brought us a mini-loaf of Italian bread. She made a puddle of olive oil and parmesan on her bread plate and swabbed it with a chunk of the bread. "Billy would never do anything to hurt you, Dar. He worships you."

"I know. But I need to understand what he's involved in, and I think you know more than you're telling me."

She dropped her head as though she were praying. When she looked up there were tears in her eyes. "I'm really worried about Billy. I think he's in over his head."

I tore off a piece of the bread and dipped it in her olive oil puddle as the waiter brought a huge plate of antipasto to our table. Kelly plucked a green olive off the plate and popped it in her mouth. "Do you like olives?" she asked.

"Not the green ones so much. Black are okay."

She took her spoon and ladled the rest of the green olives on to her plate. "We're a good team, Darwin. I don't like the ripe ones. So they're all yours. Olives are sort of an either or thing. Just like Billy. People either loved him or hated him."

"So talk to me, Kelly. What's the deal?"

She scanned the restaurant just as Redmond had done at Walter's, but she didn't try to whisper. "Ever since I started working for him — ten years now — he's had these deals with Weidman. Something to do with selling housing to new store managers. I figured it wasn't totally legit, but they weren't stealing anything. Weidman was just taking advantage of the system. I know you didn't know anything about it."

"How do you know that?"

"Because Billy told me not to tell you. He normally didn't share much, but one night, we both had a few too many drinks and you know…"

"I know. You start making snow angels."

She smiled. "Right. He told me not to ever tell you about his deals with Weidman. He said, 'Darwin is pure. We need to keep him that way.' Those were his words."

"So what's changed?"

"About a year ago he and Weidman stopped making deals. I don't think they had a fight, but something happened. They used to talk every day, but not anymore."

I hadn't really missed Wally, but it was true he hadn't played golf with us once this last season. He was usually good for at least an outing a month. "Maybe Weidman was getting heat from his bosses. Or the legal folks."

She refilled our wine glasses and took a sip. "About six months ago, Billy started making regular trips to Chicago. Almost every week. One day my mother had a lunch date with another trainer at Tommy Nevin's Pub in Evanston and she spotted Billy there with a couple of guys in suits. She said the men appeared out of place because they were so much better dressed than the other customers. She walked over to say hi, but Billy jumped up and intercepted her before she got half way to the table. She said he acted very nervous, which is so not Billy. She got the impression he didn't want her to meet his associates."

"That's not exactly a smoking gun."

"I know. But there's something going on with that Condo Storage company. He sold all the AutoPro stock in his 401k and invested it in that company. Maybe those guys were in the Mafia."

I tried not to laugh. From all the stories in the *Tribune* about the Chicago mob, it struck me that the typical Chicago mobster was eighty years old and wore a polyester track suit. "Frank Redmond seemed to be concerned about Billy's investment in the storage company. He wanted some evidence Billy wasn't a controlling shareholder. I think that preferred stock resolution Billy sent us has something to do with that. But it's all over my head."

"And you think Stephanie knows all this?" Kelly asked.

"She knows about the Weidman deals. That seems to be her focus. I could ask her about this mysterious Chicago connection."

Kelly's squinted at me. "Seriously? Are you crazy?"

"That was a joke, Kelly. Stephanie is not our friend. Remember that."

"Right. Billy's our friend."

We drank to that and ordered another carafe.

## Chapter 22
*(Thursday, November 10, 2005)*

When Astra and I got home from practice on Thursday, Daina was still at work. I decided to take a shower. I usually shower in the morning but I needed to decompress. I had a lot on my mind — Kelly's revelations, Stephanie's accusations, the mysterious partner Billy didn't want anyone to know about — but despite all those serious matters at that moment what I was most apprehensive about was Fariba's upcoming visit. She was supposed to stop by around 7:30 for her discussion with Astra on the Iranian revolution. There was no reason for me to be nervous about Fariba. I figured a good hot shower would help me actually believe that.

Most evenings after work I would lounge around in sweatpants and an old tee-shirt. I couldn't do that with Fariba coming over. I didn't want to wear the new Wranglers I just bought last month so I put on my 501s, which had been my going-out jeans before I bought the Wranglers. I was going to wear the Merino wool grey sweater Daina had given me last Christmas, but it was too itchy. I had never actually worn it before and this definitely was not the day to break it in.

I suppose I was trying to look good, without it appearing that I was trying to look good. Not that Daina would be suspicious — more than likely she wouldn't even notice or care what I was wearing. And I really wasn't trying to impress Fariba. I just didn't want to look like a dumpy over-the-hill ex-jock. I decided on a navy blue V-neck sweater that fit snug, but not too tight. I'd worn it enough that it wouldn't appear that I was going out of my way to dress up.

When I walked into the kitchen, Astra had just pulled a tray of brownies out of the oven. Daina was sitting at the kitchen table reading the *Chicago Tribune,* eating a slice of leftover pizza, and drinking the second-to-last can of Bud. "Those brownies smell great," I said. I hovered over Astra as she cut them into squares.

"You have to wait, Dad. They're too hot."

I popped open the last can of Bud, grabbed the last slice of pizza and sat down across from Daina. On the front page of the Trib, there was a photo of the carnage from a terrorist bombing in Amman. I leaned across the table to read the caption on the photo of a blown up taxi. "'Sixty-seven killed in three suicide bombings.' Jesus Christ. That's crazy."

Daina put the paper down. She looked at me funny, like maybe I had pizza sauce on my face. "You showered?"

"Tough practice," I said.

Astra snorted. "Tough? You didn't have to run all those suicides."

"I worked up a sweat watching everyone work so hard."

Daina squinted at the photo of the burned out taxi and scoffed. "Muslims are even crazier than Christians. Banning religion was the only smart thing Soviets did for Latvia."

Daina was an equal opportunity disliker of all religions. I don't know if that made her an atheist or not. She defied labels.

"Mom, you're not going to start talking about religion when Fariba gets here, are you?"

"What do you mean? I don't talk about religion."

"Calling Muslims crazy is sort of a religious comment," Astra said.

Daina shrugged. "Is true."

Astra had arranged the brownies on a plate. I grabbed one. "These are great. Perfect with pizza and beer."

The doorbell rang and Astra ran to the front door to answer it.

Daina gathered up her case files from the kitchen table where Astra had set up her laptop for the interview with Fariba. She looked me up and down. "Finally going to meet your coach. I hear very popular. With girls."

I thought about Kelly's snow angels comment. I was overthinking this whole situation and besides nothing had happened so I needed to stop acting guilty. "She is. The girls love her."

Astra brought Fariba back to the kitchen. "Let me take your coat," I said. "Fariba, this is my wife, Daina. Daina, Fariba."

Daina set her files back on the table and shook Fariba's hand. "Very nice to meet you," she said, sounding as though she had been rehearsing that line. "Did you have trouble finding house?"

Fariba grinned, embarrassed. "Yes. Astra gave me very good instructions, but I still missed the turn. But I was only lost for a few minutes. Fortunately, I started early." She was not nervous or the least bit self-conscious. More evidence that the incident in the parking lot was so trivial to her that she had already forgotten about it.

"Darwin says you are excellent coach," Daina said. An observation I agreed with, but I'm quite certain I never shared with her.

"It's been a fascinating experience. Mr. Burr has been very helpful."

I winced. "Stop calling me Mr. Burr," I said.

Astra grabbed the plate of brownies off the kitchen counter. "Do you want a brownie, Miss Pahlavi? Fresh from the oven."

Fariba took one of the fat ones. "Oh, these are wonderful, Astra. They are so rich. We'll have to run extra tomorrow."

"Hey, no fair,"

Daina started to gather up her case files.

"I hope we are not displacing you," Fariba said.

"No, not at all. I appreciate your helping Astra."

Fariba and Astra sat down at the kitchen table and Fariba picked up the newspaper. Her face darkened. "Islam is a grotesque faith." She flinched, surprised by her own comment. She put her hand to her mouth. "I'm sorry. I should not be so opinionated."

"See, Astra, I'm not only one," Daina said.

Astra rolled her eyes. "My mom is down on religion. But she doesn't discriminate. She hates them all."

"Not all. Buddhists seem harmless. At least not slaughtering people for having wrong beliefs."

"Or no beliefs," said Fariba.

"Exactly." Daina set her files back on the table and grabbed a brownie. "Oh, these are good. But not with beer. I need cup of real coffee." She turned to me, with that look she used to give the boys back on Rush Street, twenty years ago. "Darwin, since you are all dressed up anyway, could you run to Walter's and get us his special brew?"

It was a twenty minute drive to Walter's even without traffic, but I was glad to get out of that house. Who would have believed that Fariba and Daina would have so much in common? When I left they were sitting at the kitchen table and Daina was asking Fariba about her immigrant experience. I had expected that Daina would retreat to the dining room and leave Astra and Fariba alone, but when I returned an hour later, after listening to my new best friend Walter blather on and on about Fariba's awesomeness (the man was obsessed), they were still all at the table, and to my great surprise, Daina was talking about her life in Latvia. She never talked about Latvia.

"My parents — Anna and Juris — worked for Pegasa Pils. It was seaside resort and spa. Very popular with Comrade Brezhnev." She turned toward Astra. " He was president of USSR."

"So a very posh resort?" Fariba asked.

Daina shrugged. "For Soviets, posh. My father was tennis pro and mother masseuse. She was beautiful. Favorite of Soviet lapdogs who come with Brezhnev."

"Did your dad teach you how to play tennis?" Astra asked.

"Not like your father has done with your basketball. Juris taught me enough so I could play game. He wanted me to get education. Become engineer. He sat in tiny living room drinking his vodka and say to me, 'Soviet Union always have work for good Soviet engineer.' More he drank more he believe my future set if I get into exclusive Soviet schools with sons and daughters of men he give lessons to." She shook her head. "Never going to happen. My mother had practical plan. Not a dreamer like Juris."

"Mothers can be pushy," Astra said. "Hey Dad, did you bring me a coffee?"

I set the tray of coffees on the table. "Yep. I even got Walter to give me sugar packets, despite his warning that it would ruin his coffee."

Fariba giggled. "Walter has strong opinions about his coffee." She lifted the lid off one of the cups and inhaled the rich coffee aroma. "Thank you, Darwin. Walter's coffee is perfect with Astra's brownies." She grabbed another brownie.

"Strong is the only kind of opinion Walter has," I said. "Didn't mean to interrupt." I grabbed the paper and another brownie and my coffee and went into the TV room. I didn't close the door. I wanted to hear what Daina had to say.

"What was your mother's plan?" Fariba asked.

"She slept with headmaster of Soviet Tennis Academy. Got me into his program."

"How old were you?" Fariba asked.

"Ten. They sent me to Moscow suburb. Eleven months a year, all I do is play tennis. My father knew I would hate it."

"Why did your mother do that?" Astra asked.

"She was clear thinker. My father all caught up in bullshit of worker's paradise. Mother saw rot and corruption. When I make National team and start touring, she says to me, 'Daina. One day you have chance to escape. Don't hesitate. Go. And never come back. Save yourself.'"

"Your parents must have loved you very much," Fariba said. "That had to be a heartbreaking decision."

From my chair in the TV room I could barely hear Daina's reply to Fariba, which was very un-Daina like. She usually spoke to me like I was deaf. "My mother was tightrope walker, like your father. What do you do when you have to choose between people you love? My mother knew escape would break father's heart. He had heart attack, died, the summer after I vanished." She cleared her throat. "I will let you get on with interview, Astra. Sorry for being blabbermouth. Nice to meet you, Fariba." She gathered up her files once again and I could hear her push open the swinging door to the dining room.

Daina never told me that story. I asked Daina how she escaped, but never why. I wondered what Fariba told them about her father but didn't want to ask Daina. Fariba wasn't a subject I wanted to discuss with my wife.

## Chapter 23
*(Friday, November 11, 2005)*

Stephanie was not at work on Friday morning and when she hadn't shown up by noon, I figured we were home free, no Stephanie until at least Monday.

Fridays are typically slow days — most of the inbound and outbound deliveries are scheduled for earlier in the week and by the afternoon there was not much going on. Kelly and I idled away the late afternoon swapping Billy stories. For the last five years, Billy had mostly been a pain-in-the-ass, but now that he was gone, all I seemed to recall were the good times. And there were a lot of them. It was the same with Kelly. We shared our stories and I realized we were talking about Billy as though he were dead. Past tense again.

Kelly started to tell the story of how Billy got stopped by a state trooper after leaving a party in Galena with a local woman named Gladys. They were both drunk, but Gladys convinced the cop to let Billy spend the night at her place, which was just a few minutes away, instead of hauling his ass to the drunk tank. Only Billy could get that lucky.

We both knew that story by heart, as we'd heard Billy tell it a dozen times. Kelly had just got to the part where Billy fails his sobriety test (he had no problem counting backwards from one hundred, but he couldn't walk in a straight line, stand on one foot, or touch his nose with his finger with his eyes closed) when Stephanie clip-clopped up the stairs to the bullpen and stuck her head in my office.

"I'm back gang. Did you miss me? Don't answer that."

She was in far too good of a mood. Why was she returning to Claxton at three p.m. on Friday? "Didn't figure you'd be coming back today," I said, scrupulously following her orders not to answer her question.

"I didn't want to miss your game,.."

Kelly raised her eyebrows and stared at me with mock surprise. "Darwin's predicting a victory tonight," she said. She picked up her coffee and slipped past Stephanie who continued to hang in the doorway.

"What time is the game?"

I hadn't thought she was serious about going to our game. "Seven."

"Great. That will give me time to check into the Holiday Inn."

"You're really going to stay there?"

"I have a lot of work to do this weekend, and it'll be easier to work from here. Not so many distractions."

"That's for sure." I really wanted to know what was so important that she was going to spend her weekend in Claxton, but there was no way I was going to ask. Or volunteer to come in to work. "Everything is buttoned down out in the warehouse. If you don't need me for anything, I was hoping to take off early so I could go over the game plan for tonight with Fariba." That was somewhat of an exaggeration — we didn't need to meet for another hour, but I wanted to get away from Stephanie. I guess that was a form of denial. If I didn't see Stephanie I didn't have to think about all the problems with Billy and I could forget that Stephanie and Poindexter and maybe even the FBI were out there trying to bring him down. Failure to face reality was another of my character defects.

Stephanie waved her hand at me. "Go. I'm sure with Kelly's help I can manage any crisis that comes up in the next hour. Good luck tonight."

The Dillon Devils and Claxton Eagles had been the doormats of the league for the last three years. Sometimes the crowds on both sides of the court were so small you could hear the squeak of the girls' sneakers as they ran up and down the court. This game wasn't going to be like the Claypool game where Claypool had brought four buses and filled the bleachers with their vocal supporters. Last week there had been less than a hundred Claxton fans, mostly parents and friends of the girls. But the town must have heard about the girls' gritty performance against Claypool because there were a lot more spectators on the Claxton side, including a half dozen Black students who I had not seen at any of the games in previous years. Astra would have been annoyed with me for thinking this way, but I didn't figure it was a coincidence that they showed up at the first game Toni played.

Unlike the Claypool game where the girls had a deer-in-the-headlights look as they came out of the locker room, tonight they raced on to the court as though they were on a mission.

"I was so excited I couldn't sleep last night," Fariba said as she joined me on the bench. We'd spent an hour going over our strategy. She was as well-prepared as any veteran coach. She didn't need me sitting behind her, but I was happy to be there. "We're going to win tonight. I can feel it."

I patted her on the knee in a what I intended to be a fatherly gesture of reassurance. "You've done your job. Now it's up to the girls. Take a deep breath. You stay calm and they'll stay calm."

She nodded her head vigorously. "Yes. Yes. Precisely. It is just like when I was getting ready to go in the water for my Ironman. My coach says, "Fariba you can't win the triathlon on the swim, but you can lose it if you get too excited." He was an excellent coach, just like you. I will do as you say. I will keep my excitement in here," she patted her chest. "Bottled up."

She gave me that Fariba smile that made me wish I were twenty years younger.

There was an excited murmur from the crowd as Toni began the team layup drill with a slashing reverse layup. "I think the fans have discovered our new addition," I said. So had the Dillon Devils. Three of the girls were standing on their side of the court watching with worried expressions as Toni drove to the basket.

"Hey, Darwin, you got room over there?" Stephanie Washington, was quick-stepping it down the sideline in her high heels and a shorter version of her corporate skirt and a tight black sweater that was drawing a lot of attention from the men and boys in the crowd. Fariba too.

"Who's that?" Fariba asked. She acted almost annoyed. Or if not annoyed, definitely not happy.

I hadn't been expecting Stephanie to come to the game and I for sure didn't expect to sit with her. I waved to her and she continued walking toward me. Most of the seats in the first six rows were filled but she could have found a seat farther up. Maybe she didn't want to sit that high with that short skirt on. Or maybe this was part of her strategy to continue to harass me.

"Hi, Stephanie." I patted Fariba on the shoulder. "Fariba, this is my new boss, Stephanie Washington."

"Not really. I'm just temporary. Nice to meet you, Fariba. Darwin has told me all about your team. I'm anxious to see your girls in action." As before, I felt much more off-balance in the presence of Nice Stephanie.

"Pleased to meet you," Fariba said. She smiled in a manner I would describe as unenthusiastic. Definitely not the warm, sincere smile I had come to associate with her. I suspected her lack of enthusiasm was because she knew Stephanie was investigating Billy. Fariba was a loyal friend.

The horn bleated, indicating warmups were over. As Fariba gathered the team around her, Stephanie stepped over the first row of the bleachers — not an easy task in heels and a tight skirt — and sat down next to me. "Number 7. Is she your daughter?"

"Yep. That's Astra."

Fariba was animated but controlled as she reminded the girls of the game plan. "Defense. It starts with defense. Don't let them go where they want to go. Keep a hand in their face when they shoot. Box out. And when we get the ball: RUN. RUN. RUN. Run these girls ragged, ladies. Don't save yourself. We have plenty of fresh legs. Now let's go!"

"She resembles you," Stephanie said as the starting five arranged themselves at center court and Astra and the other subs returned to the bench.

"Who? Fariba?"

"No, silly. Your daughter. That stubborn jawline; the long legs. The smart-ass grin,"

Smart-ass grin? "Don't tell her that. It'll ruin her day."

Toni jumped center for us and easily directed the tip to Dede. The girls broke toward their basket and Dede fired a cross court pass to Toni who drove in for an easy layup.

"That girl's got game," Stephanie said. "Good start for your team."

"That is going to be as close as Dillon gets." It was a cocky thing to say, but I could see they were no match for us. We scored on our first five possessions. They didn't get the ball past half court until the score was 10 to 0.

At the half way point in the first quarter, Fariba put in Astra's unit with the score 17 to 4. I was a little disappointed the score was so lopsided before Astra had a chance to play. After the substitutions, Boo Boo brought the ball up. Fariba's coaching had paid off. Boo Boo's ball-handling was much improved. But as she crossed half court she telegraphed her pass to Astra and the Dillon point guard stole the ball. The girl was heading in for what she thought would be an uncontested layup not realizing Astra had sprinted after her. As she was about to launch her shot, Astra caught up to her and stole the ball.

Astra wheeled around and dribbled hard up the court toward the Claxton basket. With four Dillon defenders packed into the key, she nailed a three point shot, stole the inbounds pass, made a layup, and when the gal taking the ball out for Dillon tried to pass it deep down the court she intercepted and sank another three-pointer. Eight points in eight seconds. The Claxton crowd roared as the Dillon coach called timeout.

Stephanie high-fived me, cheering as loud as anyone. "Awesome. Did you teach her to shoot like that?"

If this had been a boxing match the refs would have stopped it mid-way through the second quarter. With four minutes to go and Claxton up by thirty points, their coached called timeout just to give his girls a break from the massacre. He didn't have any answers either.

Fariba looked back at me, not sure what she should do. "Put in Linda, Jane and Krissy," I said. They were the three girls who were not on either the first or second units. "Don't play Astra or Toni for the rest of the game. And tell the girls no shots until they've passed the ball four times."

"But on defense, no mercy, right?" Fariba said.

"Exactly."

With the third string subs and Boo Boo as the point guard, Dillon held their own for the rest of the quarter. It was 39 to 11 at halftime. As Fariba led the girls into the locker room, Stephanie patted my knee. "I think I'll take off now. I have a lot to do this weekend. Your team looks great. And Toni and Astra — they're college-ready. You've done a great job, Coach."

"Fariba's the coach. She's been really impressive."

Stephanie smiled at me as though I had said something very foolish. "Be careful, Darwin. That girl has stars in her eyes."

"What?"

"Oh come on. Can't you see she has a crush on you?"

I could feel my face getting warm. I thought about Pam, the Clarkie's waitress, warning me to be careful. Fariba just had a funny effect on some women. I shook my head and managed to laugh. "I'll see you on Monday, Stephanie. Enjoy the Holiday Inn."

She game me another knee pat. "You're a good coach. This is what you should be doing. Not that other stuff."

Did she mean Billy's deals or working for AutoPro? Volunteer coach wasn't going to pay any bills. Stephanie stepped down from the bleachers and marched along the sidelines to the exit, drawing almost as much attention as when she entered.

Fariba had Toni and Astra sit the entire second half. She played a number of different combinations. It was rewarding to see how tenacious all of the girls were with their defense. Nothing better for a player and a team than to see the benefits of hard work. The final score was 65 to 27. An impressive way for Claxton to return to the win column.

As I waited for Fariba and Astra to come out of the locker room, several of the parents came up to me to offer their congratulations. I spotted Frank Redmond across the gym and nodded at him, but he acted as though he didn't see me, which was fine with me.

Astra, Toni and Marcia came out of the locker room together, laughing and chattering with each other. "Dad, we're going over to Delforte's for a pizza. Marcia will drive us home," Astra said.

"Is that okay with your dad, Marcia?" I asked.

Marcia sighed, but good naturedly, not like she did when she was a brat. "Yes. The Reverend has blessed this event and given me the car keys." She held up the keys and waggled them in front of me.

"Great game, girls. Have fun. Don't stay out too late." Pizza at Delforte's had been an after-game tradition for decades. No liquor license so it was a good teenager hangout.

The rest of the girls trickled out. Gretchen Frantel, with her elaborate Farrah-Fawcett hair was always the last to leave. "Nice game, Gretchen. You were great on defense," I said.

"Thanks, Mr. Burr. I wish I could've scored."

She had a terrible jumpshot and had missed a couple of uncontested layups. "Keep working on it." I stared at the locker room expecting Fariba to emerge. "Is Coach Pahlavi still in the locker room?"

"She was in her office, talking on the phone. We could all hear her. She was yelling in Iranian." Gretchen flipped her hair back and did her beauty pageant strut as she walked toward her boyfriend waiting by the exit. "See you Monday, Mr. Burr."

The gym had emptied out and I was debating whether to stick my head in the locker room when Fariba came out. She saw me and smiled, but she didn't look as happy as I would have expected.

"Everything okay?" I asked.

"Oh yes. I thought the girls played splendidly. I keep a journal and I was recording my thoughts and feelings while they were fresh in my mind." She held up her spiral pad which she carried everywhere. "You were pleased, Darwin?" She had a peculiar look on her face. Like a poker player trying to read an opponent. I wondered who she had been talking too and why she didn't mention it. Not that it was any of my business.

"The team played great. I wish Dillon had offered a little more resistance. St. Charles will be tougher."

"I was surprised to see your boss at the game." She said boss like it was a curse.

"Me too. Stephanie's unpredictable."

"I hadn't expected her to be so beautiful."

I couldn't think of anything to say to that. "I thought you would be happier about the victory. You should be proud. You did a fantastic job."

She forced a smile. "I am happy. Maybe it's a postgame letdown. And I'm a little worried for you and Billy. I don't trust this Stephanie woman. You're not going to help her are you?"

Kelly, Pam, Stephanie, and now Fariba. It seemed as though the only woman in my life who wasn't trying to give me advice was my wife.

"Billy's my friend. Nothing has changed." Billy was my friend and that would never change. But I had this feeling that everything else was changing and I was powerless to do anything about it.

## Chapter 24
*(Monday, November 14, 2005)*

Stephanie and a rotund little man who was too poorly dressed to be from AutoPro corporate were waiting for me in front of Stephanie's office when I arrived at work on Monday.

"Darwin, can you come in here, please?" Stephanie said. Something in her expression — a seriousness tinged with a look of concern she had not exhibited before — made me decide this was not a good day to exercise my independence and keep her waiting. Also I was curious about the rumpled guy standing next to her.

"What's up?" I asked.

"This is special agent, George Hildebrand. He's from the Peoria office of the FBI."

I suspect investigating the nefarious activities of a couple auto parts executives was not a plum FBI assignment. Agent Hildebrand did not resemble the clean cut, well-dressed flat-belly we see on TV. He had a bowling pin body with a lackadaisical comb-over and was squeezed into a Sears-quality blue suit that he couldn't button.

He stepped toward me, his right hand extended as his left hand rearranged the strands of hair on his nearly bald head. "How do you do, Mr. Burr." He smiled and made good eye contact and then his eyes drifted down to the patch on my jacket. "Miss Washington mentioned you were a basketball legend around here. I see you're still playing." He pointed at the patch on the jacket that read, *AutoPro Basketball Championship.*

"It's an old jacket. Haven't played in ten years."

Stephanie turned and walked into her office. "Come in, gentlemen." She parked herself in Billy's old chair. "Darwin coaches the girls high school basketball team," she said, as though this were a job interview and she were promoting me.

Hildebrand nodded enthusiastically. "That's wonderful. Giving back to your community."

"I just help. I'm not the coach."

Stephanie frowned at me. I was not following her script.

Hildebrand rubbed his hands together and I was pretty certain the chitchat segment of our meeting was over. "I have a few things I want to go over with you. Could you sit down?" He walked over to Billy's coffee table and sat down in the only office chair. Stephanie remained seated at the desk. That left the sofa for me.

I slipped off my jacket and draped it over the sofa arm. I sat down and waited.

"Do you want coffee?" Hildebrand asked.

"No. I'm good."

"All righty then," he said.

He rubbed his hands together again and opened his worn briefcase. He pulled out a beige file and placed it on the table. Across the top it read, AUTHORIZED PERSONNEL ONLY and below that was the FBI crest and the words, FBI CLASSIFIED INVESTIGATION FILE. George's props were far more impressive than Stephanie's.

"Darwin," he said and then he paused, "is it all right if I call you Darwin?"

"That's my name."

"All righty. Darwin. You know who Walter Weidman is, correct?"

"Yes."

Hildebrand's eyebrows lifted slightly. He waited to see if I were planning to elaborate and then he continued. "And of course, you also know, William Rourke."

"Yeah, I know Billy."

"Are you familiar with The Racketeer Influenced and Corrupt Organizations Act? Commonly referred to as the RICO act."

"Just what I've learned on *Law and Order*."

Hildebrand grinned. "Love that show. Feds never come off too good, but eh, we get our own shows." He opened the file folder and frowned as he flipped through the pages. They were fastened together like a high school book report. He shook his head sadly. "Excuse my language, but this RICO legislation is…" he lowered his voice to a whisper and leaned across the table. "…a prosecutor's wet dream. Hard to believe the courts haven't thrown it out. It has just about put the mob out of business." He sighed. "Of course the folks who have taken their place are far worse." He shook his head. "Be careful what you wish for, eh Darwin?"

I couldn't tell whether this was all an act, with Hildebrand pretending to be a hapless Inspector Clouseau type, or if he was actually a stumblebum from Peoria. Whatever he was, I wished he would get to the point. "Okay," I said.

"Here's the bottom line." He picked up the file and began to read. "The Racketeer Influenced and Corrupt Organizations Act is a federal law that provides extended criminal penalties and a civil cause of action for acts performed as part of an ongoing criminal organization." He stopped and stared at me. "Extended criminal penalties. That's the key phrase. RICO convictions bring serious jail time. Twenty years. Sometimes more." He acted frightened, as though I were threatening him with jail instead of the other way around.

Stephanie walked over from her desk and sat down carefully at the end of Billy's sofa. "Explain what you mean by a criminal enterprise, George."

"Ah yes. Good point. Everyone hears racketeers and thinks this just applies to the Mafia. Not so. Under RICO a person who has committed at least…," he stopped reading and made air quotes figures with his doughy fingers, "…two acts of racketeering activity drawn from a list of 35 such crimes within a 10-year period can be charged with racketeering if such acts are related."

Stephanie leaned in, unable to stay on the sidelines while Hildebrand meandered toward the finish line. She tapped the table and stared at me. "Crimes such as embezzlement, fraud, securities violations and," she raised her voice and spoke more slowly, "money laundering."

Hildebrand jumped back in. "Here's the real kicker." He picked up his folder again. "When the U.S. Attorney decides to indict someone under RICO, he has the option of seeking a pre-trial restraining order or injunction to..." he paused and raised his voice for the punchline. "...seize a defendant's assets and prevent the transfer of potentially forfeitable property."

I wasn't sure why that was the kicker. It seemed like the twenty years in prison was pretty hard to top.

"I know that sounds like legal mumbo-jumbo, but what this means is the accused has all his assets frozen so he can't even pay for his own lawyer." He threw the folder back on the table. "It's practically un-American."

"George," Stephanie said, giving the agent her faux humble smile. "I think it would be helpful to explain the situation with Weidman."

Hildebrand nodded his head vigorously. "Yes, yes. Weidman. Good point." He fumbled through his briefcase and pulled out another folder. It had the same cover as the one he had been reading from. He scanned the inside cover and closed it again. "The U.S. Attorney made it known to Mr. Weidman that they planned to indict him under the RICO act. They laid out for him and his attorney in very stark terms what that would mean. Forfeiture of all his bank accounts, retirement accounts, property. And of course a prison term that could very well be a life sentence for a man of his years. That got his attention, as you can imagine."

"I can imagine." Weidman loved the good life. His mansion in Lake Forest. Golf, tennis, Caribbean cruises, the yacht. People sucking up to him. I suspected he would sell Billy out in a heartbeat. He was an entitled prick who had been born on third base but thought he hit a triple.

"The U. S. Attorney has proffered a plea agreement for Mr. Weidman. In exchange for his cooperation and the forfeiture of all his bank accounts that were fruit of the poisonous tree." He smiled at me with his folksy, I'm just a simple guy from Peoria shtick. "That's a legal term. It means we take back all the money he stole."

"What about jail time?" Stephanie asked, playing the straight man.

"To be determined. If he's candid and continues to cooperate he might get off with a very light sentence. Maybe even probation."

"He's a domino, Darwin," Stephanie said.

Domino horseshit. Whatever went down between Weidman and Billy, I didn't see how anyone could figure Billy was the Kingpin and Weidman just a fucking domino.

Hildebrand bent down and picked up a pile of file folders. These didn't have the FBI logo on them. They were the same files Stephanie had shown me when we were meeting with Stu Granger. "Now here's the bad news. Here are a dozen Rourke-Weidman real estate deals. Each one of them is an indictable RICO offense. That's two hundred forty years of jail time. Your signature is on every one of these."

"It makes it look like you're part of Rourke's criminal enterprise," Stephanie said in case I couldn't figure that out on my own.

The FBI and AutoPro were just playing games with me. I might have been a lousy employee who didn't know shit about auto parts but I knew how to play games. Hildebrand's threat to send me to prison for the rest of my life probably should have scared me, but mostly it pissed me off. Put me into game mode. "I don't see any criminal enterprise. Whatever was going on, I wasn't part of it."

Hildebrand smiled indulgently. "Your signature as an officer says otherwise. You're too intelligent to use a defense of ignorance. But Miss Washington does not believe you are in fact part of Mr. Rourke's criminal enterprise and I am willing to be persuaded."

"Darwin," Stephanie said, leaning forward and looking at me wide-eyed as though she really had my best interests at heart. "Billy is on the run. And his funds have been cut-off. He's going to be reaching out to you."

"Okay. What if he does?" I wasn't going to get anywhere stonewalling them. I needed to know what their play was.

Hildebrand moved forward in his chair rubbing his hands again. "Well this isn't the movies. I'm not going to ask you to wear a wire." He laughed derisively. "We don't have the budget or the manpower anyhow. And there's so much red tape these days it would take two weeks to get approval." He shook his head, pining for the good old days of J. Edgar.

"So…?"

"We have a simple, airtight case. We just need the body, so to speak. If Rourke contacts you, and we are certain he will, set up a meeting and let us know where he is. We'll pick him up."

"That's it? That's all you need from me?"

Hildebrand reached into his briefcase and pulled out a dispenser of yellow tape similar to what the police use to mark off a crime scene. The difference was his tape had PROPERTY OF FBI printed on it. "I would like permission to seal the file cabinets in your storeroom. I will have one of my analysts start going through them in the next couple of weeks."

"They could get a subpoena," Stephanie said. "But we want to cooperate with the FBI any way we can. That won't disrupt operations, will it, Darwin?"

I shrugged. Why was she asking me? "Sometimes Kelly needs to retrieve bills of lading or shipping documents if there is a dispute. It's mostly the recent stuff."

Stephanie pursed her lips. She said to Hildebrand, "Rourke hasn't been in the office since early October. You don't need any of the files that were created after that, right? Couldn't you leave them unsealed?"

Hildebrand nodded enthusiastically. "Yes, by all means. We don't want to make your lives any more difficult than necessary."

Of course he didn't. Except for that part about sending me to jail for 240 years and taking all my money. Hildebrand acted as though he really wanted my permission. I nodded toward Stephanie. "She's the boss. If she's says it's okay, I'm fine with that." But of course I wasn't. I was trying to figure out how long it would take for

Hildebrand's analysts to discover Billy's stash of cash. Not long enough.

Hildebrand smiled. He loved it when we could all play nicely together. "There is just one more thing."

For some reason, purveyors of bad news always save the worst shit for last. I don't know why. I would rather get the unpleasantness out there as soon as possible.

Hildebrand inhaled sharply and took the plunge. "You will have to testify for the Grand Jury. Mostly just affirming you were asked to sign these deals. If you're not involved in his criminal enterprise, you'll be fine. I can probably get the U.S. Attorney to give you a limited immunity on these deals."

Stephanie jumped in like an anxious schoolgirl who knows the answer. "I worked with Sean Fitzpatrick for four years," she said, giving me the soulful look again. "I guarantee he'll give you limited immunity."

Stephanie and Hildebrand were like two scam artists, piling on the promises, trying to get their mark to commit.

"Limited doesn't sound very good." It didn't. It sounded like a loophole big enough to hang someone.

It was Hildebrand's turn. "If you are as pure as Stephanie assures me you are, then you just testify about these files and you are home free. No indictment, no jail time. You walk away a free man."

"So why is it limited immunity?"

"If it were to be revealed that you were more involved than just a passive signator, what we in the business like to call a fool with a pen," he grinned nervously, "if in fact you knew you were part of his criminal enterprise, that would be, uh problematic."

Problematic. The FBI way of saying, 'you're fucked'. I scowled at Hildebrand. "You guys keep acting as though you've caught him. What if you don't find him? What happens to me then?"

Hildebrand sighed. "We're going to find him."

"If you found everyone you were looking for the Post Office wouldn't have anything to put on its wall. And most of those wanted dudes don't look like they have half the brains of Billy Rourke."

Hildebrand actually seemed offended that I had suggested the FBI might not be infallible. "Well, Darwin," he said speaking slowly, as though I might be too dumb to follow him. "Let's just say it is definitely in your best interests that we find him. We're on the same team here."

I turned to Stephanie. "Do I get to keep my job?" I needed to know badly they wanted my help. They were trying to play as few of their cards as possible. "And my retirement plan?"

Her face pruned up. "I'm not sure I can guarantee your job. But your retirement assets — no one will touch them."

"So even though I didn't do anything wrong, I have to help you put away a friend and I get thrown out on my ass from a place I've worked for twenty years. I don't like that deal."

It was a bluff, but Hildebrand fell for it. With a look of exasperation he said to Stephanie, "I think we could probably persuade your bosses that Mr. Burr should not lose his job for assisting in an investigation. What kind of message would that send?" He turned back to me. "The FBI can be quite persuasive in these kinds of situations and AutoPro Corporation has certain reasons to keep us satisfied." He tried to wink, but he ended up closing both his eyes.

Lots of empty promises was mostly what they were offering. "Can I get this in writing?"

Now it was Hildebrand's turn to look constipated. "Again, problematic. Red tape. Lawyers. Approvals. Policies and procedures."

I was wondering how many nouns he could string together without actually saying anything coherent, but Stephanie interrupted his floundering.

"You really don't want it in writing. That raises your profile in the prosecutor's office from someone who is helping with an investigation to more of an unindicted co-conspirator."

"I wasn't asking the U.S. attorney to put it in writing," I said, even though I was. "What about AutoPro? Can I get it in writing, Stephanie, that I'm not going to get my ass fired or have someone fuck with my family's retirement assets?"

"No need for that kind of language, Mr. Burr," Hildebrand said. He seemed almost as offended as when I defamed the Bureau.

"I can give you a letter on your retirement assets," Stephanie said. "You're employed at will so a letter giving you comfort on employment would be meaningless and I honestly doubt Randall Judd would ever agree to it. I'm being straight with you."

I actually believed her. It didn't matter what kind of job assurances they gave me, job protection for me was non-existent. I decided I had had enough of the dynamic duo. "Okay. Get me that letter." I pushed myself up from the sofa.

Hildebrand, startled, stood up also. "So we can count on your cooperation?"

"I will always cooperate with law enforcement. Billy was a boyhood friend. I'm not going to jail for him." It was the least responsive answer I could come up with on the spur of the moment. I suppose technically someone might argue, that since I didn't have any intention of betraying Billy, my statement to Hildebrand was a lie. But who could really see what's in a man's heart?

**Chapter 25**
*(Monday, November 14, 2005)*

While George Hildebrand called the Peoria office to arrange for an analyst to come out and start reviewing the files, Stephanie walked down the hall with me to my office. "Darwin, this is going to work out. We're fortunate. I've dealt with the FBI before and most of them are pricks. But George is a straight-shooter. He'll be fair."

We? Stephanie acted as though we were on the same side, but I didn't see her being threatened with prison and financial ruin. "I hope so," I said.

She put her hand on my forearm as I stopped at the door to my office. "And Darwin...?"

I stopped, waiting for another of those one-more-things.

"You are a good coach. I've seen dozens of high school basketball teams. Very few as well-prepared as your team. They didn't get to that level because of that sweet-faced Arab girl. You did that. Own it."

I hitched my shoulders. "Thanks." I could have and maybe I should have stood up for Fariba, but I had the feeling it wouldn't do any good. I thought Stephanie's praise was sincere, but I also had the nagging feeling she was trying to persuade me I should look to a future outside of AutoPro. "I better get to work."

She let go of my sleeve. "I've got to drive back to Chicago for a meeting. I'll be back here on Tuesday. George is hoping to get his analyst up here tomorrow."

George was still in her office talking on his phone as she left for the parking lot. I had just started to go through the paperwork on my desk when Kelly appeared in front of me, with her now familiar panic look. "I don't think I want to know what you're going to tell me," I said.

She sat down in the chair in front of my desk and leaned forward. "I just got a text from Billy," she whispered.

"Maybe it would be better if I didn't know anything. That fat guy talking in Billy's office is from the FBI."

"I know. And Billy doesn't want me to get you involved. He's trying to protect you."

I almost laughed. Billy had such good intentions. "Yeah, that's not working real well."

"I know. I'm sorry." She looked drained. The Billy crisis had been tough on her. "He needs more than the diamonds now. He wants me to bring the NPC cash to my mom. But I don't know where you put the package."

So in trying to protect Kelly I had put myself in a box. "Fuck."

"My sentiments exactly. Just tell me where you put it and I won't say another word about Billy. I promise."

It was quiet in the office and I could hear the murmur of George Hildebrand talking to someone in his office. "I can't let you do that. If you or your mom get caught up in Billy's mess you could get twenty years."

Her eyes went wide. "Jail? I can't go to jail. What am I going to do?"

"Give me your phone and the diamonds. I'll take care of it."

"You can't call him back. It was a burner phone. No caller ID."

"I'm not calling him. I'm going to get rid of your phone. You lost it. Okay?"

She nodded. She was smart enough not to ask a lot of questions. "Now give me the diamonds."

She pulled the envelope out of her jeans pocket. "Here." She appeared slightly less frightened. "Thanks, Darwin."

George Hildebrand stuck his head in my office. "Sorry to interrupt. Where can I get a cup of coffee? He had his FBI tape dispenser clutched in his hand, ready to go to work.

"George, this is my office assistant, Kelly Craven. Kelly, Agent George Hildebrand with the FBI."

George semi-bowed. An old-fashioned gentlemen. "Pleased to meet you."

I gave Kelly a broad smile to get her attention. "Kelly, will you take George out to see Felipe for some of his special coffee? I don't think he'll find his way without a guide. You can show him the operation. Give him a feel for what we do here."

George beamed. "Excellent idea. I hope I'm not inconveniencing you, Miss Craven."

Kelly got the message. "No problem at all, Mr. Hildebrand." She jumped up from her chair. "You'll find Felipe's coffee to be a unique experience. Follow me."

I waited a couple minutes and then walked over to the file room. I turned on the light and my stomach clenched. The room was a mess. Over the weekend the cleaning crew had started stripping the linoleum and the file cabinets had all been pushed together. Instead of five banks of filing cabinets there was one big block, five deep. I had hidden Billy's stash in the middle file drawer in the middle cabinet of the middle row.

I figured I had no more than ten minutes before Hildebrand returned. I tried not to panic. The cabinet where I hid the NPC folder was in the fifth column of cabinets three rows back. I tugged on the first cabinet. I couldn't budge it. I removed the top two drawers and lifting up the handle of the bottom drawer I was able to tug the cabinet out of the line. I repeated the process for the cabinet behind it. Now I had access to the 1999 file drawers. I held my breath as I pulled open the drawer marked "JUNE-99". There in the middle of the drawer was the NPC folder. I grabbed it and hustled back to my office. I stuffed it in the back of my desk drawer and ran back to the file room.

Sweat trickled down my back as I replaced the drawers. I was breathing hard and I knew I must look guilty as hell. I could hear Kelly talking louder than usual as she headed up the staircase to the bullpen. I didn't have time to return the cabinets to the block. I flung open the door to the file room and started to move another cabinet out of the block.

"We've got a mess here," I said as George and Kelly entered the room.

Hildebrand's brow was seamed. "What are you doing?" he asked.

"Cleaning crew pushed all the cabinets together so they could strip the floors. I thought I could move these cabinets so you could get at them, but it's a lot more work than I expected. We better get a crew from the warehouse to help."

"Absolutely. You can throw out your back trying to do that kind of lifting."

He seemed sincerely concerned, not suspicious. I wiped my brow. "Man. I'm sweating like a pig. Guess I'm not use to hard labor any more. I'll call Meron in the warehouse and have him bring some muscle up here. Do you want to direct them?" I asked.

"They just need to spread them out so I can put our official seal on each drawer. We have our procedures you know." He tried to wink again, but still couldn't pull it off.

"I'll make sure the cleaning crew holds off on the floor until after your guy is done with his inspection. I see you got your coffee."

"Yes. Thank you. Haven't tasted it yet. It's a little hot."

# Chapter 26
*(Thursday, November 17, 2005)*

I didn't know what to do with Billy's cash. My first thought was that as long as it stayed in the office, I hadn't really crossed a line. Maybe tiptoed up to the edge, but not crossed it. But the more I thought about it, the more I realized that if this all came crashing down, I wouldn't get any credit for my caution. Everyone would just assume I got caught before I had a chance to move it.

Hildebrand brought in two agent-trainees from his office. Art and Rollie — with their crewcuts and short sleeved white shirts — could have passed for those door-to-door Mormons who came by once a year. They were thorough and meticulous and seemed to have a clear notion of what they were looking for. They ignored the huge volume of documents generated by the motor oil companies like Pennzoil and Valvoline or the large auto parts suppliers like Federal Mogul and concentrated on the transactions with the specialty suppliers like Spartan Engines and Jasper Transmissions. Billy, not corporate, made the purchase decision and negotiated the contracts for those small, regional suppliers. Thursday afternoon they spent two hours in my office questioning me about procedures and controls.

Art reviewed a stack of invoices from Spartan Engines. Billy selected Spartan as the supplier of remanufactured engines and crankshafts last July.

"Mr. Burr, do you have a copy of the supply contract for Spartan?" he asked. I decided not to ask him to call me Darwin. Familiarity was not going to help.

I pulled open the Pendaflex desk drawer where I kept a copy of all the supply contracts. Billy made all the deals, but when there was a problem, I was the one who had to fix it. What Billy promised after a night of being wined and dined was not always what made it

155

into the supplier's contract. He rarely covered the unpleasant details like warranty policy and AutoPro's right to unlimited returns.

I got that tight feeling in my stomach as I thumbed through the file folders looking for the Spartan contract. Billy's NPC folder was in the back of the drawer.

As I handed the contract to Art he glanced at the bank of files. "Are those all supplier contracts?" he asked.

"Mostly," I said.

"Could I have the drawer? I'll go through all the contracts and get them back to you by the end of the day."

Fuck. I shook my head. "Can't do that. I need authorization from the boss lady to release any files that aren't from the storeroom. I get in big trouble if I violate procedures."

The agents nodded earnestly. They understood procedures.

"Here's what you do, " I said, trying my best to act as though we were all on the same team. "You call your boss and have him call my boss and then she'll give me the authorization." I was almost certain that daisy chain of approvals would buy me at least the rest of the day. And it did. Art called for Hildebrand, but he was gone for the day.

As soon as the two agents left my office I grabbed Billy's cash folder and stuffed it in my gym bag. At four thirty I packed up and headed out of the office. I stopped in front of the desk where Art was making notes on the Spartan contract. "I've got basketball practice," I said. "The girls have a big game with St. Charles tomorrow. Kelly will be able to answer any questions you might have."

The agent stopped his notetaking and nodded. "Sure thing, Mr. Burr. We'll see you in the morning."


After practice Toni came home with Astra so they could work on their homework together. On Thursdays, Daina's office closed at three p.m., so with typical Daina-efficiency she used the free afternoon to cook up a week's worth of food for family dinners. When we got home she had just finished grilling a batch of skinless chicken breasts and cooking a large pot of red beans and rice. If Daina had cooked all my meals I'd still weigh 180. But she didn't and I didn't.

She smiled warmly when Toni and Astra walked into the kitchen. "Toni, hi. Join us for supper."

"We need to study, Mom," Astra said. "Can't we take it upstairs?"

"Smells great, Mrs. Burr," Toni said.

In an odd sort of way, Toni and Daina seemed to bring out the best in each other. I think Daina was secretly pleased Astra had a friend. And Toni, who always had her guard up, at least with white folks, seemed to accept Daina. Maybe it was Daina's no-bullshit approach to her work.

"Sit, girls. Easy meal: chicken, beans, rice," she said. She handed me four dinner plates. "Set table."

So as usual, we did things Daina's way and it was fine. Toni was an appreciative (and hungry) dinner guest. She and Astra inhaled four chicken breasts and two glasses of milk and half the rice and beans Daina had prepared.

"I loved that chicken, Mrs. Burr. How do you get that flavor?" Toni asked.

"Teriyaki. Simple. Soy sauce and ginger. Soak for half hour. Broil five minutes. Lots of protein, no fat. Great meal for athletes."

Toni had her wide-eyed-taking-it-all-in look. I could tell she was making mental notes.

"Hey, Mom. Will you come to our game tomorrow?" Astra asked. "It's over in St. Charles. We need a big cheering section."

My immediate reaction was that I wished Astra hadn't asked her. It had been such a pleasant, Ozzie and Harriet kind of experience – the four of us having family supper together — I didn't want it to end on a sour note.

Daina looked at her daughter quizzically, and I thought she was trying to come up with an excuse but instead she smiled and nodded. "Okay. I can do that." She turned to me and said, "Can I ride with you, or are you on team bus with Fariba?"

It sounded like a casual inquiry, but it didn't feel like it. "I am definitely not riding on that bus. I'll pick you up here at five thirty." I wanted to get off that subject quickly. "What are you girls working on?" I asked.

They grinned at each other. "We're going to do a dramatic reading for Lit class on "The Bluest Eye," Toni said.

"We're using a photo of Mom as a prop," Astra said.

Daina looked at Astra, her brow knitted. "What photo?"

"The one from your twentieth anniversary party," Astra said. "You're staring right into the camera. It's scary."

Billy had made himself official photographer for the party and by the time he captured that image Daina was about to strangle him. With her icy blue eyes, she was hot and chilling at the same time. It was a great shot.

"You have the bluest eyes I've ever seen," Toni said. "Percola, the main character in the novel wishes she had blue eyes. That would make her beautiful, she thinks. Beautiful like you."

"That's crazy," Daina said. She was truly oblivious to her beauty.

"It's a story of racial identity," Toni said. "Society made this girl believe she had to have white features to be pretty. Black skin, kinky hair weren't cool. The book was written in the sixties, but it's still true today. I know lots of girls who want to look white."

"What do you do with my picture?" Daina asked.

Astra laughed. "Percola — played by Toni — will have it next to her as she stares in the mirror—"

"—at my ugly brown eyes," Toni said, laughing and batting her eyelashes. Her phone vibrated and she stared at the screen. "It's Grandma. Excuse me." She pushed back from the table and walked into the TV room to talk to her grandmother.

The call was obviously bad news. I could hear Toni's voice rise and we all heard snippets of her conversation: "Are you kidding me?...Grandma that's crazy...I don't... Such a waste..." She returned to the kitchen, clearly shaken.

"What's wrong, Toni?" Astra asked.

She collapsed back into her chair. "Bedelia's boyfriend Ray was arrested today for tagging. Grandma bailed him out and now he's staying with us." She acted like she might cry. Or hit someone.

"Ray? The guy who was messing with all the Gangster signs?" I asked.

Daina looked up, alarmed. "Doing what?"

"He's a Vice Lord and they're trying to move in on Gangster territory," Toni said. "He's beyond stupid and he's going to get us all killed."

This was clearly a serious development. Daina went into total action mode. "Toni, call your grandmother. Tell her you're staying here tonight. After game tomorrow night, we'll go to your place and get your stuff. You can't live there while that man's in the house."

It wasn't a suggestion. Toni followed instructions and the girls went upstairs to study.

Daina stared at her phone, thumbing through her directory. "Monique has put those girls and baby at risk." She stood up from the table. "I have to make calls." She walked into the dining room and I realized I had dropped my gym bag with the Billy cash beside the dining room table. I grabbed the bag and took it upstairs to our bedroom. I wrapped a somewhat used towel around the folder and put it back into the gym bag. I threw the bag in the back of my closet. I always did my own laundry so Daina wasn't likely to discover it there.

## Chapter 27
*(Friday, November 18, 2005)*

Given the crisis with Toni's family, I expected Daina to cancel her plan to go to the girls' basketball game. I wouldn't have blamed her if she had, but when I rolled into the driveway at 5:35 she was standing on the porch talking on her cellphone.

I could tell by the strained look on her face as she climbed up into the pickup, that the call wasn't going well. The other party seemed to be doing most of the talking. Daina could intimidate most bureaucrats with her icy glare. That didn't work so well on the phone. It was a man talking — I could hear his voice as Daina had stopped listening and held the phone in her lap waiting for him to finish his monologue. It was twenty miles to St. Charles and we were nearly halfway there before he finally stopped bloviating.

Daina put the phone back to her ear and said with icy contempt. "Thanks for help, Stan." She hung up the phone. "Fucking *peza*."

It was a bad sign when Daina started swearing in Latvian. "Anything I can do?" A dumb question, but well-intentioned. It was really just an invitation for her to talk.

"Toni cannot go back to that house until we get that boy out of there."

"I agree. She can stay with us forever as far as I'm concerned. Do you really think the family is in danger?"

She nodded grimly. "Yes. I talked to new gang-crimes coordinator. If Vice Lords try to take over Gangster territory it will spark gang war and there will be civilian casualties. He didn't think danger was imminent, but he doesn't know."

"Fuck. What do you hear from Monique?"

"Nothing. Not answering her phone. Bedelia either. I drove over knocked on door but no answer. Maybe they're hiding. That would be smart thing to do, but Monique not always smart. DCFS can take baby away temporarily but they're backlogged and don't see this as an emergency situation. Won't go there until Tuesday."

"So what do we do?"

"After the game we can drive over let Toni get her stuff. If Monique or Bedelia are there I will convince them to let me take baby for the weekend."

I didn't care for the idea of driving over to East Claxton on a Friday night. Or any night for that matter. "Why don't you and Astra ride back on the team bus and I'll drive directly over from the game with Toni. It's on our way back. That will save us an hour." I didn't say it, but I'm sure Daina understood my intent. It would be better to show up at 9 p.m. than to wait until 10 or 11. And we would draw less attention if there were fewer white faces in my truck.

Daina shook her head. "No. I have to accompany. But plan makes sense."

She punched a number into her cellphone. "What are you doing?" I asked. We were almost to the high school and I knew it would be a waste of time to argue with her about her decision.

"Calling Ed. He can pick up Astra at school and bring her home."

One advantage of having an eccentric neighbor like Ed Mackey is that he's usually home. Survivalists don't have a terribly active social life. He answered on the first ring, and since it was Daina who was making the request, he readily agreed to pick up Astra, no questions asked. He assured Daina he would be at the school when the bus returned from St. Charles waiting for Astra in his '89 Ford pickup.

The St. Charles Saints were a much better team than the Dillon Blue Devils. They would be a good test for just how much we had improved. They had won their first two games easily and last year had beaten Claxton in both games by nearly twenty points. They had an All-State point guard, Connie "The Jet" Carter, who led the league in scoring and assists last year and had averaged thirty points a games so far this year. When Daina and I got to the gym the teams were already on the court going through their warm-ups.

Fariba was standing in front of our bench studying her clipboard of plays. She spotted us as we entered the gym and waved. Daina waved back. "I'm going to sit here by the exit in case I get a call from Monique or department. You go do your coaching thing."

I had expected her to sit with me, but I wasn't really surprised or disappointed that she didn't want to. Even after twenty-five years of marriage I couldn't always read Daina. She didn't appear to dislike Fariba, and I'm sure she wasn't jealous, but she acted different around her. More friendly than normal, but more aloof, too.

"Okay. I'll let Astra and Toni know our plans after the game. No need to distract them now."

I walked across the court to where Fariba was waiting.

"Astra told me Daina was coming to the game."

She seemed genuinely happy. I had told her it wasn't likely Daina would attend any of our games.

"She's not sitting with you?" It was a statement that sounded like a question.

"She's waiting for a call." I didn't want to try and explain the Monique — Bedelia — gangbanger mess to Fariba. We had other stuff to deal with. "Are you ready?" I asked.

Her teenage girl excited smile returned. "Yes. I. Am," she said. "WE are ready. This will be a great test of our defensive prowess. Dede is especially excited."

We had a strategy for stopping The Jet. Dede would hound her as she brought the ball up the court and try to force her to one side or the other. As soon as she crossed half-court our nearest player would double team her, trapping her against the sideline. She wasn't going to score thirty points against us as she had her last two opponents. If she was going to beat us she'd have to find the open player.

It was close for a while, but mostly because Toni was off her game. She made a couple of stupid fouls on her double teams and missed her first four shots. But by the second quarter the constant defensive harassment of The Jet started to take its toll. Astra stole the ball from her on back-to-back possessions and then Toni returned and found her groove. We were up by ten points at half time and by the end of the third quarter, Fariba had inserted the backups.

Midway through the fourth quarter a dark, sullen man in an expensive suit and a well-dressed woman in a headscarf sat down in the front row near the door, a few rows from where Daina was seated. They didn't seem all that interested in the game — the man was talking to the woman who kept nodding her head and looking over at our bench. She appeared to be looking at Fariba. Maybe I thought that because they looked like Iranians, but a few moments later when we took the ball out under the basket near where they were seated it was clear to me that Fariba had spotted them and was noticeably unsettled. Her confident smile had vanished and her face was etched with concern. She tried to remain focused on the game, which didn't require much attention, but she kept looking over at them.

We won the game by twenty-five points and it was apparent to everyone in the gym that the Claxton Eagles were a team to reckon with. I leaned over and patted Fariba on the back. "Congratulations, Coach. Great game."

"Thanks, Darwin." She forced a smile, but she couldn't hold it. "Can you excuse me for a moment?"

She walked quickly across the court without further explanation. Very un-Fariba like. I huddled up the girls as they came off the court. "Great game, ladies. Go take your shower and Ms. Pahlavi will be back there in a few minutes. Toni, Astra, I need a word."

The girls filed on into the locker room. Toni and Astra waited impatiently. "Toni, I'm going to drive you back to your place from here so you can get some extra clothes. You'll be staying with us until they get the Ray situation figured out. Astra, Mr. Mackey will give you a ride home from the school."

Astra squawked. "Are you kidding me? In that stinky old pickup? It'll take an hour to get home the way he drives. Why can't I come with you?"

I knew that would be her reaction. I was deciding whether to use the lack-of-room in the truck or the school policy excuse, both of which were seriously lame, when Toni rescued me.

"You don't want to be down in that neighborhood after dark. Not the way you look."

Astra frowned. "The way I look?"

"White. Blonde. Deadly combination, girl."

Astra rolled her eyes, but didn't push it. They ran off to the shower and I looked over to see if Fariba had finished her business with the mysterious strangers. She was nowhere in sight. Daina was walking across the court. She seemed as serious and distracted as Fariba had. "Your friend had to go with those Iranians," she said.

'Friend' was an unusual way to describe a woman she spent hours talking with just a few days ago. "How do you know they're Iranians?"

Daina shrugged. "They were speaking Farsi. She says she will call tomorrow to explain. Says she is sorry to run out."

Daina paused, debating whether to be more helpful or not. "They seemed upset with her even before she came over to talk to them. They mentioned her name several times. Their tone was unpleasant."

Fuck. There was too much going on. One of the reasons I loved coaching was that it was the only time I had some semblance of control over things. In the basketball world we could plot a strategy and execute it and if it didn't work perfectly we could make adjustments. And at the end of game, we either won or lost and that was it. Everyone went home. Out here in the real world, plans, at least my plans, weren't for shit. Everything was out of control. Out of my control anyway.

We waited for all the girls to shower and get on the bus. Daina hugged Astra and told her she played a great game. I could tell by Astra's smile that that meant a lot to her. She was in awe of her mother. Me too. Sometimes. At least when she wasn't pissing me off. Astra impulsively hugged Toni as she was about to step up into the bus. "Don't forget your piercing kit," she said, giggling.

Toni laughed too. "You got it, girl. I've got some black rings that will look totally hot on your pasty skin."

Twenty minutes later I had exited the interstate and was heading into East Claxton. I lived in Claxton all my life, but today I felt like a stranger. A foreigner, actually. On Saltonstall, the old Rib Pit from my youth was now a club blasting music out on to the street so loud it felt as though my truck were vibrating. It was warm for November and the street was crowded with clusters of young and not-so-young, talking, walking, taking it easy. I glanced over at Toni — I had asked her to sit up front to help me with directions, but the real reason was I preferred to keep Daina, with her shocking blonde hair, out of sight in the back.

"Folks having a good time," I said.

Toni nodded as she scanned the neighborhood from one side of the street to the other, like a point guard sizing up the defense. "Everything looks cool tonight."

For a few minutes I relaxed, but that everything's-going-to-be-okay feeling ended the moment I pulled into Monique's driveway. The house was covered with Gangster Disciples graffiti. And I mean covered.

"Fuck me," I said as I put the truck in park in front of the garage door, which had a five foot tall Star of David spray painted on it, bracketed by a large G and D.

"Shit," Toni said, breathing rapidly. "This is bad."

Daina leaned forward in the truck so she could see what we saw. "Okay, Toni. Let's just get in and get out. Five minutes."

I thought about staying in the truck. I wasn't going to be any help to Toni so the right move would have been to stay in the truck with the engine running. Maybe if I had, things would have turned out different. Maybe when Melvin Thigpen, the notorious Gangster Disciple assassin walked up the driveway planning to kill Ray

Tunney, the father of Bedelia's child, he would have spotted me sitting there and run off.

Sure. That was a possibility. Middle-aged white guys are so scary. More likely, everything would have been different because Melvin would have clipped me first, before moving on to his primary target.

Anyway, I didn't stay in the truck because I was scared. Scared for Daina and Toni and scared for myself. I followed them inside. I was relieved that Monique and Bedelia and the baby were not home. Daina would have tried to take the baby and I know that wouldn't have gone down smoothly. But our good luck ended there. Ray was in the alcove to the living room, sprawled like a dead man on the sofa, his crack pipe on the floor next to him.

Daina walked over to him. "Ray. Wake up. Where's Monique? Where's Bedelia and the baby?"

Toni, with a snort of disgust said, "Just leave him be. He's not be going to be able to tell you anything. Fucking loser." She ran past him into her bedroom.

Ray groaned and slurred something unintelligible. He turned away from Daina and covered his head with a pillow. Toni returned in less than three minutes, lugging a large duffel. I took the bag from her and hooked the strap over my shoulder. "Come on, Daina. That kid can't help us. Let's get out of here."

Just as I said those words, Melvin Thigpen pushed open the door. In his right hand he held a 44 Magnum. He gripped it firmly, but it was pointed to the floor, not at us, as though he didn't want to frighten anyone. He smiled pleasantly. "I'm sorry. I wasn't expecting company." His voice was gentle, not much more than a whisper. Melvin was slender and was wearing khaki cargo pants and a black turtleneck. He could have been a Gap model. While the gun got our attention it was his voice that was terrifying. "Put the bag down, please," he whispered politely to me.

I did as he said. He scanned the room. Daina had moved away from the sofa and stood next to Toni. He was trying to figure out who we were. He stepped closer to Toni. "Are you Bedelia?" he asked.

Toni glared at him. "No!"

"Bedelia's not here," Daina said. She was cool and professional. "We don't know where she is."

Thigpen hadn't noticed Ray, passed out on the sofa in the side room. He seemed to be considering what Daina had said. Daina exuded competence and people tended to believe her when she told them something. She didn't lie, and she didn't bullshit, and I suspected that Melvin Thigpen had heard plenty of both in his brief life.

Thigpen smiled sadly and tilted his head and I really think he was about to let us leave, when Ray groaned. Thigpen looked over at Ray, surprised and a little embarrassed that he hadn't noticed him on the sofa. "Ray, Ray. So good to see you again."

Ray, even as stoned as he was, had some sixth sense that warned him he had to do something. He swung his feet on to the floor and struggled to rise from the sofa. Thigpen, who was standing next to me and Daina, perhaps as a courtesy, took a few steps away from us before he raised the Magnum and fired two shots into Ray's chest, knocking him backwards to the floor.

I had never heard anything that loud. My whole body seemed to be vibrating and the ringing in my ears drowned out my screams. Thigpen walked slowly over to where Ray had fallen and even though he was obviously dead, fired a third shot into his face, following some hit man gangbanger protocol I suppose.

He stared down at his feet as Ray's blood soaked into the dirty beige carpet. He sighed and turned slowly toward Toni. He acted sad, as though he sincerely regretted what he had to do. He raised his gun, and as Toni screamed, I squeezed my eyes closed.

Pop. Pop. Pop.

This time the sounds were more like a cap pistol than a that Toni's troubles would follow her out to canon.

I wanted to pray, but I didn't have time. When I opened my eyes, Melvin Thigpen was face down on the carpet, his gun still clutched in his hand. Daina walked quickly over to Ray and wrapped his blood-splattered hand around the grip of her Luger LC9.

"Let's go," she said. Toni, like me, was frozen in place. Daina took her by the hand. "Come on, Toni." She spoke softly and waited for Toni to look at her. "Nothing more we can do here tonight. Darwin, get the bag."

Numb, and in a fog, I stumbled out to the truck. Daina crawled into the backseat with Toni, who was sobbing softly, and wrapped her arms around her. I fumbled for my keys. My hand was shaking so badly I couldn't put the key in the ignition.

"Breathe, Darwin. Just breathe," Daina said. Her voice was soothing, as though we had just survived a minor fender bender, instead of a gangland hit.

I took a deep breath and managed to get the truck started. My arms kept shaking and I was having trouble steering.

"Loosen your grip. We're almost to the highway."

She was right. I was trying to strangle the steering wheel. I turned left on Saltonstall away from the crowds and looked for the signs for the highway. It was grotesquely dark and I could barely see the road.

"Turn on your lights."

I made it to the highway and as everything started looking more familiar I could feel my muscles relax. I took a deep breath and a sob escaped my throat. Hot tears rolled down my cheeks. I was too scared to be embarrassed.

Daina leaned forward from the backseat and whispered in my ear. "It's okay, honey. Everything's going to be okay."

## Chapter 28
*(Saturday, November 19, 2005)*

As we turned into the long driveway to our home, Daina told Toni how she wanted to explain this situation to Astra, and, I guess, the rest of the world. "When police investigate, they'll figure two gang members killed each other. Not interested in what. Not interested in why. Not interested in who. They don't care. You know that, Toni."

Toni whimpered and it appeared from the rearview that she nodded her head.

"I don't want Astra to know I shot that man. We know nothing about shooting. It happened after we left. Is okay, Toni?"

"You saved my life. I'll do anything you want."

"That's all I want."

I was relieved Astra was asleep when we got home. Daina saved all of our lives, but I was still in shock and not ready to face my daughter. Not ready to start lying to her as Daina must have lied to me all these years. Where did she get the gun? How did she learn to shoot? Why didn't she tell me? Who was this woman I've been married to for twenty-five years?

We put Toni in our guest bedroom. Daina helped her get settled in and then she went in and talked to Astra. I took a long shower and then collapsed on our bed. Fear is exhausting. I must have fallen asleep almost immediately, but I woke up when Daina slipped into the bed. I stared up at the ceiling, waiting to see if she would say anything. Offer me an explanation, something. Anything. But she remained silent, as though this were just another night like all the others.

"Where did you get the gun?" I asked finally.

"I thought you were asleep."

"No. I'm not."

She took a deep breath and exhaled like she used to do when she was a smoker. "I got it from Ed Mackey. Last summer. After Stacey got mugged."

One of her co-workers had been assaulted after leaving a house call. Hospitalized for two weeks. "He offered it or you asked him for it?"

"He offered many times. I always refuse. But after Stacey, I changed my mind."

"Not registered, I'm assuming?"

"No. And Ed's guns untraceable. He's careful man."

"Right. Ed's famous for that." I rolled on to my side, away from her. I felt like I was sleeping with a stranger. We all have our secrets and I have accepted for years that Daina has more than her fair share, but this was hard to process.

Daina snuggled up to me and I could feel her warm breath on my neck. "Are you okay?"

"No, not okay, but I'm alive."

It was still dark when I woke. Daina was already up and dressed for work, even though it was Saturday. "Hey," I said. She flinched, as though she had been planning to sneak out undetected.

"Didn't want to wake you. I'm going into work. Have to find Bedelia and Tamara."

"Tamara?"

"The baby."

"Okay." I pulled up the covers and turned away. It thought it was a bad idea, but she wasn't interested in my opinion.

I slept till nine. When I walked into the kitchen Astra and Toni were at the table both texting on their phones. Toni appeared surprisingly normal. Astra looked up from her phone and frowned. "Hi, Dad. Did you hear about the shooting?" she asked. "You guys were sure lucky. It must have happened right after you got Toni's stuff."

I nodded. "Mom told me." As a general rule, I don't mind lying. People who tell the truth all the time make life difficult for everyone. But I hated lying to Astra. "She left early to see if she could find Bedelia and the baby. And Monique," I said. That was more for Toni's benefit.

Toni scowled. "They need to stay lost."

I agreed with Toni, but didn't say anything. I poured a cup of coffee and sat down at the table. The *Tribune* ran the story on page 8, "Two killed in downstate Claxton shooting." No details, but an unnamed spokesmen indicated that the victims appeared to be affiliated with rival gangs.

"Dad, your phone's ringing." Astra said.

I hadn't had many calls on my cellphone since Billy had disappeared. The phone was on the counter, vibrating. Astra picked it up and glanced at the screen. "It's Miss Pahlavi," she said as she handed it to me.

I didn't want to talk to her in front of the girls but it would look suspicious for me to walk out of the kitchen to take the call. As usual, I was overthinking things when it came to Fariba. I took the phone from Astra and pretended I was trying, ineffectively, to answer it. The phone stopped ringing. "Damn, this phone's defective," I said. Technically that was a lie, but it's one of those lies that makes everything work a little smoother. And the price I had to pay was modest.

"Jeez, Coach. You don't know how to answer your own phone," Toni said.

Astra giggled. "Dad, you need to take a course like 'Cellphones for Dummies.'" The girls high-fived each other, celebrating my technical incompetence. Like I said, a small price to pay for preserving my privacy.

I grabbed my AutoPro championship jacket. "I'm going to take a walk. Better cell reception outside," I said, continuing my charade of cellphone ignorance. The girls shook their head at my cluelessness and then went back to their own phones.

As I walked down the driveway the sun was warm on my face, but the air cold and the jacket didn't keep me from shivering. The snow from last week had mostly melted except at the base of the larger trees. All the leaves had fallen and covered the ground like a soggy blanket. I was about to call Fariba back when the phone dinged, indicating a voicemail message. I listened.

> Hi Darwin. Sorry I had to run out without any explanation. Family matter that I need to address. I will be out next week, but I will plan to meet you on Friday at the Orrington for our Bobby Knight clinic. Very much looking forward to that. I hope you and your family have a wonderful Thanksgiving. I'm about to board my plane and have to turn off my phone now. See you Friday.

I could tell from the PA announcements in the background that she was at the United terminal at O'Hare. With that clever sleuthing I had limited her possible destinations to most of the free and not-so-free world. I hoped her family matter didn't require her to return to Iran.

I continued down the driveway, hoping the cold air would clear my head. It needed a lot of clearing. As I reached the end of our driveway, I heard a dog barking. I looked down the road toward Ed Mackey's place and there was Ed, tromping through the field with his dog.

As always, he was wearing his fatigues and the same army jacket he wore when he left the army. Good quality, I guess. His head was shaved and a more normal person would have been shivering, but Ed, a double-barreled shotgun cradled in his arm, seemed impervious to the cold. He was one of those men who projected toughness without ever acting or talking tough. Even in his baggy army jacket it was obvious he was lean and strong. He approached me with the special grace of a soldier: balanced, alert, with a light step. He was accompanied by his golden retriever, Emerson, who was named after Ed's idol, Ralph Waldo Emerson — the dean of self-reliance.

"Thanks for picking up Astra," I said as he drew near. I suppose I should have thanked him for giving Daina that gun, but even though we'd probably all be dead if Daina hadn't acted, I still couldn't come to terms with her having the gun and me not knowing about it.

He nodded and shook my hand. His hands were large, but his grip was gentle, as though he were afraid of crushing my soft basketball hands. "Happy to help. You got her friend out, no problem?"

"We did. Toni's staying with us for a few days."

"I heard there was a gang shooting on the east side last night," he said. I remembered Billy's comment that Ed was the craziest Black man he knew. He made it sound like Ed was a hermit, living off the grid, but Ed seemed to know what was going on.

"I saw that in the paper."

Ed leaned over and rubbed Emerson behind his ears and along his throat. "A senseless goddamn 'turf war.' Nothing changes."

"Are you hunting?"

He patted the dog's flank. "Wild turkey. You folks have any plans for Thanksgiving?"

We usually went out to dinner for the holiday. Daina was always too busy to prepare an elaborate meal. With everything going on, we hadn't even discussed it. "Not that I know of. Daina's not much for cooking. She doesn't like turkey."

Ed smiled, as if I'd challenged him to a duel. "She ain't never tasted my special deep-fried turkey. Y'all come over and I'll serve you a Thanksgiving feast for the ages."

"We got company. Astra's friend is staying with us."

"I know. That's no problem. I serve all races," he said, winking.

There were any number of good reasons why I should have turned him down. But he seemed genuinely excited about the idea and I didn't want to disappoint him. Maybe, I was a little intimidated. And maybe a little curious about the arsenal Billy claimed to have seen. And maybe it was my way of saying 'fuck you' to Daina. Whatever my reasons, I accepted his invitation.

"What time do you want us? And what can we bring?"

"Just your appetite. Come over about two."

## Chapter 29

*(Sunday, November 20, 2005)*

Daina spent all day Saturday looking for Monique, Bedelia and the baby. I was pretending to be asleep when she got home. She undressed quietly and slipped into bed. I remained in pretend sleep. I didn't want to talk to her. She was up before daybreak on Sunday, and with the room still dark, she probably figured I was still asleep. I knew she would hunt all day for Bedelia and her baby and there was no point in giving her my opinion about that mission.

That afternoon I told Astra and Toni we would be having Thanksgiving dinner at Ed Mackey's.

"Is that the old Black dude with the ugly pickup?" Toni asked.

Astra giggled. "It took him over an hour to drive me home. He's not what I expected though. I figured he'd be all Rambo-like."

"Dude looks like Mr. T," Toni said.

"He's actually read 'The Bluest Eye.' Astra said. "We talked about it all the way home from the school. He doesn't have a TV, so he reads a lot."

"That's cool. Are we going to have a real turkey?" Toni asked.

"As opposed to a fake turkey?" Astra said.

"No. I mean a turkey that's, you know, still all together with stuffing inside it. I ain't never had one."

"We're going to have wild turkey," I said. "That's what he was hunting for yesterday."

"Neat," Toni said. "How about pie? Is he going to have pie?"

I was surprised at how excited Toni was at the idea of Thanksgiving with Ed Mackey. Astra too. "He didn't say anything about pie," I said.

Astra jumped up and grabbed a cookbook from the kitchen counter. "We should bring pies," she said.

"Make our own?" Toni asked.

"Yes," Astra said. "What kind should we make, Dad?"

They both grinned at me, as though this were going to be another opportunity for me to show my ignorance. But I knew pies.

When I was a boy I used to ride along with my dad every Saturday when he did his road inspections. We'd always end those trips at Vivian's Pie Shoppe where I would play video games for an hour while dad had a cup of coffee and a slice of pie. It was years before I realized that Dad's interest was in Vivian, not the pies.

"Your best bet is pecan pie," I said. "It doesn't require a top crust which is the trickiest part of pie-making and the ingredients are sugar, butter, molasses and pecans. Those are idiot-proof ingredients. Even rookie pie-makers can't screw it up."

They laughed. "But we should practice, right Coach?" asked Toni. She looked at Astra. "We need to make a practice pie today. And the real pie on Thursday."

And that's what they were doing when Daina walked in the door at 6 p.m. She looked beat, and I should have felt sorry for her, but I didn't. I didn't want anything bad to happen to her clients, and I know I was being selfish, but I didn't want them showing up here. We had enough going on.

"What are you doing?" she asked the girls.

"Practice pie, Mom," Astra said. "We're going to Mr. Mackey's for Thanksgiving."

It wouldn't have been the way I would have let Daina know, but it did prevent her from trying to get out of the invitation.

With her back to the girls she glared at me. "Why?"

"He invited us," I said, shrugging. "Can't turn down Rambo."

The girls laughed. "We're going to have turkey, Mrs. Burr," Toni said with genuine glee.

"Mom doesn't like turkey," Astra said.

A week ago I wouldn't have made the Rambo crack, but something had changed. I was tired of avoiding all the subjects that annoyed Daina. If Ed Mackey was good enough to be her handgun supplier, he ought to be good enough to sit down and have dinner with. Even if she didn't like turkey.

## Chapter 30
*(Monday, November 21, 2005)*

I canceled basketball practice for the week. I wouldn't have been able to focus on the team, and with Fariba out, and only three days of school because of the holiday, I had a convenient excuse.

Daina was in the shower when I woke up. She came out of the bathroom towel-drying her hair and gave me a look I interpreted as, "I'm pissed at you, but we have to talk."

"What?" I said.

"You will probably get call today from Mark Sanchez. He investigates gangs."

"I thought you already talked with him."

"I told him we were at house with Toni to get her stuff. He wants to know what you saw. Different perspective." She shrugged. "He has your work number."

"Okay." Not much I could say to that. "Those women must be in hiding, right?" I know we were both thinking worst case scenarios. Hard not to after seeing what the Disciples did to Ray. And probably would have done to us, if not for Daina.

"I hope so. Monique has family in Alabama. Maybe…" She sighed.

Daina was visibly upset. Sad, even, which was not a natural emotion for her. Part of me wanted to wrap my arms around her and tell her everything was going to be okay. But I couldn't do that. Things weren't going to be okay. Not for a long time. Maybe not ever. Still, I hated to see her hurting and I felt shitty that I couldn't do anything about it.

When I got to work, I had a message to call Mark Sanchez. I called him back and agreed to meet him at the Claxton police station on Main Street at 9 a.m. I wanted to get it over as soon as possible. Kelly told me Stephanie would be coming in tomorrow with the "FBI dork."

"I assume she didn't call him that," I said.

Kelly smiled. "No. But that's what she meant."

Something in the way she said that made me believe Kelly had more conversations with Stephanie than she was letting on. But maybe I was just paranoid. Imagining secret rendezvous. "I'll be here."

Kelly bit her lip. "Did you, uh, you know, take care of that file?"

I glared at her, trying to imagine where they might hide a wire on someone wearing a tight tee-shirt and painted on jeans. Maybe in her bra. Or the belt buckle on her cowboy belt. "I don't know what you're talking about."

Her mouth twisted into an uneven frown, as if she had something stuck in her teeth. "Are you going to bring that stuff to him on Friday?"

"You're starting to annoy me. I have to go to a meeting. I'll be back before noon."

Her face fell. "I'm sorry, Darwin. I can't help it."

I smiled and opened my arms for a hug. "It's okay, Kelly." I held her tightly and gave her a quick butt cup to show we were still friends. Also to see if I could detect any kind of monitoring devices.

She shoved me away good naturedly. "You asshole. You're worse than Sleepy. But you don't smell as bad."

Mark Sanchez had spent twenty years with the Chicago P.D. He worked from a battered gray metal desk in the corner of the Claxton police station. The two chairs in front of his desk were piled high with files.

"Sorry, Mr. Burr. I'm a little short on space." He grabbed a stack from one of the chairs and set them on the floor next to his desk. He shook his head, ruefully. "This was supposed to be my pre-retirement job. Not working out the way I planned. You want some coffee? It's not very good."

Sanchez had Semper Fi tattooed on his left forearm and had the build of a middleweight boxer. Dark hair with streaks of grey and a Chicago accent with a trace of his Mexican roots. His easygoing manner made him appear to be a nice guy, but one who could turn nasty if he had to. I didn't plan to let that happen.

"I already had my bad coffee for the day. Thanks." I looked around his desk. "This is all gang-related stuff?"

"I'm afraid so. And it's going to get worse." He dug through a pile of papers on his desk and pulled out a dog-eared manila folder with the tab heading scratched out. "I talked yesterday to…" he scanned the folder, "Dina? That's your wife?"

"Daina. D, A, I, N, A. It's a Latvian name."

He nodded. "Got it." He scratched out the name he had written and rewrote it. "Nice lady. Sounds as though you folks were very lucky. That hit went down right after you were at the house."

I nodded and shook my head trying to express my disbelief without saying anything. If I could get away without lying to a police officer I figured that would be a good thing.

"You all were there to fetch some clothes for that girl …" he looked at his folder again, "Toni Wallace?"

"Right. She's staying with us."

"Why is that?" Sanchez asked. He was nonchalant, but I figured he had to know the answer.

"Daina thought it was dangerous for her to be in that house with her cousin's boyfriend living there."

Sanchez chuckled humorlessly. "That's got to be one of the best social worker calls of all time." He shook his head as he looked at the file again. "I just don't get it."

Against my better judgement, I played along with him. "What's that?"

"This guy Ray is a lightweight loser. A goof. But somehow he manages to get off three shots before Thigpen — who is a stone killer; a primo assassin — clips him." He shrugs. "I want to believe it. Two bad guys kill each other, that sounds like a win-win. But it bugs me. Just doesn't smell right." He shuddered and closed the file. "Sorry. Enough of my cop angst. So when you were there, Mr. Burr, did you see anything? Do you think it is possible Ray was there, maybe hiding?"

I sat back in the folding chair and ran my hand over my head as though I were trying to think back to that day. "We were only there a couple minutes. I was scared."

"Why was that?"

"The gang graffiti on the house."

"That was new?"

This guy was sharper than Hildebrand. I reminded myself that I only needed to lie when there was no other option. Tell the truth as much as possible, because the truth is easier to remember. "Wasn't there when I took Daina to the house a week ago."

"That's when you met Toni?"

"Right. She was playing ball in the driveway. Got her to come out for our basketball team."

Sanchez nodded and wrote something on his notepad. "Did you know she had a gang affiliation?"

Fuck. "Toni?" No way was Toni involved in a gang. "No. That's hard to believe."

"Why?"

"Because she was so upset when she learned that that guy Ray was tagging Gangster sites."

"Her father was in the Vice Lords."

"I don't know anything about that." He was like a boxer. He'd get me looking for his right and then he delivered a left to the gut.

"He was killed by a Gangster Disciple in one of their turf wars. Ten years ago. In the projects."

"Like I said, I don't know anything about that."

He grunted as though he didn't necessarily believe me. "So you didn't see Ray when you were at the house?"

"No."

"But he could have been hiding?" Sanchez asked.

It was one of those intentionally stupid questions meant to trigger smart-assed responses and I wasn't going to fall into that trap. "Sure

179

it's possible. I didn't look around the house. We just got in and got out as fast as we could."

Sanchez tilted his head from one side to the other as if he were weighing all of my fascinating answers. "Toni's staying with you folks now?"

"Just temporarily."

"I'll tell you what I told your wife. That's not a good idea. She should be a ward of the court. If she's got troubles with the Disciples it's going to follow her. Right out to your safe little house in the country."

I pushed back from the desk. "That's Daina's call, not mine. Do you have any more questions for me?"

Sanchez stood up and shook my hand. "Just be careful, Mr. Burr. These folks don't play by any rules."

I heard what he didn't have to say. Toni staying with us, even though she was innocent, was putting my own daughter at risk.

## Chapter 31
*(Tuesday, November 22, 2005)*

I had a lousy night's sleep trying to figure out what I should do. I couldn't talk to Daina. She was wearing herself out trying to find Monique and Bedelia and the baby. Each day that passed without word made it more likely she was never going to hear from them. Whatever happened to them, it wasn't Daina's fault. But she wasn't interested in hearing that, and if I told her about my meeting with Sanchez it would make things even worse. If Daina knew Sanchez suspected Toni, I'm certain she would confess to killing Thigpen. I didn't want her to do that.

I finally fell asleep just before dawn and when I awoke an hour later, Daina had already left for work. It was windy, and icy sleet pounded me as I walked from the kitchen to my truck parked in the driveway. Looking back, that was the high point of my day.

When Stephanie and Poindexter showed up looking for Billy four weeks ago everything started to go to hell. We finally reached that destination today, about five minutes after I sat down at my desk. It was just after eight, and neither Stephanie nor Kelly had shown up yet. That was unusual, but not unwelcomed. I was enjoying the tranquility as I waited for Felipe's coffee to become less scalding. The solitude was short lived.

At ten minutes past eight, with a loud bang, the door to the bullpen was flung open and a phalanx of men and women wearing blue windbreakers with FBI plastered across the back, poured into the office with guns drawn. Three of them surrounded the two data entry operators and screamed at them to step away from their computer consoles as if they were about to launch cruise missiles instead of coding inventory tickets.

The first agent through the door, who I assumed to be the leader of the contingent, was clutching an official looking document instead of a handgun, like the others. He yelled in my direction, "Who's in charge here?"

Stephanie's office was dark. So was the conference room. I stood in the doorway of my office wondering where in the hell was nice old George Hildebrand.

The document-waver quickly assessed that I was the only management type on the floor. "Sir? What's your name?" The agent was blond with a bad military haircut. He had a pumped up look, like a weightlifter.

"Darwin Burr."

He looked down at a sheet which contained a list of distribution center employees. "You're assistant to the Distribution Center Manager, correct?"

"Yes."

"Where is your manager?"

"I don't know."

He frowned. "That's Stephen Washington, correct?"

"Stephanie."

He frowned again and looked back at his sheet. "Correct. Are you expecting her?"

I expected that Stephanie and George Hildebrand would be in the office waiting for me. They were both early bird types. "I expect her soon."

The agent looked around at his squad. They seemed to be frozen at strategic locations around the office waiting for a signal. "Okay." He handed me the document. "This is a court-ordered warrant to search the premises — office and warehouse. We can handle the office without assistance. I want all your office personnel to remain in the conference room." He pointed to the trucker's coffee room where I first met with Poindexter and Washington. "I request that you ask your warehouse personnel to assist us with our search of the warehouse. We need to move pallets and open cartons."

I was about to offer to call Paul Meron, the warehouse manager, when Stephanie burst through the doors almost as loudly and dramatically as the FBI had. "What's going on?" she asked the agent with the search warrant. It was Bad-ass Stephanie, and she looked exceptionally pissed. She marched up to him and squinted at the badge he was wearing on a leather cord around his neck. "What are you doing here, Agent Beatty?" She said Beatty like it was a curse.

"Executing a search warrant, Ma'am. What is your name?"

"I'm Stephanie Washington, Manager of the Claxton AutoPro Distribution Center."

"Good. Always best to deal with the boss." He took the search warrant back from me and handed it to Stephanie.

She quickly flipped through the pages of the document. "This didn't come from George Hildebrand," she said, waving the document in the agent's face.

"This case has been transferred to Chicago. It's no longer Agent Hildebrand's responsibility."

"Why?"

It was a good question.

"Chicago has jurisdiction. It's an international case. I was asking Mr. Burr to instruct his warehouse personnel to assist us in the search of the warehouse. Moving crates and opening packages."

International case? How did Billy's real estate deals turn into an international case?

Stephanie's face tightened around the mouth, but that was it for any emotion. She stayed cool. "Darwin, will you please assist the agents with their warehouse search. The quicker we help them, the quicker we can get back to normal."

Nothing was going to get back to normal anytime soon. And for me, probably never. They had started to cart off the files from the store room. Everything, sealed or unsealed. Kelly would have had a fit, but she wasn't here. Although I felt a little guilty about it, I was having bad thoughts about Kelly.

I walked out to the warehouse where a different swarm of agents surrounded Meron, who had stepped down from his forklift when they stormed the warehouse.

Meron was an ex-Marine. A tough nut like Ed Mackey. I valued him because he told the truth and didn't worry about sucking up to authority. But the FBI was a totally different kind of authority than some suit from AutoPro and Meron, while not cowed, was not spitting tobacco juice on the floor either.

I put my arm around his back and yelled over the forklift noise, "Give them whatever they want. Full cooperation is the order of the day."

Meron nodded. "They're only interested in the shipments from Spartan, L&B and Jasper," he yelled in a voice that was easy to hear even with all the background noise. Those were all specialty supplier deals that Billy had set up in the last six months. I remembered the performance crankshaft I had asked Meron to stow for Billy. Maybe there was something more illicit than a steel crank in that carton.

Meron could have had one of his drivers help them, but he did it all himself and I was grateful for that. He was the world's fastest forklift driver. In ten minutes he had pulled eight pallets holding a hundred crankshaft boxes off the shelf and in another ten minutes he had used his box-cutter to slice through the packing tape on the cartons, so all the agents had to do was flip open the box. Each one was supposed to contain a crankshaft, a set of bearings and a tube of installation lube.

Meron printed out an inventory register for all the pulled stock which he gave to the two FBI agents. Before they opened each box they methodically checked it off the inventory register. The first forty-five cartons all had a crankshaft, bearings and lube. Nothing out of the ordinary. The forty-sixth carton was the performance crankshaft.

"This one is not on the list," the senior of the two agents said to Meron. "And it doesn't have a barcode."

Meron frowned and looked over the inventory list. He shrugged. "Sometimes we miss one," he said. He had that air of authority; a competent guy doing his job just like the agents. They nodded and wrote the product on their inventory sheet. The two agents looked at each other grimly and then the younger agent stepped back while the more senior one kneeled next to the carton and carefully lifted up the lid, as though he were defusing a bomb. I held my breath.

Inside was a shiny steel crankshaft, with bearings and lube. Nothing else. I was relieved, and let down. I had really expected that there would be something more dramatic.

It took them almost three hours to open all the crankshaft, transmission and oil pump crates and cartons we had inventoried. I didn't ask them what they were looking for and they didn't volunteer that information. When they started the hunt, they had a bounce to their step. They were confident they were going to find something. Something big. But by the start of the second hour their enthusiasm had waned considerably. And by the third hour, they were playing out a game where the outcome is no longer in doubt and everyone just wants to get it over with and go home.

It was after one o'clock and I was starving by the time I made it back up to the bullpen. There were no agents in sight and the office looked as though we'd hired a very bad moving company. Desks had been opened, manuals rifled through, and the store room had been emptied. Literally. The filing cabinets were all gone.

Stephanie came out of her office holding a slice of pepperoni pizza, with a take-no-prisoners look on her face. But she lightened up when she realized it was me and not another FBI stormtrooper. She even smiled. Sort of. "Hey, Darwin," she said with a sigh. "Fuck of a day, huh?"

"Where did you get that pizza?" I asked.

"The Feebs bought a dozen from Delfortes. Didn't eat half of them. They're in the conference room. Come on."

I followed her into the break room that usually smelled like trucker BO and burnt coffee. It still did, but now there was the added aroma of melted cheese and Italian sausage. I grabbed a slice of sausage and mushroom and plopped down in the folding chair. I'd been standing out in that warehouse for three hours and my knees and back were killing me. "They took all the filing cabinets?" I asked.

She shrugged. "They were making such a mess, trying to pull out the folders and rebox them, that I suggested they take the whole cabinet. Then maybe we won't have to re-file everything when we get the stuff back. If we get it back."

"Why did they yank the case away from Hildebrand?" I thought of him as a sort of a stumblebum but with decent impulses. The same with those junior analysts with him.

Stephanie grabbed another slice of pizza — she was definitely a pepperoni fan. She looked around the conference room. "I wish we had some beer."

"Billy had a bottle of Jim Beam—"

"Those assholes took it," Stephanie said. "Grabbed all of Kelly's party photos too. You're lucky she gave me your Ray Charles pic. They'd probably arrest you for politically incorrect costuming."

"It was Stevie Wonder. I can get us beer."

"Great. I'll even drink it warm."

She was clearly stressed by the FBI invasion, but she was dealing with it. I had to admire that. "We're not that desperate, Hold on." I picked up the phone and dialed Meron in the warehouse.

"What do you need?" Meron said, with his usual growl.

"Feds leave yet?"

"They just drove off. We're putting the stuff back now. Fuckers didn't offer to help with that. They seemed pretty disappointed."

"Too bad for them. The Feds left a bunch of pizzas up here. How about I trade you, a cold six-pack of Bud for four Delforte pizzas."

"You drinking alone?"

"No." I winked at Stephanie. "I'm having lunch with the boss." Stephanie gave me the finger, which I thought was cool.

"Beer for pizzas? Sounds like a good deal. I'll be right up."

I grinned at Stephanie, unreasonably proud of my shrewd negotiating ability. "Meron says the Feds went away disappointed. What were they looking for?"

She sat down across the table from me and eyed the last slice of pepperoni. "I have a call into Sean Fitzpatrick — he's the U.S. Attorney I worked for. Something had to change for Chicago to take over Hildebrand's case. Sean will know. Oh, I almost forgot." She hustled out of the coffee room and returned a minute later with an envelope. "Here's your letter from Randall Judd, assuring you that your retirement assets are safe and secure. I'm impressed. You've got almost two million dollars in that account. You might want to diversify a little."

My whole 401k was invested in AutoPro stock. With company matching contributions and the twenty percent plus growth of the AutoPro stock, the account had grown impressively, which was why before the Billy fiasco I figured I would be in good shape to retire in another seven years. "I'm a company man. I thought I might take one of those 401k loans. Redmond said I can get up to fifty thousand."

Stephanie stared at me as if she were wondering if I were kidding. "You're not planning to run off, too, are you?"

"Can't run very far on fifty grand. I might give it to my attorney, just in case AutoPro changes their mind and I can't get at my money when I need it."

Stephanie nodded. "That's not going to happen. But it's not a bad idea either. I didn't know you had an attorney."

I didn't, but Stephanie didn't need to know that. "Isn't everyone supposed to have an attorney these days?"

Meron appeared in the doorway holding two six-packs of Michelob.

I stood up. "Stephanie, this is Paul Meron, our invaluable warehouse manager and world class stock car driver. Paul, this is Stephanie Washington." I didn't bother with her title. He knew she was the boss.

Meron gestured like he was tipping his hat to Stephanie, but he wasn't wearing a hat. "How do you do, Ma'am. I thought if you were drinking with Darwin you better have an extra six pack, because that boy can pound them down when he gets going."

Stephanie stood up and reached for the six pack Meron held out for her. "How thoughtful," she said, grinning broadly. "And Michelob. I'm impressed."

"Yes Ma'am. That's our management beer." He set the other six pack on the table.

I picked up the four pizzas that hadn't been opened yet and handed them to him. "For you and the crew. Thanks for all your help."

Stephanie nodded her assent. "Sorry that you've had your day all messed up. I'm hopeful we'll get things back to normal soon."

"It's not a problem, Ma'am." He turned toward me. "Nothing from Billy?"

I shook my head. "No. Nothing." *And I hope I don't hear from him. Not now.*

Stephanie's phoned buzzed. She stared at the screen and then answered it. "Sean? Can you hold for one minute?" She looked at me. "I have to take this call. Don't drink all the beer." She grabbed the last slice of pepperoni and a Michelob. "Thanks for the beer, Paul."

Meron looked over his shoulder at her as she walked out of the conference headed for her office. He gave me his she's okay look. "Billy's fucked, isn't he?"

"Looks that way. Maybe not just Billy, either."

Meron frowned. "You need anything done, just let me know. Anything." That was not a trivial offer. Paul Meron was a man who could get things done.

"Thanks. I will."

Meron gathered up the four pizzas, gave another salute and walked out the door, headed in the opposite direction from Stephanie, back to his crew in the warehouse.

I sat back down and twisted the cap off a Michelob. It was icy cold and I must have been thirsty because I had nearly finished a second beer before Stephanie returned from her call. I could tell that whatever she learned from her ex-boss, it was worse than she expected.

She sat down at the table and grabbed a fresh beer. She looked at me and then studied the beer bottle as if there might be some answer written on the label. She started to speak and then stopped. She started again and stopped.

"Just tell me, Stephanie."

"Sean says the Feds think Billy is involved in some kind of terrorism."

"What!" I pounded the table with my fist, bouncing the second six-pack on to the floor. The bottles didn't break, which was the first good thing that had happened today. "You gotta be fucking kidding. That's crazy."

Stephanie held up her hands. "They apparently have a confidential informant who has linked Billy with a Shia sect. Different from Al Qaeda. Iranians. This is high profile now."

Iranians? I remembered Walter telling me about Fariba's uncle and how he was worth "billions." I was sure Billy had some involvement with the uncle. But there was no way Billy would ever be involved with terrorists. "How do all those real estate deals you grilled me on having anything to do with terrorists?"

She shook her head. "I don't know. I don't think it does. This is something new. They have Interpol involved. They don't think he's in the country anymore."

Not in the country. But according to Kelly, he was still in Chicago, waiting for his cash. "So what now?"

"I don't know. But if you hear from Billy, let me know immediately. And don't, whatever you do, go see him. Don't help him. He's toxic, Darwin. They think he's a terrorist, and they are not going to fuck around. You get swept up in this and you could disappear down a hole so deep know no one's ever going to find you."

But I was already swept up in it. And now I realized that it didn't matter if Billy were involved with terrorists or not. It only mattered that the government thought he was involved.

## Chapter 32
*(Wednesday, November 23, 2005)*

Daina was at the kitchen table reading the *Tribune* when I came downstairs. This was the first morning since the shooting that she had not been off to work before I woke up. I didn't ask her about her missing clients. If there had been any good news she would have mentioned it.

I poured myself a cup of coffee. Eggs, bacon, flour and a large tub of sour cream were staged on the kitchen counter. "Are you making Piragi?" I asked.

She looked up from her newspaper and smiled wearily. The stress of the last week was evident. Worry lines were etched in the corners of her mouth. "I'm going to teach girls. We make for Ed Mackey."

"Sounds great. Where are the girls?" I asked. I had been dropping them at school on my way to work, but they were nowhere to be seen.

"No school, so they sleep late."

"No school?"

She put down the newspaper and took a cleansing breath, as though she were trying to push through labor. "There was brawl yesterday so principal closes school until Monday. Cooling off period." She made a face that made it clear she didn't agree with the decision.

"Who was fighting?"

"Toni said started as argument between pledges of Vice Lords and Gangster Disciples."

"Pledges? Those aren't fraternities."

"That's what she called them. She is worried."

I sat down across from her and grabbed the paper. In the center of the front page was a photo of an FBI agent in a blue windbreaker carting off a file carton. For an instant, I thought they were reporting on the raid on AutoPro yesterday. But that would have hardly been *Tribune*-worthy news. The caption revealed that the agent was in Manhattan removing files from The Free Iran Coalition — an Iranian dissident organization.

"Toni should be worried. Do you think she's tied in with one of the gangs."

Daina set her coffee cup down on the table and stared at me as though she were trying to decide whether to tell me the truth or not. This time she went with the truth. "Her father in Vice Lords. Killed by Disciples. She has no love for gangs. Especially that gang."

If Daina knew that, so did the Disciples. "We need to get her out of there."

"I know." Her hand trembled as she held her cup of coffee. "I don't know what to do."

I didn't know either. All our plays were bad. We needed a new game plan.

The day before Thanksgiving is one of the slowest days of the year at AutoPro. I thought that would be a good thing. I figured we would need some time to regroup. But when I arrived just after eight, in the warehouse, everything was business as usual — Paul Meron was not about to let his organization get disrupted by a couple of FBI agents — and in the office the two data entry operators and the three bookkeepers had been at work since seven getting the bullpen back in shape. Other than the empty file room, there was no evidence of yesterday's fiasco. Even the pizza boxes and beer bottles had been disposed of.

I knew Stephanie was not coming in. She had told me last week that her son's bail had been reduced. She and her husband were posting the bond and were bringing Devante home this morning. Her family would be together for Thanksgiving. I felt good for her. We were not on the same team, but she treated me fair. She was a stand up woman and I respected her.

I didn't hear from Kelly yesterday. I suspected she wouldn't show up today and I was right. She had called in before I arrived and left a message that she was sick. I didn't believe her, but I was glad she wasn't coming in because I didn't know what I would say to her.

When Billy was around, I checked my cellphone all the time, because he was always texting me. And while most of his texts were bullshit, I had to keep checking because sometimes he was alerting me to the imminent arrival of some vendor or customer he had promised something. After Billy disappeared I got out of the habit of checking for texts. This morning, as I hung up my coat, I glanced at the phone as I pulled it from my coat pocket and saw that Fariba sent a text at 3 a.m.

Greeting from Basel . We have moved  mother here. Getting her settled. Will explain on Friday. Arriving late to hotel. But will knock on your door. Okay? Miss you very much. Difficult week. Love F.

I didn't have to look in a mirror to know I was grinning like an idiot. Everything was falling apart around me but one cryptic message from Fariba and I get all giddy like a teenager. I knew love didn't mean "love," but it meant something. I composed a half dozen different replies. They all sucked. Finally I got tired of trying and typed: *Hell yes, knock on the door. Doesn't matter how late. I miss you too. Love D.* But the text didn't go through. I tried to find someone at AT&T who could help me, but after five minutes on hold I gave up. My message was lame anyway. I reminded myself to leave a note at the Orrington for her when I checked in on Friday.

There was a long queue of voice mail messages on my office phone. Most of them were from vendors who heard about the raid. They didn't need to hear from me today. There was a message from Mark Sanchez. I didn't call him back, either. I wasn't ready to talk to him again. I figured with the flare-up at the high school there was nothing good that he was going to share with me. He couldn't solve our problem. The last message was from Stephanie. She sounded happy and I hoped that was because she had sprung Devante. She had a criminal lawyer — a former colleague — she wanted me to contact. "Even innocent people need criminal lawyers," she said. She reminded me of her son's plight and told me to call her ASAP.

I knew she was right. If I'd learned anything from watching all those years of *Law and Order* it was that a good lawyer makes a huge difference. My money was all tied up. I needed good financial advice and the guy I always relied on for that, Billy, couldn't help me now. I called Frank Redmond. His office gal said he wasn't in, which I didn't believe. I called his cellphone and he didn't answer. I called it again. And again. On the third try he answered and despite his misgivings, he agreed to see me in his office.

They weren't going to miss me at AutoPro today. As I headed down to the parking lot, I routed myself through the warehouse so I could let Meron know I was leaving. He was, as usual, on his forklift, organizing stock, like a cowboy herding cattle. I waved to him and he dismounted and walked over to me.

"What's up?" he asked.

"Taking off for the day. Keep an eye on things. You can close up early, if you want."

"Sounds good. The crew will appreciate that. Y'all have a good Thanksgiving."

I thanked him and started to walk away, but then I had another of my brilliant ideas. "Hey, Paul. You know that performance crank Spartan shipped to Billy?"

"What about it?"

"Is that something you could use?"

He scratched his head. "Hell yes. That's a 4340 forged crank. Put it in one of my small blocks it could handle seven hundred horses no problem."

I laughed. He might as well have been speaking Farsi. "You know I have no fucking clue what you're talking about, right? Take it. Billy's not going to use it and we don't need it around when our auditors start doing yearend inventory."

Meron actually smiled. "Thanks, boss."

As I waited outside Redmond's office for him to get off the phone, I got a text from Sanchez.

NEED TO SEE YOU ASAP

I guessed that the caps was his way of telling me he was pissed. In my playbook, it's not good to have the cops pissed at you. I texted him back that I would see him when I was out of my meeting. *Okay,* he texted instantly, but at least he dropped the caps.

Redmond hung up the phone and waved me into his office. I knew he feared I would bring up another Billy project so when I told him I wanted to execute a 401k loan he was all smiles and good ole boy again. The old Frank. He pulled out a form and started writing on it. "How much do you want?"

"Fifty thousand."

He raised his eyebrows, but wrote the figure on the form. "You've got plenty of equity. That's not a problem. Going to buy a boat?" He belly laughed.

"Actually, I want to buy some diamonds. Where did you get that last bunch?" He stopped laughing and dropped the pen on his desk with disgust. "Come on, Burr. Don't fuck with me."

I stared hard at him. "I'm not. And I need them today."

He folded his hands on his desk and took a breath like Daina had done earlier today. A try-to-stay-calm breath. "Okay. You need this loan. I can do that. But diamonds?" he shook his head. "Not going to happen."

"Why not?"

"It would take me at least a week. And the discount is obscene. For fifty thousand dollars you'd get maybe twenty thousand dollars of diamonds."

I didn't think he was lying to me. I hadn't thought about where the diamonds would come from. It didn't seem likely there were any freewheeling diamond merchants in Claxton.

Redmond rubbed his chin and looked around his office. He picked up a plastic-sealed coin that was on his desk. His eyes got wide. "I have an idea." He handed me the coin. "This is better than diamonds. No discount."

I looked at the coin. "A Krugerrand?"

"That's right. And…" He punched some numbers into his desktop calculator. "Gold is selling today for $504 an ounce. A Krugerrand is an ounce of gold and tracks the spot price. For fifty thousand dollars I could get you ninety coins. Carry them in these little plastic tubes. Easy as pie. Wouldn't weigh more than six pounds." He pulled from his desk drawer a tube that looked like it held about twenty coins.

"At five hundred dollars an ounce, I should get a hundred coins," I said.

Redmond smiled, like a carnival barker. "Five hundred and four dollars per ounce. And there's commissions and handling fees and a lot a red tape if you go to a bank and try to buy them. But I happen to be a collector and I can sell you out of my private stock."

Ninety Krugerrands would be worth close to $45,000. That should be enough to retain an attorney and have something left over for other emergencies. I made the deal with Redmond and stuffed the five tubes of Krugerrands into my jacket pockets. I was weighted down, but not noticeably. I would stop by and see Sanchez, but I wasn't planning on taking off the jacket.

I didn't have to. I literally ran into him as I hiked up the steps of the Claxton police station. My head was down and my arms were snugging my Krugerrand jacket to my body as a blustery prairie wind threatened to blow my fifty thousand dollar loan down the main street of Claxton. Sanchez was headed down the steps clutching a Big Mac and a large coke. It looked as though he hadn't slept in two days.

"Watch it," he shouted. And then "Oh, hey, Mr. Burr," We stood nose to nose on the steps. Nose-to-nose because he was on the step above me. He tilted his head back to the entrance. "Step into the lobby. I got something I need to tell you."

I followed him up the steps, grateful to get out of the wind.

He set his burger and coke on the receptionist desk. "All hell is breaking loose here so I don't have much time. You heard about the incident at the school yesterday?"

"My wife told me."

"We're trying to head off this turning into a full scale gang war. We got too much going on right now, putting out fires — metaphorically and real — but Monday I want you or your wife to bring in Toni Wallace. We need to talk to her and she needs to be put in some kind of foster care."

"Why do you want to talk to her?" It was obvious he wasn't telling me everything.

He took a slurp of his coke and fought back a burb. His phone buzzed for the third time since we had started talking. He glanced at it and shook his head. "Man I don't have time for this. Here it is as plain as I can make it. The Gangster Disciples figure Toni whacked their boy. It couldn't have been that dipshit Tunney. I know that. And they know that too. They've got Toni pegged as the shooter. Like father, like daughter. I can protect her. We're not going to arrest her for offing that creep. I'm sure it was self-defense. I can get her sent someplace where they won't reach out. If she's stays with you, you're all at risk." He sucked up the last of his coke and threw the cup and the remains of his Big Mac in the trash. "Fucking food is going to kill me."

I didn't say anything because I didn't know what to say.

"You understand, Mr. Burr?" He stared hard at me and for a moment I was worried he was going to make his point by poking me in the Krugerrand. But his phone tweeted again and he stepped back to answer it.

"I understand." I said. I waved at him and walked down the steps to my car.

## Chapter 33
*(Thursday, November 24, 2005)*

The girls spent all morning in the kitchen with Daina preparing their desserts. Daina showed them how to make Piragi and how to roll out the crust for the pecan pie and how to flute the edges. It was a surreal experience, as though I were in some episode of the Twilight Zone where I go to bed in a world of gangs, terrorists and FBI investigations and wake up in Norman Rockwell land. All that was missing was for Daina to be wearing an apron, instead of her baggy Cubs sweatshirt, which was splotched with floury fingerprints.

The house was so much more lively with two girls. Daina and I were only children. I wanted Astra to grow up with a brother or sister. It was one of the few domestic issues where I knew I was right. But Daina didn't want another kid — she didn't have time — it would mess with her Daina Plan. I used to tell myself in the years after Astra was born, that I gave it my best shot, trying to convince Daina to have another kid. But that was a lie. I could have and should have tried harder.

I try not to play the wish game. You can't win. Life doesn't give mulligans. They say eighty percent of life is just showing up. That's what I did. My life was unexamined and that was fine with me. Adam and Eve before they took that bite. I never thought my life was perfect, but it was good enough.

I kept everything on track until last month when the wheels started to come off. First, Billy fucks up my easy-as-pie job, then Fariba makes me desire something I can never have, while Stephanie tries to convince me I could be something I'm never going to be, and then, if all that's not enough, I discover Toni and she shows me what we could have been if I'd just had the guts to change Daina's mind.

I watched Daina as she showed Toni how to roll out the pie crust and I have to believe she must have seen it too. We would have been a better family if we'd had another kid. For an instant, watching them, I thought it might still be possible. Maybe we could, if not adopt Toni, keep her. A guardianship or something? But I quickly came back to reality. A month from now I could be in jail, Toni would still be at risk, and with Detective Sanchez on the case, who knows what might be in store for Daina. Norman Rockwell wasn't happening.

I walked back into the kitchen to pour another cup of coffee. Astra and Toni were giggling. "You ask him," Astra said.

"Shut up, Astra," Toni said with a stage-whisper.

"What?" I said.

"Daddy?" Astra said. She never called me Daddy. Not a good sign. "Could you drive to the Farmer's Market and get us some sweet potatoes?"

I expected something far worse than a minor shopping errand, so I was relieved. "What for? Mackey will have potatoes, I'm sure."

"I want to make sweet potato pie," Toni said. She was smiling as if that was some kind of joke I didn't get.

Daina walked back in to check on her Piragi which was in the oven filling the kitchen with the mouth-watering smell of bacon and fresh pastry. "She wants to be represented," Daina said. She seemed to be in on the joke.

"Mrs. Burr is bringing a Latvian dessert, Astra is bringing a white-folks pie, so I want to bring sweet potato pie, the dessert of my people." They both laughed.

I stared blankly at them. I felt like the only sober guy in a roomful of drunks. "You like that pie, Toni?"

They laughed some more. I was killing them with my one-liners.

"She's never had it," Astra said. "Her family dessert was HoHos."

"Shut up, Astra." Toni punched her in the arm. "It was Twinkies."

"I know, but I like saying HoHos." Astra stopped laughing, but her chin was trembling. "We looked it up, Dad. According to Wikipedia, sweet potato pie is the favorite dessert of the African-American community."

Daina pulled the Piragi from the oven and set the tray on the counter. "Is simple pie. We can make it easy. But need potatoes," Daina said.

I had already grabbed my jacket. "I'll be back in twenty minutes. How many do you need?"

"Enough for a pie," Toni said and they all burst out laughing again.

The farmer's market — it was actually just a self-help vegetable stand in front of the McGrady farmhouse — was five miles north on Hoover Road, a few hundred yards before the intersection with the interstate. As I pulled on to Hoover, the road was empty. But, surprisingly, a black SUV pulled on to the highway ahead of me from one of the dead-end snowmobile trailheads. They had to be lost. The county didn't do a good job of marking the roads, and kids were always stealing the signs. The SUV pulled away from me, but a quarter mile farther up the road it turned into another dead end. As I passed that intersection I glanced over and I could see the driver had figured out it was a wrong turn and was ready to pull back on to the highway.

The SUV closed on me fast. It was an MDX just like Billy drove, only this one was black and all the windows were tinted. I couldn't clearly see the driver or his passenger, but I could hear their sound system. It was cranked up to full-volume, blasting some kind of hip hop thing. The bass was heavy and I could feel the reverberation in my head. I slowed down and they blasted the horn and then swung out and passed me going at least eighty. They had Illinois plates: DGB 747: Darwin Good Boy 747, like the passenger plane; I said it out loud, which usually helped me to remember stuff. I would write it down when I got home, just in case.

At the next intersection, also unmarked, they turned east again. But this time they had pulled on to Grennan Road, which would take them all the way to Vivian's Pie Shoppe just outside of Geneva. I don't think they were looking for pie.

A week ago, if I had spotted this SUV with two Black guys driving it (I was guessing they were Black) I wouldn't have given it a second thought. But now, after Sanchez's warning that Toni's troubles would follow her out to the country, I was worried. As I passed the intersection I looked east, but the road was deserted. Maybe they had found whatever it was they were looking for. I wanted to believe that, but I didn't.

# Chapter 34

*(Thursday, November 24, 2005)*

I wasn't going to tell Daina about the SUV. I told myself it was because I figured she would just dismiss it out of hand, but the real reason was I was afraid she wouldn't dismiss it. I was trying to ignore the threat, hoping it would go away. But hoping hadn't worked so well for me lately, so while we sat in the truck waiting for the girls to come out, I told her. And she didn't dismiss it. Her face was pinched.

"We need to get away. They'll find our road eventually."

"I could skip the basketball clinic. We could go someplace for the weekend."

"If you don't go to clinic, girls will figure out. I don't want to scare them."

Toni and Astra emerged from the house. Dressed in jeans and sweaters like they often wore, but more stylish. They had done something to their hair. Maybe combed it. Whatever they did, they looked nice.

Daina sighed. "You go to clinic. I can take somewhere. We'll figure out when we get home tonight."

Ed Mackey lived on Rourke Road a mile beyond our place. His home was deep in the woods at the end of a long and winding driveway that was unpaved and potholed. I was glad I drove the Silverado, as Daina's Corolla would have had trouble navigating the rough terrain. His house was a Cape Cod design, much like the house where I grew up. It had fifties-vintage dark green asphalt siding that had the effect of camouflaging his home so it was nearly invisible to spot until you were almost at his front door. The driveway wrapped around the side of the house to a carport, which was tucked in behind the house. Ed's truck was parked on the side of the driveway as the carport space was occupied by two shiny red three-wheel ATVs. That was my first surprise of our visit.

The second surprise was that Ed was wearing khaki pants and a red-checked flannel shirt instead of his usual army fatigues. He was on the back porch stirring a steaming pot on a large stone grill. At the far corner of the clearing behind his house there was a chicken coop with four or five birds and in the other corner a vegetable garden and a dog house. In the middle of the clearing he had a giant witches pot suspended over a crackling fire. As we got out of the car, Emerson loped over to greet us.

"Emerson!" Astra cried. She loved dogs. Emerson put his paws on her shoulders and tried to lick her face.

Toni took a step back and slipped behind Astra. "Damn. You keep that dog off me." She didn't love dogs, but that didn't deter Emerson, who, tail wagging, squeezed himself between Astra and Toni and started licking Toni's hand.

"He likes you," Astra said.

Toni giggled. "No he don't. He's just tasting me to see if I'm worth eating."

Ed turned around, looking genuinely pleased that his guests had arrived. "Emerson, behave yourself," he said. He had a rich voice, like a radio announcer. "That ain't no way to greet company." He walked over to the edge of the porch. "Good to see you again, Astra." He extended his hand to Toni. "You must be Toni. I'm Ed Mackey."

"Nice to meet you, Mr. Mackey." She shook his hand bashfully as Daina stepped on to the porch with the two pies.

"Girls made pies, Ed. I'll put in kitchen." She opened the backdoor and walked in the house. She seemed to know her way around.

"You gals play basketball AND make pies?" Ed laughed warmly, and I couldn't help but feel as though this were a completely different man than the one most folks saw tromping around the brush in his army jacket, brandishing a double-barreled shotgun.

"Want a cold one, Ed?" I held up the twelve pack of Heineken I had bought on the way back from the farmer's market.

"Don't mind if I do." He nodded toward the picnic table that had an array of cooking implements on it. "Should be a bottle opener there."

I opened two bottles and handed one to him. Toni walked over and looked in the pot. She frowned like she did when things didn't make sense to her. "That's turkey?"

Ed picked up his huge ladle and stirred the pot some more. "No. That's rabbit stew. The turkey's out there." He pointed to the witch's cauldron.

Toni leaned over the pot. "I don't see the rabbit."

Ed dipped his ladle in and scooped out a chunk of meat. "Taste it," he said.

Toni grabbed the piece with her fingers, blew on it and popped it in her mouth. She smiled. "Tastes like chicken with some kind of funky seasoning. It's good. Did you kill the rabbit?"

Ed nodded. "It's not nice to throw those bunnies in the pot when they're still alive." He laughed. "Got it this morning. I was just going to have vegetable soup, but Emerson got excited about the rabbits traipsing through his yard so we went for an early morning hunt."

"You use that big gun I saw you carrying last week?" she asked.

"The shotgun? Nah. That's for bigger game. I got a 22 pistol I use just to keep myself sharp. Rabbits aren't that hard to hunt. Them turkey are a different story."

Daina had come out of the house and helped herself to a beer. She peered into the pot.

"It's rabbit stew," Toni said.

"Toni!" Astra had walked out to the dog house. "Want to play Frisbee with Emerson?" She hurled the Frisbee toward the chicken coop and Emerson took off and caught it before it reached the birds.

"Damn, that dog has moves," Toni said.

Emerson brought the Frisbee back to Astra. Toni jumped off the porch. "Throw it, Astra!"

She flipped it across the yard, right over the sizzling turkey cauldron. Emerson raced after it. "Look out!" I yelled. But Emerson didn't need my help as he swerved effortlessly around the pot. Toni grabbed the disc just before he reached her.

"Don't throw it over the pot, girls," Ed said. "That dog gets excited he'll run through a window. Don't want him ruining my turkey. Worked too hard to get that bird."

The three of us stood on the porch sipping our beer, as if we were at a swanky suburban cocktail party instead of having Thanksgiving dinner with a crazy survivalist. "Turkeys hard to hunt?" I asked, feeling a need to break the silence before it became awkward or I asked some less lame question, like, 'Did Daina mention that she had a chance to use that gun you gave her?'

"Toughest game I hunt. Those birds have really good eyes. You have to wear camo. Very hard to sneak up on a turkey. Took me five hours to nail that girl. Even old Emerson was beat."

"Thank you for invitation," Daina said. She sounded as if she really meant it. I'd almost forgotten she had that talent.

Ed chuckled. "If I hadn't made the invitation, I'd probably given up on that turkey after three hours." He paused. "Or worn a disguise and gone shopping at the Safeway. Don't want to ruin my reputation as that crazy-ass soldier."

Despite all the things that couldn't be talked about, the pre-dinner conversation kept flowing. Ed Mackey, who hid behind the façade of an angry Vietnam Vet was actually charming, educated and good company. When the turkey was ready, he had me help him retrieve it from the cauldron, while Daina and the girls set up the table he had moved out of his kitchen into the living room.

There was a roaring fire in the fireplace providing warmth and soft lightening. We took our places and Ed brought the whole turkey in on a platter. It looked perfect — a crispy golden color — and I was thinking that we were in another Norman Rockwell painting.

Everyone applauded.

Astra nudged Toni. "There's your real turkey, Toni."

Ed set the platter on the table in front of his chair. "Let's have a prayer before we start." He raised his hand like a Baptist preacher and with a deep baritone said, "Our father, bless this gathering of neighbors. Let us give thanks for this day and this food and watch over us all, especially the children. Give us the strength to resist evil and the courage to defend ourselves from the forces in this world that would seek to rob of us life and liberty. In Jesus's name we pray. Amen."

And with that call to arms, Ed, with frightening efficiency, carved up the turkey.

"Damn. Was that your Army knife?" Toni asked.

Ed carried the platter around to Daina, who was seated at the other end of the table. "Ladies first." He held the platter for her as she speared a few pieces. "That's a Kabar. Saved my life many times in Nam." He walked on around the table serving each of us.

When he was seated, Toni asked the question each of us wanted to ask but didn't. "How did it save you?"

Ed held the pot of rabbit stew and was walking around the table ladling some into each person's bowl. He sat back down, acting as though he hadn't heard her question. He reached into the center of the table where there was a fresh loaf of sourdough bread. It looked very much like the loaves they were selling at Safeway when I stopped for the Heineken. He took the carving knife and sliced the bread, with the same efficiency he employed on the turkey.

"When I was in Nam, they'd give us bread that came in sealed tins. You know how frustrating it is to be hungry and not be able to get the damn food out of a can? But this Kabar here did the trick. Pried those biscuits out and sliced them up like nobody's business. Yessir, that knife was a lifesaver." He smiled so hard his eyes almost disappeared.

Toni stared at him, expecting there to be more to his life-saving knife story.

"How's that turkey, Daina?" Ed asked. "Darwin told me you weren't a turkey fan."

"Is good," she said. "Very moist. Not what I expected from fryer."

For someone who had lived alone most of his adult life, Ed Mackey was a skilled conversation manager. He appeared to be genuinely interested in what his guests had to stay and clearly did not want to be the center of attention. Toni asked him a question about his Marine training and he segued that into having Toni an Astra talk about their basketball training. The smooth way he turned that conversation reminded me of how skillfully Fariba always deflected my attempts to get her to talk about herself. As Toni described all of the training drills Fariba put them through, I wondered what she was doing tonight. And despite all of the turmoil, or maybe because of it, I was looking forward to seeing her tomorrow night.

The girls started talking about *The Bluest Eye* and Astra told Toni about her conversation with Ed on the way home from the game.

"How did your dramatic reading go?" I asked Toni.

"She was awesome," Astra said. "You should have seen her staring at Mom's picture, wishing she could have those spooky blue eyes, too."

Daina gave her patented frown. "That doesn't sound like good school project. What is purpose?"

Ed peered across the table at Daina, as though he had never noticed her before. "You're right. Those are spooky eyes."

"Public speaking," Astra said. "So we learn not to be afraid to talk in front of a group." They both giggled at that notion.

Daina scowled and then stood up and dropped her napkin on the table. "Talking not your problem. Help me get pies ready."

They returned a moment later carrying plates with large slices of pie topped with a dollop of whip cream on each one. Astra set a huge piece in front of Ed. "This is for you, Mr. Mackey. Sweet potato pie. It's the favorite pie of the African-American community."

"Thank you. I always try to support my community. Even if they do change their name every five years. When I was in Nam some of us were still Negroes."

Astra frowned, uncertain if he was kidding her or not. "Why did you go to Viet Nam?" she asked.

The difference between Ed and most men his age, other than the obvious survival skills, was that he treated young people like Astra and Toni with respect. He didn't dismiss their questions or ideas. He took a big bite of pie and wiped his mouth with his napkin. "Delicious. Mmm," He looked at Astra. "They drafted me. I was eighteen and Uncle Sam said he wanted me. I didn't even think about not going."

"Doesn't seem right that all the Black dudes got drafted and the white boys got to stay home," Toni said. "Why fight for them?"

Ed looked at her. It was a kind look, like a father would give his daughter. "Lots of things not right in the world, Toni. That hasn't changed. We didn't fight for them. We fought for each other. Blacks and whites. Just to stay alive. I was no hero. Just not a coward. Couldn't desert my buddies."

When dessert was over, Daina volunteered the girls to do the dishes. "Thanks a lot, Mom," Astra said.

"Welcome. I will scrape. You and Toni clean. Like old days before dishwasher."

"I appreciate that, ladies. Darwin and I will check the perimeter, smoke a cigar to keep those rabbits out of Emerson's yard."

I turned down his offer for a cigar, but joined him on the back porch while he lit up. We stood next to the stone grill looking out at Emerson's dog house as Ed puffed on the cigar, the tip glowing cherry red. It had a peculiar aroma of pepper and eucalyptus that was strangely familiar.

Ed tapped the ash over the porch rail. "It's Cuban," he said. "Got it from Billy Rourke."

"When was that?" I asked.

"Just before he disappeared. Showed up here one night. Wanted a gun. Had the idea I was some kind of free-lance gun merchant.

Told him no, but he gave me a case of cigars anyway. Said he'd given up smoking."

"Why did he want a gun?"

"Didn't say. And I didn't really want to know."

I'd never hunted. I didn't even have a BB gun growing up. My dad had his fill of guns and violence during the war. He said there was always a better way, but that was twentieth century thinking. I thought about what Detective Sanchez said. The bad guys don't play by any rules.

"I need to protect my family. Can you help me?"

"You mean with a gun?"

"Yes. Things are getting hairy around here."

"I know. Not a good situation. Not good at all." He watched as a puff of smoke drifted toward the heavens. It was a starry night and the moon was full. "Can't do it, Darwin."

I stared at him but he kept looking out at the yard, as if he were a sentry keeping an eye out for the enemy. "You gave one to Daina."

"Good thing, too."

So Daina had told him about the shooting. I wondered if he replaced the gun she left in Ray's bloody hand. "Why Daina but not me?"

He turned and looked at me. We were close and he had to look up to eyeball me as I had at least six inches on him. "It ain't in you, Dar. You're not like Daina. She's got ice water in her veins. I knew the minute I saw her, that if she needed to shoot, she wouldn't hesitate. And she didn't. But you would have. That ain't a rap. You're a good man. Most folks hesitate. That's why civilians with guns usually end up getting other people killed. It just ain't you, man."

I didn't want to hear that, even though I didn't disagree. About me or Daina. I could have just let it go, but I was angry, not just at him and Daina, but at the whole clusterfuck my life had turned into these last few weeks.

Ed shifted back to his sentry posture, gazing out at the perimeter. He was done talking, but I wasn't. I leaned over and rested my elbows on the porch rail close to him looking out at the yard as though I were one of his soldier buddies. "You know, Ed, everyone sees you roaming the countryside in your thirty-year-old Army jacket and they think they know you. But they don't. You don't want to give me a gun, that's your business. But don't act like you know me, cause you don't. And if you give Daina another gun, you're going to have a problem with me."

He grunted. I couldn't tell if he was surprised or not. He wasn't one to tip his hand, and I'm not sure what he would have done or said, because at that moment, like the cavalry arriving in the nick of time, Toni and Astra bounded out from the carport where they had been dumping the remains of the dinner in the garbage pail. Daina was right behind them.

"How come you got two of them dune buggies?" Toni asked.

Ed stepped away from the railing and walked over to the girls. "What? You don't think I have any friends?" He laughed, happy to be the gracious host again, instead of the reluctant gun dealer. "But don't call them dune buggies. Those are three-wheel ATVs."

"Where do you ride them?" Toni asked.

"Lots of places. There's some really good trails at Coogan's Park, it's about three hours south of here."

"Can you see us riding those, Toni? That would be a blast," Astra said

Daina looked at me, still standing over by the grill, and for the shortest of moments her face had that Daina-worry look. Then she turned her attention to Ed Mackey and smiling coyly said, "Maybe you could take girls and me to ATV camp for the weekend. Darwin has basketball clinic in Chicago. It would be good chance to get away."

Another gut punch I hadn't seen coming. The girls whooped. Astra pleaded, "Could we, Mr. Mackey?" as if she needed to help her mother persuade our neighbor. If Daina had asked Ed Mackey to drive to the North Pole, all he would have said was "When do you want to leave?" In this case he looked back at me, pretending I had some say in this plan. "That okay with you, Darwin?"

I shrugged and turned away from him, pretending I was the guy on sentry duty now. "Not my call."

I could see out of the corner of my eye that he was still staring at me, waiting for me to say something more, but I was done talking to him and to Daina.

"Hmmph," he grunted at me and then turned back and said to Daina and the girls, "I'd be happy to. I'll load the ATVs on the truck tonight and we can get an early start tomorrow. I'll have to bring Emerson. Is that okay, Toni?"

## Chapter 35
*(Friday, November 25, 2005)*

Maybe if we had all sat down and talked it through, I would have seen that the ATV road trip wasn't a bad plan to get Toni and Astra and Daina out of Claxton for the weekend. It didn't bother me that Ed Mackey had an old man's crush on Daina. She wasn't going to be taken advantage of by Ed or me or any other man. What blinded me to any dispassionate analysis of the option was that it was one more development I had no control over. I was tired of being threatened and tired of being played.

I didn't realize it until later, but that moment standing out on Ed Mackey's porch gazing up at the starry sky, was the moment I decided to get my life back.

As we got ready for bed, Daina tried to explain to me what she'd done. "Is good plan. Gets Toni away from gang. Monday we can talk to Sanchez. Find a safe place."

I suppose it was ironic that I had always chafed at Daina's refusal to discuss her family decisions with me and now when we faced the crisis of our life she wanted to talk and I refused to listen to her. "I'm going downstairs to watch the Bulls game," I said and walked away. When I returned two hours later she was asleep. She got up at six and woke the girls, but I pretended to be asleep. When I finally did get up an hour later she and the girls had already left with Ed Mackey.

I packed a small rollerboard for the weekend at the clinic. I put the Krugerrands in a sock and stuffed them into my running shoes. From the closet I retrieved my gym bag with Billy's cash and covered it with clean workout clothes. I got dressed and stuffed the envelope of diamonds into the front pocket of my Levi's. With Billy's cash, my Krugerrands and the diamonds, I was carrying over three hundred thousand dollars. I didn't know what I was going to do with it, but I liked having the resources. Whether it was true or not, I felt like it gave me options.

We had only a skeleton crew at work on Friday. Most businesses were on holiday and there were few deliveries or shipments scheduled. I was surprised to see Stephanie's Lexus in the parking lot. When I got to the bullpen her office light was on but the door was closed so I continued down the corridor to my office.

Usually, the first thing I would do in the morning is return calls, but most of the vendors had the day off so I made a list of the calls I would make on Monday. I put Detective Sanchez at the top of the list, but I wasn't sure I would call him. He was a wild card. He could help us protect Toni, but at what risk? What if he kept digging into the shooting of Thigpen. I didn't want that.

Stephanie had asked me to update my management development plan. Billy had always considered those a waste of time, but I figured if Stephanie wanted it, I would comply. Most of it was easy to complete. The last question on the form was to recommend your replacement. I had always listed Kelly. She could easily do the job and deserved a promotion. But now I had my doubts. I was disappointed she was trying to play all sides of the game. I decided to nominate Paul Meron as my successor. It didn't mean anything. If things continued to go sideways, a recommendation from me was meaningless at best.

I had just put the form in my outbox when Stephanie appeared in my doorway. Normally I have a warning, as I can hear her clip clop down the hall in her heels. But today she was wearing running shoes. Instead of the skirt and silk blouse uniform, she was wearing an untucked white shirt and jeans. She still looked hot.

"Hey, Darwin. How was your Thanksgiving?"

"Good. Did you bring Devante home?"

She beamed. "It's so wonderful to have him back." She sat down in the chair in front of my desk. "I forgot how much I missed him."

She sighed and gazed distractedly at an imaginary hangnail. I could tell she hadn't popped into my office to talk about the holiday.

"Sean called me last night. He said the FBI is pushing to have you indicted on those RICO violations. They're expediting. It could happen as early as Monday. I'm sorry, Darwin."

A month ago if she had told me that, I might have collapsed. Now, it didn't even faze me. Everyone was taking their shot. There is one advantage when life keeps slamming doors in your face. It's a lot easier to pick the next door when there aren't many left. Most folks might not consider that much of an advantage, but I always liked having a plan. Even a bad one.

"Why the rush?" I asked.

"They had a tip you might be trying to flee. Probably because of that 401k loan."

"So Redmond told them about that?" If he had, I wondered if he told them about the Krugerrands he sold me. And the five grand he made on the deal.

Stephanie nodded. "Probably. Or he had to make some filing disclosure and they're on alert for anything that pops up with your name on it."

"Great to be popular, I thought they weren't interested in those real estate deals."

"Sean doesn't think they are. He said it's just a way to contain you, while they gather their terrorist evidence. They have a bead on Billy, by the way. And pictures."

"Doing what?"

"He's meeting with a man named Saeed Larijani. Larijani is the head of the Free Iran Coalition, which has been designated by the State Department as a terrorist organization."

If I had learned anything in the last four weeks, it was that everyone had secrets. At least secrets from me. Maybe Astra and Toni were right – I was clueless. But I refused to believe that Billy had anything to do with terrorism. Even for money. No fucking way.

"Billy's not a terrorist," I said.

Stephanie sighed. "At this point it doesn't really matter." She handed me a slip of paper. "Here is the contact info for Vikas Karode. Goes by Vik. We worked together in the U. S. Attorney's office. He is out on his own now. An excellent criminal defense lawyer. I told him you might be calling. With his connections to Sean's office, he'll be invaluable to you."

I took the paper and put it next to my phone, as if I were planning to call. "Thanks," I said.

"Do it right away. They're going to get a search warrant for your house. Nothing you can do about that, but have your lawyer with you." She glanced over her shoulder and then whispered, "If you have anything in your house you'd rather they not find, get rid of it now." She paused. "I never said that."

"Thanks, Stephanie. I appreciate it." I looked at her and I could tell there was something more she wanted to say. "I like your outfit,"

She smiled sadly. "I'm leaving AutoPro."

I actually felt worse hearing that than her news about the Feds planning to indict me.

"If you had told me that three weeks ago, we would have had a party. After you left. But now I feel bad. What are you going to do?"

She sniffed. "I know the timing sucks. I hate to abandon you at a time like this, but I have to. For my son." She sighed and looked at me and this time I didn't doubt for a moment her sincerity. "Devante's a prisoner in his own home. There's a full-scale gang war going on out there. Two assassinations on Thanksgiving. It doesn't matter that he's not in a gang. They think he is. Trey's taking a sabbatical to Nigeria and we're all going. We leave next week."

I walked around to the front of my desk and hugged her. "I'm going to miss you. You are one stand up woman, Stephanie."

She dabbed at her eyes. "Damn you, Darwin Burr. No one makes me cry."

I smiled, even though I didn't feel like it. "I didn't think any more wheels could off, but I guess I was wrong again. I'm still planning to go to that basketball clinic this weekend. That's crazy isn't it?"

"That's what you should be doing. I'm praying for you. I believe everything is going to work out and when it does, coaching, is what you should be doing. Now I'm going to pack up my stuff and go home and I'm not going to cry again, dammit. You take care." She kissed me on the cheek and hustled back to her office.

Stephanie was packed up and gone in ten minutes. Another door had closed. I took the paper with the lawyer's name and slipped it into my wallet. I wouldn't need it today. I needed legal help, but not the kind I could get from him. I pulled Mark Sanchez's card from my wallet and dialed his cell. It went straight to voice mail, but a minute later he called me back.

"Mr. Burr? This is Mark Sanchez. Sorry I missed your call. Couldn't get the phone out of my pocket."

"We're going to bring Toni in on Monday so you can talk to her." I still wasn't certain that was the right play, but I wanted him to believe I was cooperating.

"That's good. Hold on." More paper shuffling. "Can you be here about nine o'clock?"

"Okay," I said. Now it was my turn to pause. If I really meant it when I told myself I was going to take charge of my life then I had get on top of the gang problem. "There was a suspicious car driving around our area yesterday. I think they were gang members."

"What were they driving?" Sanchez's voice was animated. "Did you get their license?"

"2005 MDX. Black, with tinted windows." What was my license prompt? Darwin Good Boy. Wide body jet. "License number DGB 747. Illinois plates,"

"Hold on a minute," Sanchez yelled to someone in his office to bring him the surveillance report on the Gangsters. "Yep. There it is. That's definitely one of their rides. Where were they?"

I had a cold feeling in my gut. I had been hoping that I was just being paranoid. "Hoover Road, They kept turning onto dead ends. I thought they might be looking for our road. It's hard to find."

I could hear a tapping sound and I visualized Sanchez drumming on the desk with his fingers. "I'll notify State Police to keep an eye out for them on Hoover, If you see them call 911 immediately. Don't try to be a hero."

I remembered the paralyzing fear I had when Thigpen shot Ray. "No chance of that," I said. "Thanks. I'll see you Monday." I didn't want to tell him no one was going to be home all weekend. Sanchez might be able to help us, but I didn't trust him. I didn't trust anyone anymore.

Except Fariba. It was time to head up to Evanston. There was nothing more I needed to do here today.

I had brought my rollerboard and the gym bag up to my office. I didn't want to have some knucklehead decide to steal that junky Silverado and drive off with my fortune. I swung by the warehouse to let Meron know I was leaving. He was talking on his office phone when I walked down, with a serious frown on his face. "Hold on," he said to whoever he was talking to. He muffled the receiver against his chest. "That's Hank at the gate. The Feds are here. They want to talk to you."

"The office is locked. Tell them I'm here in your office."

He gave the message to Hank and then said to me, "They're on their way."

More doors closing. Decisions getting easier. "I need a favor. You don't have to do it if you don't want to. I understand completely."

"Jesus. Just tell me what the hell you want."

I handed him the gym bag and my suitcase. "Find a safe place for these before they get here."

He turned around and stowed my luggage in the ancient Diebold safe in the corner of his office.

I stared at him incredulously. "I thought the combination to that safe had been lost long ago."

Meron grinned. "I often forget that I know the combination. Yesterday was one of those days. The agents weren't interested in the safe. If they change their minds it will take a day to find someone who can open it."

The two agents walked across the warehouse, still wearing those annoying windbreakers. The lead agent, the same one who had brought in the search warrant yesterday approached me. "Mr. Burr, I'm here as a courtesy to let you know we are about to execute a search warrant of your house at," he looked down at his paper, "3245 Country Road HH." That was the official name of the road we lived on. Rourke Road would have been a better name. "You have the right to be present while we execute the warrant, but you may not interfere with the agents. Do you wish to be present?"

"I appreciate the courtesy, Agent Beatty. Yes I want to be there. I'll be over in a few minutes. Do you want my keys? I don't want you to break down the door."

"We have keys, sir. So we will see you over there. Correct?"

I had no intention of accompanying them. They could take hours and I didn't want to hang around while strangers trampled through my home as they had just done to our office. But if I told them I wasn't going to go with them they might be suspicious and detain me. "It will be a few minutes but I'll be there. You don't have to wait for me," I said.

"Correct." He turned and the two agents scampered down the loading dock steps to their car.

Meron watched them go, a disgusted look on his face. "I'd like to correct that motherfucker. What else you need, boss? And skip the part where you tell me I don't have to do it."

"I need the rollerboard. Keep the gym bag for now. And I need another vehicle." I was afraid that once I didn't show up at the search, the Fed would become suspicious and start looking for me. I was just being extra cautious. Not paranoid.

Meron opened the safe and yanked out the rollerboard. He handed me his keys. "It's the black F-150. Diesel. Five hundred horsepower. That ought to work for you."

"Are you sure?"

"You bet. I don't want you driving one of those sissy S-10 pickups with AutoPro signage all over it, like you're some kind of delivery boy. Not good for your outlaw image."

I laughed. "I guess not. Thanks."

Ten minutes later I was on the interstate headed toward Evanston.

## Chapter 36
*(Friday, November 25, 2005)*

As soon as I got on the interstate I called Daina to let her know about the FBI search. I was certain Ed Mackey had given her another gun, but I was also certain she would have taken it with her so I wasn't too worried they'd discover something like that. Even so, I was relieved when the call went right to voicemail. I left her a message, and I know when she heard it she'd be pissed. From Daina's perspective this would just be another Billy fuckup. And I guess she'd be right about that.

It took me over two hours to make it to the Orrington Hotel. I somehow forgot that the day after Thanksgiving was a huge shopping day. The interstate was rush-hour busy and when I got off, Golf Road, the main drag to Evanston, was bumper to bumper. I was glad to have Meron's truck — comfy seats and elevated suspension that put me above the traffic. There had been two calls on my cellphone from blocked numbers. I suspected they were from the FBI wondering what happened to me. I don't think I broke any law by not hanging around to watch them search my home. I wasn't worried about them finding anything. I just hoped they didn't trash the house, like they always seemed to do on *Law and Order.* That seemed wrong, even when the perps were guilty.

I turned off Golf on to Asbury and then made a left on Church Street. As I waited at the traffic light to cross Ridge Avenue, I noticed the sign on the building across the street: 1717 Ridge. That was the building where Billy owned the condo he made available to Kelly's mom.

Billy's condo was only three blocks from my hotel. My room, according to the solicitous young woman at the front desk, was prepaid through Sunday. She confirmed for me that Fariba's reservation was also prepaid, and that she had the room adjoining mine. Since she hadn't yet checked in, I left a note with the clerk to give to Fariba. She gave me a fat envelope with my pass for the clinic, along with an itinerary and an official Bobby Knight coach's whistle.

I unpacked and looked over the itinerary. There was a cocktail party scheduled for six tonight in the Grand Ballroom. The actual clinic would begin tomorrow morning at nine at Evanston Township High School. I had four hours to kill before the cocktail party.

In basketball I always let the game come to me. I didn't try to force the action, I looked for my opponents' weaknesses and took what they gave me. I followed the same philosophy in life. I went with the flow, tried not to make waves — Billy created enough turbulence for both of us. But today was different. Instead of waiting to see what happened, I pushed the action, and it worked out well. I managed to elude the FBI, secured a safe place for Billy's cash and even had the police out looking for those gangbangers who were after Toni. I was on a roll and there was no point in stopping now.

I brought the lambskin leather zip jacket Billy had insisted I buy for the big AutoPro store convention in New York a couple years ago. It was a cool-looking jacket, but I never got around to wearing it after that weekend. I guess I was waiting for a special occasion. A weekend in Chicago with Fariba seemed about as special as I was going to get.

I started walking west on Church Street. The sidewalks were crowded, and everyone was walking fast. Not New York fast, but faster than Claxton. I was swept along with the tide of shoppers and the next thing I knew I was back on Ridge. I walked north, and two minutes later I was standing in front of Billy's condo building.

The FEDEX package Billy sent us was shipped from unit 508. I stepped into the entryway. There was a phone for visitors to ring the apartment they were visiting. To find the code I had to scroll through the names of the residents. There was no Rourke listed. I couldn't remember Kelly's mother's name. Craven was Kelly's married name. She always signed the phone message slips, "KCC".

I scrolled through the Cs. There it was: Heather Carter, unit 508. I pushed the button and it rang like a phone. After several rings it went to a regular voicemail account. The voice on the phone said, "This is Heather Carter, please leave a message." Small town rube that I was, I had never experienced a doorbell that forwarded to a cellphone.

I was holding the receiver, still trying to figure out what was going on, when the computer-voice operator, sounding irritated, asked me if I wanted to leave a message. I left my name and cell number and told her I was a friend of Billy Rourke's and that I was outside her building.

I was standing on the curb watching the traffic race by and pondering my next move, when my phone buzzed. A text from an 847 number. GO TO TOMMY NEVINS PUB. I remembered passing that bar on my way to the condo. That was the place Kelly's mother saw Billy meeting with those Mafia types.

It was a popular spot. The Black Hawks were playing tonight and there were a swarm of hockey fans getting prepped for the train ride into Chicago. The tables were all taken, but there was a seat at the end of the bar next to a beefy, grey-haired guy wearing a Hawks sweater. I ordered a Harps and nursed it while I watched the Hawks pregame show.

They were showing highlights of previous Hawks games and I marveled at the athleticism of the players. I could barely skate, and I couldn't imagine racing down the ice, trying to control a puck and elude big dudes trying to take your head off. My hockey fan neighbor cashed out and a moment later a guy in jeans and a turtleneck took his seat. He was tanned, unusual for this time of year, and his head was shaved, a common look for hair-challenged middle-aged guys. I was glad I still had my hair. I wasn't anything special in the looks department, but I would have been a dog-ugly bald man.

I waved to the bartender for another beer. Baldy wrapped his arm around my shoulder and slapped a twenty down on the bar. "I got it, buddy." I didn't have to look at him. He could change his looks all he wanted, but after listening to his bullshit for forty years I'd recognize Billy Rourke's voice anywhere.

"I don't know whether to kiss you or kick your ass. What the fuck, Billy." In addition to the shaved head and the tan, he had lost at least twenty pounds.

The bartender brought me another Harp's. He nodded at Billy. "What'll you have?"

Billy shook his head. "Just some tonic and a lime wedge."

"I heard you quit smoking. Drinking too?"

He patted his stomach. It wasn't flat, but he'd lost the beach ball. "It's a special macrobiotic diet. I've lost thirty pounds."

"Getting in shape for prison?"

He lifted the sleeve of my jacket that was draped over the back of my chair. "You never wear this jacket. Don't tell me your developing a fashion sense. Wait a minute. You're here with Fariba. That's why your stylin'." He snort-chuckled and I was ready to kick his ass.

"You didn't lose any of your asshole pounds."

"True that, brother." He closed his eyes as he sipped his tonic water. "I ain't going to prison," he whispered. "Neither are you."

"Good to hear. The FBI has other ideas. They want to send me away for 240 years and they have you pegged as a terrorist."

His face scrunched up, as if he couldn't be bothered with such petty concerns. "They're just trying to scare you."

"It's working. Being called a terrorist doesn't scare you?"

"What? I'm supposed to be a terrorist because my partner is Saeed Larijani? Do you know who he is, Darwin?"

"How the fuck would I know?"

"He's Fariba's uncle! Part of that Pahlavi family. They're fucking royalty. He's an Iranian patriot, not some Al Qaeda schmuck. Typical dipshit bureaucrats in the State Department add two plus two and get twenty-two. They're idiots. It's going to get cleared up, pronto. We're both going to be fine."

I had gone from Norman Rockwell back to the Twilight Zone. "You're crazy. You take off for some fucking fat farm and leave me to clean up your goddamn mess." I grabbed Billy's forearm as I was making my point. His bulky turtleneck had masked how thin he really was. His arm felt like a twig.

The bartender stepped closer, eyeing me suspiciously. "It's cool," I said. I let go of Billy's arm. "What's wrong with you, Billy? Talk to me. I'm your friend, not some mark."

He sighed and stared at the bottles of booze stacked up behind the bar. "Okay. It wasn't a fat farm. It's a special cancer clinic in Honduras — Nunca Te Rindas — run by Dr. Ramon Flores."

Shit. "You got cancer, Billy? What kind?"

"It doesn't matter. Look at me. I'm being cured. I was dying and I'm not anymore. I don't cough. No night sweats. I feel great. Doctor Flores is a genius."

I didn't want to puncture his balloon, but he didn't look all that great to me. He just had a nice tan. But he was wasting away and he was bald. It wasn't a good look.

"What does this have to do with that Iranian guy?" I asked. How was Fariba involved? That's what I really wanted to know.

Billy sipped his tonic water. "It's complicated. I was doing all those real estate deals with Weidman — and they are totally legit so don't let the FBI give you that RICO bullshit. Weidman's a pussy. He confessed to something he wasn't guilty of and then tried to pin the rap on me."

"And me." For a guy who was supposedly out of circulation, Billy seemed to know everything that was going on. It had to be Kelly.

"I'm sorry you got dragged into this. I never wanted that to happen. You gotta believe me. Timing sucked. I worked on that condo storage deal for years. Refining it. Figuring out how to make the numbers work. I wanted to do it with Weidman, but he pussied out. He thought he was going to be the next CEO of AutoPro. Bad luck for Wally, good luck for me, because Saeed is a hundred times better partner. And a fucking billionaire, which doesn't hurt."

"So what's Fariba got to do with all this?"

Billy smiled. "Ain't she something? I love that gal."

If I wasn't afraid he would shatter like Humpty Dumpty, I would have knocked him off his barstool right then.

He looked at me, and his eyes widened. "Damn. You got it bad, dontcha?" He held up his hands in defense. "Okay. Okay. Relax. I was looking for a partner and Saeed was looking for investments, but he's superrich so everyone's coming after him with bullshit proposals, most of them cons. I would have never got close to him. I needed a way in, and when I heard that Fariba's job in Chicago got eliminated at the same time Duby Laurence took a powder, it was kismet, man."

"Kismet?" In the forty years I had known Billy I never heard him use that word.

"Fate, dude. I got her a job and she was grateful enough to introduce me to her uncle. That's all. She doesn't know from nothing about his business. They weren't close — I don't think Fariba's mother was a big fan of Saeed. But anyway, she just got me the audience. I pitched him on the deal and he loved it. He had tons of property already and with this concept he can leverage that investment a hundredfold. I'm serious as a heart attack. This company is a goldmine. Once I had it launched, I was going to bring you in on it. You and me. And Saeed. And it's still going to happen. I just gotta get this other thing finished."

"What do you mean finished?"

He crunched on his ice and waved at the bartender for another round for both of us. "I have to go back to Honduras and finish the treatments. I'm about halfway through. Those FBI fuckers froze my accounts so I need that money I stowed with Kelly. The clinic's not cheap."

"How much?" I didn't really want to know.

"Half million now, another half when I'm completely cured. Dr. Ramos says the next round of treatments should do the trick. Another six months."

I was wondering how a wheeler-dealer like Billy could fall for such an obvious con. But maybe I would do the same thing if it were my only option. I didn't want to be the one to say he was wasting his time and money, but I had to say something. "A million dollars? Are you sure about this guy? Aren't there any specialists in Chicago who could help you? Or New York?"

He shook his head so hard it made me dizzy. "AMA has its head up its ass. They'd rather I die than get treated. It's that not-invented-here bullshit. My doctor sent me to a specialist at Mayo. Bloodless motherfucker told me I had no shot. Fuck that. There's always a shot. You know that better than anyone." He shrugged as though all of it were beyond his control "I know it's a lot of money. But I can't take it with me. Damn sure don't want to leave it for the exes." He laughed like the old Billy. "I got almost two hundred k, so with the money I had Kelly holding and those diamonds I should have enough. You brought the cash, right?"

His smile was forced and it didn't cover up his desperation. Despite all the hell he had put me through, if I'd had the cash on me, I'd have given it to him right then. I reached into my pocket and pulled out the envelope of diamonds. "Here's the stuff from Redmond. I couldn't bring the cash, Billy. The Feds were all over the place so I hid it."

He slipped the envelope into his pocket. He stopped trying to smile as he put his hand on my sleeve. His whole arm was shaking. "Doctor Flores has a plane coming for me. He flies out of a private airstrip in southern Missouri. I gotta be there by Sunday night. Before midnight. I need that money, Dar."

The smart thing would have been to lie to him and tell him there was no way to get the money. That was the best cut-my-losses option on the table. But I didn't take it. Maybe that was kismet, too. "I'll get you the money. I need to make some calls. How do I reach you?"

He took a deep breath as if I had just saved his life. He wrote down a number on the bar napkin. "Call this cell when you're ready." He slipped off the barstool and slapped me on the back. "We got a day and a half. I got to run now."

There wasn't any run left in him. He walked like every joint in his body ached. It hurt to look at him. I wondered if I would ever see him again.

## Chapter 37
*(Friday, November 25, 2005)*

I ordered another Harps and pondered my next move. There were no good options. My best friend was dying and the only way I could help him was to give him his money and let him get conned by some quack doctor. But what was I supposed to do? Tell him, "Sorry, Billy, I can't help you. You're fucked." I couldn't do that. Billy was right. There was always a shot. Sometimes the longshot won the race. If Billy wanted to place that bet, it should be his call, not mine. I walked out to the street where it was quiet and phoned Paul Meron.

He answered on the first ring, as if he had been waiting for my call. "The FBI find you yet?" he asked.

"Are they looking for me?"

He scoffed. "That agent with the bad haircut came back here and wanted to know what you were driving. I told him I had no clue. He wasn't too happy."

"I need you to call this number." I gave him Billy's cell number and the details on Billy. The cancer, the cash in the gym bag, the plane waiting in southern Missouri. "Can you drive him there?" I asked.

There was no drama with Paul Meron. No bullshit. He was just flat-ass dependable. "You got it. I'll call Billy and we'll figure out the best place to pick him up. I'm sorry he's sick, Dar. He's an asshole. But a good one. Are you all right?"

"I don't think it's sunk in yet. I've known Billy since we were kids."

"I know." He'd never admit it, but Paul liked Billy, too. "What the fuck, Dar. The dude's always been lucky. Maybe he'll beat this thing."

That's what I wanted to believe and it felt good to hear someone say it. But deep down, I knew this wasn't going to be a buzzer beater. "Call me when you've got him on that plane, okay?"

"You got it, boss."

It was a little after six when I made it back to the hotel. I didn't really want to go to the reception, but I figured they'd have appetizers, and I was hungry. I'd had four beers, but hadn't eaten anything since breakfast. The grand ballroom wasn't too crowded. The registrants were mostly high school coaches, men and women. More women than I expected. But it made sense. Most all the schools had girls basketball and unlike when they first started playing, now most of the coaches were women.

After Billy's last marriage broke up five years ago, he started dragging me along to the supplier cocktail parties where he was always a VIP guest. Daina refused to come along so it was just me and Billy. And as soon as we hit the floor Billy would be surrounded by senior managers, all treating him as if he were royalty. They weren't interested in me and I didn't want any part of that suck up parade, so I would slip away to the open bar, grab a beer and find a spot where I could just hang around and watch people. It wasn't bad duty. Some folks, Billy for instance, can't stand being alone at a party, but it never bothered me.

I had spent all day not being the typical, laidback Darwin, but it was time to revert to form. It was a cash bar, so I bought a Bud for five dollars and parked myself in a strategic crossroads where I could be certain that the waiters bringing around appetizers would have plenty of opportunities to serve me.

There was a murmur from the crowd as Coach Knight entered the ballroom. He walked across the room to the tables that lined the perimeter, a gaggle of coaches following in his wake. I admired Bobby Knight. He was a tough, no-nonsense, passionate coach. Throwing-chairs-passionate, which occasionally got him into trouble. I would have liked to hear what he was saying to the group, but he had drawn so many of the participants over to that corner of the room that I now had a chance to feast on all the good appetizers:

stuffed mushrooms, bacon-wrapped scallops, mini-quiches, chicken skewers, and my all-time favorite, little pigs in a blanket. I scarfed down six of those little wienies and then went back and bought another beer.

"Are you still hungry, Darwin Burr?" A tall redhead, about my age, approached me, sipping from a martini glass.

I stared at her, dumbly. How did she know me? "Uh…"

She extended her hand, "Gail Andrews. Regina Dominican High." She leaned closer and stared at my chest. "Where the hell is Claxton?" she asked.

I forgot I was wearing a nametag. With **DARWIN BURR** printed in large type so even the nearsighted would know my name. Claxton was in much smaller print. "It's about sixty miles down the interstate." She was wearing a beige skirt with an emerald-colored blouse that looked great with her red hair. She had redhead freckles, like Billy, which made her look younger than she was. I glanced at her nametag above her left breast. It revealed that her school was in Wilmette, the suburb just north of Evanston.

A waiter walked up to us with a tray of bacon-wrapped water chestnuts. Not as good as scallops, but anything wrapped in bacon was worth trying. I wanted to grab two, but I didn't. "They need to make these bigger," I said. "I'm still hungry."

She smiled and drained her martini. "I was going to grab a burger upstairs at the sports bar. Do you want to join me?"

"Sure," I said. "Not eating at home tonight?" The words were out of my mouth before I realized that it might sound as if I were asking if she was staying at the hotel. That's what happens when I have too many beers and too little food.

"Are you kidding? I have three teenage girls at home and this is my weekend getaway. I'll let my husband deal with all the drama for a change. I'm staying at the hotel, same as you out-of-town folks. You're staying here, aren't you?"

Gail was, as expected, a huge basketball fan. She had been the head coach at Regina for ten years. She graduated from there and it had been a dream realized when she returned to teach English and coach basketball. She asked me about my basketball career and I think Billy would have been proud of my rendition of our championship game. I found myself talking about Billy a lot.

We finished our burgers and ordered another pitcher of beer. As I topped off Gail's glass, she said, "You keep staring at my hair. Don't you have any redheads in Claxton?"

I could feel my face getting warm. "I'm sorry. This sounds stupid, but my friend Billy used to have hair that color."

"Why are you sad? Did something happen to Billy?"

I guess one of her coaching skills was the ability to pick up on subtle cues. I hadn't even realized I was sad. "He's dying. I just found out today."

She reached across the table and squeezed my hand. "I'm so sorry. Cancer?"

While ignoring all of the criminal aspects, I told her about Billy's quest for a cure in Honduras. She was sympathetic and understanding and not judgmental. She insisted on paying for the meal. "It's my treat. You saved me from dining alone. And you've been great company."

We walked together to the elevator. She was a little wobbly from the martinis and beer, and clung to my arm as we stepped into the elevator. She was on the sixth floor, one floor below me. When the couple that was on the elevator got off on the 3rd floor, Gail leaned in closer to me and squeezed my hand. As the elevator doors opened on the sixth floor she handed me her key envelope with the room number written on it. "I'm in room 624. If you get lonely or want to talk, give me a call." She kissed me softly on the lips, stroking the side of my face with her hand.

"Okay," I said as the door closed.

Okay? There must be something about getting kissed that freezes my brain. I was now two for two on totally lame responses. As I pulled my key out of my pocket, I knocked on Fariba's door. No answer. She said she'd be arriving late on Friday night and it was only nine. I didn't want to fall asleep and miss her. In the note I left at the desk, I told her to knock on the door, no matter how late.

I was emotionally and physically drained. There had been too much drama and too much booze today. I don't know how Billy functioned like this day after day. I needed to take a week off to recover. I took a shower to wake up and put on my sweatpants and tee-shirt. I collapsed on the bed and surfed through the television stations. TBS was running a *Law & Order* marathon. Comfort food, while I waited for Fariba to arrive.

I clicked on the channel. They were in the middle of one of their interminable commercial breaks. I muted the set so I didn't have to listen to the schlock lawyer telling me how he could help me beat the IRS. The IRS wasn't my problem.

I'd seen every episode of *Law & Order* at least three times. I loved its dependably predictable format; Lenny's pithy one-liners when they visit the crime scene, Sam Waterson's take-no-prisoners moral outrage, the always beautiful and brilliant assistant ADAs, and a great collection of bad guys who beat the rap just enough to make it interesting. Sort of like watching the Bulls during the Jordan era. They didn't win ALL their games, but, win or lose, at the end of the show there was a winner and a loser. Didn't work like that in the real world.

The commercials finally ended, and the show resumed. My heart sank. It was the season finale where Assistant ADA Claire Kincaid is killed by a drunken driver as she leaves the bar where she has gone to comfort her friend, Lenny. I couldn't watch that again. I'd had too much sadness today.

There was nothing else worth watching — just shopping networks and late-night bloviators. I settled back on top of the bed and closed my eyes. With the lights all on there was no chance I would fall asleep and miss Fariba.

I was at the police station. Sanchez was sitting behind his desk surrounded by files. He grabbed a file off the stack, looked at me with disgust and pounded a staple through it. Bang! He grabbed another file and repeated the process. This time multiple staples. Bang! Bang! Bang! I opened my eyes. Someone was knocking at my door.

I jumped off the bed and bolted toward the door, my body two steps ahead of my brain. I flung open the door and there was Fariba, heartbreakingly beautiful in her long winter coat, cheeks flushed, hair tousled like she'd been running, with her fist poised to knock again.

She started to say something, but never got the chance. I grabbed hold of the flaps of her coat and pulled her to me. Kissing her hard, before she could speak. She kissed me back and we stood there in the doorway, kissing lips and cheeks and ears and eyelids.

I started to tug her into my room, but she resisted. I stopped. Confused. Mortified.

"My bag," she said. She turned around, grabbed her rollerboard, and wheeled it into my room. She let her coat fall to the floor and kissed me again, her tongue probing and teasing. She reached under my tee-shirt and ran her hands over my chest, as she danced me backwards. We tumbled on to the bed — the same choreography we had executed in Clarkie's parking lot.

She jumped up from the bed, grinning. "Too many clothes." She tugged off her sweater and then with incredible athletic skill, balanced on one foot as she tugged off first one boot and then the other. She started to unbuckle her jeans when I grabbed her.

"That's my job," I said. I pushed her on to her back, unclasped her bra and tugged off her jeans. She wasn't wearing panties. She had an incredible body. Lean and dark, with ripped abs. I took off my sweatpants and tee-shirt and bounced down on the bed next to her. We locked ourselves in another embrace, now skin to skin. I nuzzled her neck. She tasted salty and had a sweet aroma of stale airplane sweat and body lotion. My hands and lips and tongue explored her body, the body I had been imagining for weeks, never really believing it could come to this.

I lay there with Fariba, our limbs entwined as though we were one. We kissed. Deep, passionate, devouring kisses. We stopped only to come up for air. I would have been content to just kiss her for hours. Days. Forever.

Fariba finally unwound herself. She straddled me and said softly, "I love you, Darwin Burr. I know there are many reasons why I should not, but tonight I don't want to talk about them or think about them. Tonight I just want to make love as though we are the only people who matter. Let's pretend that we are the last people on earth and tomorrow the world ends."

And that's what we did.

# Chapter 38
*(Saturday & Sunday - November 26-27, 2005)*

After we made love the first time, Fariba snuggled close to me in the bed and with her head resting on my chest, told me what happened with her family.

"My mother was in danger in Tehran. My uncle's activities had upset the clerics and she was being harassed. He was worried she would be arrested, so he managed to get her out of the country."

"How did he do that?" I asked. In the hallway the elevator dinged and a group of raw-voiced coaches got off, talking and laughing loudly. I looked at the nightstand clock. It was one a.m.

"Bribes. In Iran, you can get anything if you know the right people and have enough money."

The coaches were right outside our door, heatedly debating Michael versus LeBron. "What did your uncle need you for?"

"Mother doesn't like Saeed. She doesn't trust him. They brought her to Basel, but she didn't want to stay. They needed me to convince her. Mother wants Tehran as she remembers it when she and Daddy were young. I think I succeeded, but it was not easy."

The coaches finally left the hallway and the hotel was now quiet again. Fariba wrapped her arms around my neck and pulled herself on top of me. The room was dimly lit from the light in the bathroom. I could see the outline of her body and I felt the rising and falling of her chest as she breathed slowly. Her face was in shadows, but she looked peaceful, content.

"Your uncle, Saeed, he's Billy's partner?"

She nodded. "Yes. I introduced them. I'm sorry I did that." She slipped off of me and sat on the bed cross-legged. "I know Billy's sick. Uncle Saeed convinced him to see that Doctor Flores. He's a quack. My uncle is very clever, but not very smart about some things. Like modern medicine."

234

"The Feds think he's a terrorist. Billy too."

Fariba shook her head. "He's not. My uncle has upset some people in your government. They think he is meddling. But it's his country. He told me he was certain the terrorist designation will go away quickly."

"More bribes?"

"No. But he does know the right people. He was positive he has everything under control."

"He has Billy convinced. Do you believe him?"

"Yes." She stretched her arms over her head and sniffed her armpit. "I stink. Do you mind?"

I pushed her down on the bed. I teased her nipples with my tongue and kissed down her belly to her pussy. "You smell good to me."

She giggled and stroked my cock. "I think you are ready for another event, Mr. Burr."

Our first time, we had been manic, maybe a little anxious, as though the world really was about to end. Now we were familiar lovers. We took our time and when it was over we fell asleep in each other's arms.

When I awoke, Fariba was standing at the window.

"Come, Darwin. Watch the sunrise with me. You can see the lake from here."

I joined her at the window. The sky was dawn-grey and the sun was rising from Lake Michigan, a brilliant orange ball. I ran my hand down her smooth back. She turned and kissed me and ran her hands over my body. "You have a nice butt, Darwin Burr. I have a little boy's butt."

"Your ass looks great to me. But I'm old and my eyesight is failing."

"You're not that old. How about a shower?" she whispered as she ground her hips into me.

"Are you trying to fuck me to death?"

She grinned as she took my hand and led me to the shower. "No. But it wouldn't be such a bad way to go, would it?"

After the shower, we sat on the couch in our fluffy Orrington Hotel bathrobes and had the room service equivalent of the Fariba slam. I hadn't realized how hungry I was until we started eating. I wolfed down an omelet, a side of bacon and three pancakes, barely stopping to breathe. Fariba had a similar appetite but she ate slower. "Are you worried I'm going to steal your meal, Darwin?" she asked, grinning.

It wasn't hunger, it was nerves. I set my coffee cup down. "There was a lot more going on this week, than just Billy and the FBI," I said.

Fariba could tell by the look on my face, that my news would not be good. She seemed to gather herself, like someone who had learned how to deal with the worst kind of news. "Talk to me, Darwin."

I told her about Ray and his foolish tagging and how that ultimately led to his being murdered and how Daina shot Melvin Thigpen, and made it appear as though Ray killed him.

"Oh my god!" Fariba covered her mouth with her hands. "Daina shot him?" She took a deep breath and composed herself. "That was very brave of her," she said softly, her lips trembling.

I told her the Disciples thought Toni had killed their man and that I had spotted their SUV on Thanksgiving as they searched for her. I explained about Ed Mackey and told her about Thanksgiving dinner and how Daina and Astra and Toni were now all down south with Ed on his ATVs. I told her I was supposed to meet with Detective Sanchez on Monday morning to deliver Toni.

She reached across the table and took my hands. "You've given me all the facts. But not how you feel. That's what matters." She smiled sadly. She seemed to have a magical power that I was defenseless against.

"I'm angry. And conflicted, I guess. If Daina didn't have that gun, we'd all be dead. But I can't get around the fact that I don't know the woman I've lived with for twenty-five years. I always knew Daina had secrets, but not something like this."

"You feel betrayed and that makes you feel guilty."

"Yes. Exactly."

"I know that feeling. Years after my father's death, I learned he was an informant for SAVAK. The Shah's notorious secret police. It would be like discovering that your father had worked for the Nazis. I feel guilty, responsible even, for what my father did. And I feel guilty because I still love him. I only knew the man who was kind and gentle and loved me with all his being."

"I don't know what to do."

She got up from her chair and came over to the couch where I was sitting. I draped my arm over her shoulders and she leaned in close to me. "I don't know either. But I do know this. You aren't happy. You have a wife and a wonderful daughter and a beautiful house, and a good job. Is that enough? Maybe. I know we could be happy together. Even if we had nothing."

"I can't leave Astra."

"She's sixteen. In two years, she will be leaving you. My father thought he had to sacrifice everything he believed in for his family. He lost his family and died in disgrace. He should have been true to himself. And so should you."

The clinic was a blur. I didn't even try to concentrate. As Bobby Knight was giving a wrap-up talk I received a text from Astra.

Heading 4 home Love Astra.

Attached was a group selfie with Ed, Daina, Astra and Toni all somehow squished together on Ed's ATV. Toni was hugging Emerson.

After the conference we walked over to Lake Michigan and strolled along the bike trail that ran all the way into the city. As the sun set behind us, it lit up the skyline of Chicago. The city looked magical, a dream world where everything was clean and sparkling. Where anything was possible.

I took hold of Fariba's hand as we stood there at the edge of the water. "I love you . I want to be with you. I need to make sure Toni is safe, but if I can put this mess with Billy behind me, I will go anywhere with you. I think we can have a good life together."

I said those words. And I meant them.

**Chapter 39**
(*Sunday, November 27, 2005*)

When we got back to the Orrington after our walk, I noticed I had missed a call from Daina. I didn't want to not call her back, but it felt wrong to talk to her while I was with Fariba.

"Call her back," Fariba said. "I'm going to take a shower in my room and get ready for the banquet."

There was a closing banquet in the Grand Ballroom but we had planned to skip it and order room service. "What? I thought—"

She grinned impishly. "Just kidding. We can watch *Law & Order,* or, you know..." She kissed me and stepped into her room.

I sat on the sofa and looked down at Orrington Avenue. The street lamps were all lit with white Christmas lights. I wondered where I'd be on Christmas Day.

Daina had called an hour ago, probably right after they got back from their trip. She hadn't left a message so I figured it was just a check-in call, not an emergency. I called and the phone range several times. I was expecting it to go to voicemail again when Daina answered.

"Hi, Darwin. Sorry. Didn't hear phone." In the background, Astra and Toni were laughing.

"I can hear the girls," I said.

"Rented movie from Blockbuster. Girls, turn sound down. "

"We paused it Mom. Hi, Dad!" Astra shouted. "Let Mom go, we're watching a film."

Toni yelled, "Hi, Coach. You're missing a great flic. Denzel is so fine,"

I felt odd — as though I already were an outsider. Their lives were chugging along smoothly without me. I guess that was Fariba's point. "Sounds like they're having a good time. What are you watching?"

"Fire man. Something like that. Denzel Washington," Daina said.

"*Man on Fire*, Mom. You're as bad as Dad. Dad, let Mom go so we can watch our movie."

"Did the FBI trash the house?"

The girls voices subsided. Daina must have walked back into the kitchen. "No. Didn't they reach you? They called off search," she said, her voice lowered to almost a whisper.

"What?"

"I got call from FBI agent. Obnoxious voice. Said you weren't answering your phone. Told me they were cancelling search. Didn't say why. I didn't ask. He seemed annoyed with you."

"Yeah. I have that effect on some people."

"Also got call from Detective Sanchez. He doesn't need to see Toni. He wants to talk to you. Tomorrow. Early. He said he would be there at eight."

What the hell. No search. No Toni. "Just me?"

"That's what he said."

I was about to ask her what she thought Sanchez wanted, when my phone buzzed. Paul Meron was calling.

"I guess I'll find out what's up tomorrow. I'll drive right from here to the police station. Say hi to the girls. See you tomorrow night."

I hung up, and took the call. "Hey, Paul."

"Billy's on the plane. Looks like shit, but he hasn't changed. Fucker talked the whole way down here."

"Thanks, Paul. You driving back tonight?"

"Nothing else to do. The only places opened down here on Sunday are churches. Everything cool at your end?"

"I don't know. I'll find out tomorrow."

I set the phone down and looked beyond the buildings. The lake was now a huge empty darkness. I felt less hopeful than I had an hour ago when the sun illuminated everything. My mind raced. How do I tell Daina I'm leaving? What will that do to Astra? What's going to happen to Billy? What's going to happen to me?

Maybe I won't just be leaving Daina and Astra. Maybe I'll be leaving everyone.

I felt a soft hand on my neck. Fariba had slipped into the room through the connecting doors. She had on the Orrington robe, uncinched. "I don't want to shower alone. I need company."

I kissed her. "I think a shower is just what I need."

# Chapter 40
*(Monday, November 29, 2005)*

We got up early and made it to the interstate before six, but traffic was already intense. Fariba was scribbling madly in the journal she carried everywhere.

"You're not critiquing my performance are you?" I asked.

She looked at me, her mouth agape and then grinned. "Are you worried, Mr. Burr?"

"No."

"Good. You shouldn't be. I'm re-writing the notes I took on Coach Knight's agility drills. I can't wait to incorporate some of them in our practice tonight."

"More drills. Girls are going to love you."

Her phone buzzed with a text. She set down her journal and pulled the phone from her purse. "Damn," she said. "The high school is having a special teacher's meeting tonight to discuss the gang situation. They've cancelled basketball practice."

The gang situation. Life at Claxton High was never going to be the same. "We're playing Dixon on Friday. We should be okay with three days of practice. Maybe save some of your new drills for the week after."

Fariba smiled at me and then dutifully wrote down my suggestion in her journal.

As we were approaching Claxton, I got a text. Mine were never good news. "Could you check that for me?" I asked.

I handed the phone to Fariba.

"It's from Billy. He says 'Thanks' and he attached a photo." She showed me the screen — a selfie of Billy with a big smile, wearing a Hawaiian shirt with baggy shorts and a Cubs hat. He was standing by a palm tree with a postcard perfect ocean and beach behind him.

"Well, he looks happy," Fariba said. "Maybe that doctor will work a miracle."

"Do Muslims believe in miracles?"

Fariba deposited my phone in the console cupholder. "No, but I believe in you."

That was nice to hear, but it wasn't going to do Billy any good. That charlatan doctor couldn't save him, and neither could I.

We pulled up to Fariba's apartment building just before seven. She lived a few blocks from Walter's Pancake House so I dropped her off and decided to kill an hour there. Better to face Sanchez's news — which I figured had to be bad — on a full stomach.

I ordered the Fariba Slam. Walter appeared with a pot of coffee while I waited for my meal. "The team looked fantastic last week, Darwin. You and Fariba have done a super job with those girls."

Fariba and I. Everyone thought we were a great team. I wondered what everyone would think when we were really teamed up. I always told myself I didn't care what other people thought, but that was just another thing I lied to myself about.

I was starving and devoured the Slam quickly. As I was finishing, I got a call from Stephanie. She was leaving for Nigeria today.

"Stephanie," I said, unable to contain my pleasure. I didn't think I would ever see or hear from her again.

"Why don't you ever answer your cellphone?" she said, in her Bad Stephanie voice.

"I just did."

"The FBI and the U.S. Attorney have been calling you all weekend. Sean asked me to try. He thought you might take my call."

Calling all weekend? I don't think so. I might have ignored a couple of calls. Three tops. But Stephanie probably didn't want to debate that with me. "Sean was right about that. I always take your calls. What's up?"

"Are you sitting down?"

"I'm eating pancakes."

"Okay. Don't choke on them. The FBI has decided that Billy is not a terrorist. Actually they have deemed the "Free Iran Coalition," to not be a terrorist organization. Ergo, Billy is not aiding and abetting a terrorist organization, and thus your guilt by association to Billy has gone away. Isn't that fantastic, Darwin!"

Somewhere in the course of that message, Bad Stephanie had morphed into Good Stephanie. "So the FBI is done with me? What about AutoPro? Everything cool with them?"

I could hear a flight attendant announcing that they were about to close the doors to the plane. "I've got to turn off my phone. On my way to Lagos. Yes, I think everything will be fine. AutoPro just wants this whole thing to go away, and that's sort of what's happening. If you have any questions, call Vik Karode. Bye now. Congratulations!"

Holy shit. That was a great start to the day. I was tempted to call Fariba and share the news with her, but I still had Sanchez and the gang situation to deal with. That cop was never going to buy the 'Ray shot Thigpen' proposition and that was a problem.

Sanchez was waiting for me at his desk, which was considerably less cluttered than it had been a week ago. He looked like he had actually gotten some sleep and had definitely changed his clothes. He smiled as he shook my hand, but I still couldn't read him. This wasn't his faux cordiality like on the first visit when he was trying to convince me he was just a regular guy. His smile seemed more genuine now, but maybe he was just good at keeping me off-balance.

"Thanks for coming in, Mr. Burr. Did you have a good weekend?"

As a matter of fact, I had a very good weekend, but I didn't figure he really wanted to know about my weekend. "It was okay." I wanted to ask him why he no longer wanted to talk to Toni, but I figured I would find out soon enough.

He pulled out a manila envelope from a small stack of folders on his desk. "I have some photos I want to show you." He pulled out a mug shot of a young Black man. It was only a headshot, but he looked powerful. He had a weightlifter's neck and his shoulders had muscles on top of muscles. "Ever seen this man?"

I studied the photo. "I don't think so."

He pulled out a second mugshot. This one a slender man with a goatee. He had a professorial look, except for the numbers plastered across his chest. "I don't recognize him either."

Sanchez nodded and put the photos back in the envelope. "The large gentleman is King Kelly, aka Michael Amos Johnson. The bearded one is Triple D, aka David Devon Duckworth. They're up and comers in the Gangster Disciples." He pulled out another photo. "How about this?" he asked.

It was a black MDX. "That's the car I spotted on Thanksgiving."

"Are you sure?"

I looked at the license plate. DGB 747. "Yeah. Same license plate."

"Did you notice it on the previous Friday, when you stopped at Monique Wallaces's house to let Toni Wallace pick up her belongings?"

"No." It probably wouldn't be a good idea to tell him I was too petrified to notice anything.

"Here's the thing, Mr. Burr. We picked up Triple D and King Kelly on Saturday, thanks to your tip. Had a conversation with each of them. Separately. I sweated them on the Thigpen and Tunney hits. Couldn't get anything out of Triple D. He's old school gangsta. He wouldn't piss on me if I were on fire. But King Kelly, he's a newbie. Lots of muscles, not too bright. Told him I didn't care if he didn't do it, I'd have him arrested for harassing you and I'd get him sent to Cook County along with a rumor he was cooperating with our investigation."

I wondered if Sanchez had rehearsed this speech. Maybe he just watched a lot of *Law & Order* too. "They weren't harassing me," I said.

"I know. It was a ruse. It worked, too. King Kelly said they drove Thigpen to Monique Wallace's house the Friday night when Thigpen and Tunney were killed. They heard three gunshots and then a couple minutes later, three more. Not so loud. Those quieter shots had to come from the Luger. So Tunney takes two 44 shots to the chest and a third that blows his face away, but somehow three minutes later manages to get off three shots and kill Thigpen. The dude must have been a fucking Zombie."

Sanchez was enjoying his performance. "I'm sorry, Mr. Burr. I forgot to ask if you wanted coffee. Or water? Or maybe a coke?"

"No thanks." My mouth was dry and I could have used some water, but I was afraid with the lump in my throat I wouldn't be able to swallow.

"So a few minutes later Kelly sees a tall, middle-aged white man stumble out to the truck parked in the driveway. In his words, the man looked like he was scared shitless. Dropped the keys. Couldn't get the car door open. That kind of thing. And that's totally understandable, given what he just witnessed."

I thought this whole story might have been a clever Sanchez speculation. I don't remember dropping the keys. But scared shitless was for sure an accurate assessment.

"A moment later Kelly sees a Black girl and a blonde lady come out of the house. The lady's helping the girl, who has the same frightened look as the man. But the lady, she's different. Before she gets in the car, she scans the perimeter like a pro. Looks right at Kelly, but he's in the shadows and she doesn't spot him. Ice cold, he said. A killer."

I shrugged. "It wasn't us," No reason to fall apart now. It would be our word against a couple of gangbangers.

Sanchez held up his hand, as if to shush me. "Hear me out, Mr. Burr. I'm switching gears for a moment. He pulled another photo from the envelope. It was a grainy copy of a morgue photo of a young woman. "That woman look familiar?"

I shook my head. "No."

"Interesting. That's Daina Balodis. A Latvian prostitute killed in Helsinki in July 1976."

"Balodis was my wife's name before we got married," I said. He obviously knew that. It didn't take a genius to see where Sanchez was going with this. But Daina didn't escape from her tennis team until November 1978 so she couldn't have anything to do with this girl's death.

"I've talked with some folks who have worked with your wife. Judges, cops, even some lawyers. Not everyone likes her. She's not warm and fuzzy. But everyone, and I mean everyone respects her. She's first class. A solid citizen."

"I know."

"Of course you do. Did you know that Balodis means pigeon in Latvian?"

I stared at him. He was starting to piss me off.

"Since 9-11 we have had much better cooperation with many of the so-called Iron Curtain countries. It was fairly easy to discover that your wife entered the country using a forged passport."

Fuck. We could beat the Thigpen rap — it was their word against ours. I would take our chances on that contest any day. But forged papers, that was another story. After 9-11, INS went bad-ass. There were stories in the paper every month about folks getting deported even after they lived here for decades. Solid citizens just like Daina.

I couldn't let them deport Daina. She loved America. She deserved to be here. There was only one play.

"I shot Thigpen, He was about to shoot Toni. I had no choice."

Sanchez smiled slyly. This is what he had been orchestrating all along. "That's what I thought." He took the photo of Daina Balodis and ripped it in half and dumped it in his waste basket. "INS," he said disdainfully. "Fuck them. They don't need to be bothered with something like this. They got enough to do looking for the real bad guys."

I took a breath. My heart had been racing. Sanchez had put away his papers like we were done talking. From my *Law & Order* experience, this should be when he announces I'm under arrest and that I have the right to an attorney. I tried to remember where I had put the number for that criminal attorney Stephanie gave me.

"I believe you, Mr. Burr. Self-defense. No point wasting tax dollars pursuing a case against you. I'm going to talk to Triple D and King Kelly. In fact I'm going to do more than talk. I'm going to let them go, no harm no foul. But I'm going to make damn sure they understand that if anything were to happen to you or your wife or Toni, I will arrest their sorry asses and personally see to it that they get lost in the system for a long long long time.

I don't anticipate a problem with them. The gangs steer clear of civilians, and now they know Toni had nothing to do with Thigpen's untimely demise."

My jaw ached from clenching my teeth and I had a throbbing headache from concentrating on every word Sanchez said. Incredibly, impossibly, he was letting me go. Letting us all go. I was free. Daina was free. Toni was safe. I stood up and shook his hand. "Thank you, Detective."

He smiled again, and this was definitely from the heart. "Go home, Mr. Burr. Enjoy your family. Stay out of trouble."

As I was walking down the block to my truck, I called Daina. She answered on the first ring. She was as anxious about this meeting as I was.

"Sanchez has decided whoever killed Thigpen, it was self-defense. He let the two men go who had been looking for Toni and he convinced them that she had nothing to do with it. She won't have any trouble from the gang, and the Thigpen and Tunney cases are officially closed."

"You mean—"

"It's over, Daina. Nothing more to say about it." I didn't want to say anything too specific. There might have been someone listening or recording our conversation. No point in taking a chance.

"That's good." She said it softly, like the reality of the situation hadn't sunk in yet.

"It's very good. I will see you tonight. Let Toni know she's safe."

# Chapter 41

*(Monday, November 28, 2005)*

A Krispy Kreme donut shop had opened across the street from the police station. After I hung up the phone with Daina, I pulled over to their drive-thru and bought four dozen of their specialty — glazed donuts. I inhaled two before I was back on the highway, even though I had no business being hungry after the Fariba Slam.

I bought a cup of Felipe's coffee and gave him one of the glaze wonders. "Is good, Mr. Burr. Gracias." He reached under the counter for his cash envelope.

I held up my hand. "No more rent, Felipe."

His broad smile morphed into a worried frown. *"Hice algo mal?"* When Felipe got worried he forgot his English.

"English, *por favor,"* I said.

"Did I do something wrong? That lady not like my coffee?"

"Everything's cool, Felipe. New policy. No rent. Give the employees a discount if you want."

"Ah, si. Okay, Mr. Burr."

I reached for my wallet to pay for the coffee, but he waved me off.

"My treat, Mr. Burr. For the donut!"

I didn't argue the point with him. His coffee still sucked.

When I got to the warehouse I found Meron at the shipping table matching up documents. I dropped three of the donut boxes on his table. "Thanks for your help with Billy. These are for your crew."

He grabbed one. "Still warm. Thanks, boss. Hate to ruin your day, but Poindexter is upstairs. I'm guessing he's not here to play golf."

"Fuck me. I was having a perfect day."

"Best to avoid those. They never last."

As I walked up the bullpen steps, Kelly intercepted me, wide-eyed. "Poindexter is waiting in Billy's office for you."

"Welcome back. You feeling better? Here. Take these. They're for the office." I handed her the last box of Krispy Kremes. I didn't know what Kelly's involvement in this whole fiasco was, but I was ready to just put it all behind me.

Her face flushed with what I would interpret as a guilty look. "Dar, I'm sor—"

I held up my hand. "It doesn't matter. It's over. Let's move on."

"But—"

I leaned over the box of Krispy Kremes she was holding and kissed her on the forehead. "I mean it, Kelly. We're cool. Now let me find out what the big boss wants."

Poindexter was back to his corporate uniform, which was a relief. I figured that probably meant he wasn't going to be moving into Billy's office while he searched for Stephanie's replacement. We went through the same handshake ritual and he made a halfhearted effort to engage me in conversation on the Bulls, even though it was clear he knew nothing about the team or sport. He probably had a special Human Resources cheat sheet that linked me with basketball and figured that was an appropriate small talk topic. After a few moments of chitchat he invited me to sit down.

From his suit jacket pocket he pulled out a white business envelope. At least this one wouldn't have mugshots. Or morgue photos. I hoped.

"Darwin. It's been a harried four weeks. I'm hoping things can return to normal now. As you know Stephanie Washington has left the company. Personal reasons. We all miss her, but certainly understand her situation. She was extremely complimentary about the support you provided her in her role as Interim DC Manager. And she recommended in her Management Development Questionnaire that you be her replacement. I heartily concurred with her endorsement." He reached across the desk to hand me the envelope. "Congratulations, Darwin. I know you'll do a super job."

Holy shit. I had this almost creepy feeling I must have slipped back into the *Twilight Zone*. I made a mental note to go out and buy a lottery ticket, because I had obviously opened a vein of incredibly good luck.

Harry stepped around his desk and shook my hand again. For good measure, he added the back clasp. I was now officially part of management. I immediately thought of Daina, and how pleased she'd be. And then I remembered Fariba and I felt really good and really shitty at the same time.

After Harry left, I sat down at Billy's desk and that's when it hit me. I was about to leave my wife of twenty-five years and take over the job of my best friend. I tried to pretend that I was completely dispassionate about Billy's situation. Like Billy was just some guy I worked for.

But he wasn't. For almost as long as I can remember, Billy had been a part of my life. He was the kid who had been there when my mom tried to kill herself. The friend who spent hours on the playground, chasing down my errant shots and making me laugh at all his stupid jokes while I honed my game. The teammate who had made possible the greatest moment of my life. The boss who had treated me square for the last twenty years. He was my friend.

Billy wasn't going to find a cure in some jungle clinic. He was going to die there and I was never going to see him again. That made me incredibly sad, and the idea of me taking his job was wrong. I wanted to call Poindexter and tell him to find someone else, but I knew what Billy would say to that: "What the fuck, Burr! More money, less work — what's wrong with that? What's wrong with you?"

I sat in my office the rest of the day, going through my files, as though I were preparing to move. But most of the time I was just sitting at my desk thinking about what I wanted and what I didn't want. I didn't want Billy's job. I wanted to coach. I didn't want to spend the rest of my life with Daina, who didn't really love me, who probably couldn't love anyone. I wanted Fariba. I didn't want to lose my daughter. I wanted to have more kids. Fuck. Why not add world peace to my list of impossible wants and needs?

What the hell was wrong with me? My situation was so much better than it had been just twenty-four hours ago, I should be ecstatic. What had Fariba said? You can't win the race in the first round, but you can lose it. I needed to let the game come to me. Some of this stuff would work itself out. I didn't have to make every decision today. Poindexter could wait. So could Fariba.

**Chapter 42**
*(Monday evening, November 28, 2005)*

When I walked through the kitchen door, Daina was standing next to a sizzling frying pan, shaking something in a paper bag, while Astra and Toni were at the table peeling potatoes and chopping up green beans. They were laughing and talking over each other.

"Hey, Dad!" Astra jumped up from the table and ran to hug me, as though I had been gone for a month, instead of a weekend. What would it be like when I was really gone for a month? Or six months? "Can we get an ATV?"

"Coach!" Toni said, as she chopped the ends off a wedge of green beans with Ed Mackey zeal. "Those dune buggies are sick. You should have seen Mrs. Burr driving that thing. Like one of those Fast and Furious chicks. Mr. Mackey said she could drive that thing better than any of the women he knew."

"ATVs, Toni," Astra said. "Mr. Mackey would be upset if he heard you calling them dune buggies."

"You gals must have worn old Ed out," I said.

Daina laughed. "I think he was very glad to retreat to his home after three hours in the car with the girls." She made bird mouth gestures with her hands. "Chatter, chatter, chatter."

"No fair, Mom. You're the one who told all those stories about Dad's high school basketball team."

I looked at Daina quizzically. She told the story of "The Shot"?

She smiled, almost like she was flirting, and said, "I hear Billy tell story so many times, I forget I wasn't there."

"I hope that's not one of Mackey's rabbits," I said as she dumped the contents of the bag on to a platter. It was some kind meat that she had coated with a mixture of flour and spices.

"Venison. Gift from Ed. He has lifetime supply." The venison steaks sizzled as she dropped them into the hot oil.

It was another Ozzie and Harriet meal. The addition of Toni changed our family dynamic. Astra usually didn't talk much during dinner and she seldom shared, without prompting, any news about her day. I guess I'm to blame for that. Burrs don't share. And Daina, she was so wound up in her job, it was all she ever talked about. We never laughed at the dinner table. We ate meals in a hurry and escaped to our own private domains. But now, with Toni part of the mix, we talked and laughed. Nobody was in a rush to leave the table.

We had gone from a morgue to a carnival.

"Special dessert for your return, Dad," Astra said. She grinned at Toni and they both laughed like dessert was the funniest thing they had heard of.

Toni jumped up from the table and brought me a huge slice of sweet potato pie. Everyone was grinning.

"Nobody liked the pie, did they?" I said.

Another explosion of laughter. Even Daina joined in. "Someone forgot brown sugar," Daina said.

"That was Toni's job," Astra said.

"You were in charge of sugar," Toni said.

"I do the white sugar. You do the brown sugar."

I took a bite. "This is good. Not real sweet, but tastes fine."

Both of the girls wrinkled up their faces. "Tastes too much like sweet potatoes," Toni said. "Luckily we bought HoHos at the grocery." She jumped up again and retrieved the package of HoHos.

Daina gave a good natured frown and stood up from the table. "You girls do dishes. Darwin, bring pie in dining room. We need to talk."

Damn. I had the feeling my streak of good news was about to end. I left the pie and joined her at the dining room table. She closed the door. Her face turned grim.

"There's still no news on Monique or Bedelia and the baby. Monique would have contacted me by now if…" She bit on her lip and hung her head.

"I'm sorry, Daina." I resisted the impulse to offer her some shred of hope. She wouldn't have believed me.

"I talked with Child Welfare today." She had a strange look on her face. She was studying me. "Would you be willing to adopt Toni?"

Life can change in a heartbeat: Make a last second shot to win the state championship. Stop to play HORSE with some kid you don't even know. Be in the wrong place when Melvin Thigpen comes to call. I had my lifetime road trip planned. A detour to a new life with Fariba. She was kind and funny and beautiful and she loved me. We would make a good life together. We would have kids and we would work at jobs we loved. It was a good plan.

But now this. Another shot with the family I have now. How could I say no? If I went with Fariba, it would kill any chance for Daina to adopt Toni and it would devastate Astra and Toni. With that simple question, Daina had just offered me an opportunity I had given up on long ago and blown up my new plan.

"Yes, I would be willing to adopt Toni. Would you?"

Daina nodded. "She's good person. Good for Astra. For me too. Good for all of us."

"What does she think?"

"We should ask. Yes?"

"I think so." What the hell. No reason to wait. Maybe she didn't want to be adopted by white people. I yelled through the kitchen door. "Toni! Astra! Can you come in here?"

They bounced through the door, like they had been waiting to be summoned. Their faces had a mix of excitement and trepidation. I didn't want to prolong the suspense. "Go ahead, Daina."

She looked at me and nodded. "Toni. We have no news on Monique or Bedelia and the baby. I hate to say this, but I think they were killed."

Astra covered her face, but Toni stared at Daina without expression. She had come to that conclusion long ago.

"What are you going to do with me?" she asked.

From her tone, she sounded like she was steeling herself for the worst. Expecting us to discard her.

"If you are willing, we would like to adopt you," Daina said.

Toni's jaw dropped and Astra looked at us with shock. Happy shock. Toni screamed. "Oh my god! Oh my god!" She crushed Astra with an embrace and then ran to Daina, with tears streaming down her face. "Yes. Yes. Yes. Yes." She buried her face in Daina's chest and then she pulled away and looked at me. A big grin creased her face. "Does that mean I should call you Dad, Coach?"

I swallowed trying to get rid of the lump in my throat. My eyes felt moist. "Just call me Coach."

## Chapter 43
(*Monday, November 28, 2005*)

Daina explained to us how the adoption process worked. Toni's mom had relinquished her parental rights to Monique. With Monique missing, Toni became a ward of the state. Daina, with her connections, would get herself appointed as Toni's guardian immediately. Then we would apply for adoption. The adoption process could take up to six months, but given it was uncontested, and given that Daina knew everyone involved in the bureaucracy, it should proceed without a glitch.

The girls volunteered to clean the kitchen — that would have never happened before Toni — and Daina began filling out the forms that were required for her to apply for the guardianship. We both agreed it would be better that she be the sole guardian, so that none of my Billy problems could derail the process. I watched a Bulls game, and even though they were winning, I couldn't focus on the game. I had to let Fariba know what had happened.

I texted her, "Need to talk. Can I come over?"

She replied almost instantly:

Yes. Is there a problem?

I texted her back:

Be there in 15 minutes.

Daina was buried in her paperwork. "I have to go out for a few minutes," I said.

She looked at me with the Daina-frown, but she just nodded. It was almost like she knew.

Fariba had a townhouse in Riverview Gardens. There was no river, her view was of the Junior High School across the street and the only garden was a small courtyard with a few evergreen bushes and a Weber grill that was shared by the tenants. I parked on the street and slowly walked toward the door. My hands were clammy and I was sweating even though it was near freezing and I wore my thin lambskin leather jacket. I was torn. I wanted to keep seeing Fariba and I wanted Toni to be a part of our family. And as much as I wanted both of those things, I also didn't want to hurt Fariba. She deserved better.

Her porch light was on and she opened her front door as I walked up the steps. She smiled thinly as I stepped inside. She was holding a steamy mug. "I've made some tea. Would you like some?"

I shook my head no. As pathetic as it sounds, I was actually afraid I might start crying. I had an ache in my chest. I followed her into her living room that looked out on to the school across the street. She set her drink on the coffee table and perched on the edge of the sofa. She gestured toward the arm chair opposite the sofa. "Sit down, Darwin. You have something to tell me?" She spoke softly, like I was one of her students she was counseling.

I had rehearsed a dozen ways to try and explain what had happened. They all sucked. "Daina wants to adopt Toni," I said. Fariba nodded, but didn't say anything. "That's what I want to. I'm sorry."

She closed her eyes for a moment. She opened them again and smiled. "I'm happy for Toni. That is very good news for her."

I stared down at my feet. "I'm sorry."

"You shouldn't be."

"I love you."

"I know. I love you too. Sometimes love's not enough." She sighed and clasped her hands together.

I wiped a tear from my cheek. I wanted to take her in my arms and kiss her again. Hold her tight. Never let her go.

"I think you need to leave now." She stood up and walked me to her front door.

I stood in her doorway, desperately wanting to touch her, but afraid. She wrapped her arms around me and we embraced. "Please go. I don't want you to see me cry. I will survive this. So will you. And we will become friends. Good friends. I will always love you."

She closed the door. I knew she was right. Sometimes love is not enough.

## Chapter 44
(*Tuesday, November 29, 2005*)

I had another night where I could not take my brain out of gear. The last time that happened was after I had kissed Fariba in the Clarkie's parking lot. That was just three weeks ago. It didn't seem possible. My whole world had changed in those three weeks. Something broke loose in me and I didn't think I was ever going to be the same.

Even after a hot shower I was still fuzzy-headed. I needed coffee, but I didn't want to stop at Walter's and I couldn't abide any more of Felipe's molten swill. I decided to try the food mart at the BP gas station on Hoover Road. The attendant had a television on, tuned to CNN. They always have "breaking news" trumpeted as though the world is about to end. Today's big news appeared to be an outdoor rally in New York. A swarthy young man in a track suit, walked by carrying a placard that said, "Free Iran Coalition."

That was the organization Fariba's uncle was involved with. I sipped my coffee and peered closer at the rally. According to the CNN captioning, the speaker was Saeed Pahlavi. Holy shit. He was slamming the FBI, the Bush administration, the CIA and a host of others for their "malicious vendetta," that temporarily branded his organization as a terrorist group. He was clearly not accepting victory graciously.

I was curious as to how CNN would spin his attack, but he showed no signs that he was ready to stop talking so I took my coffee and drove on to AutoPro. With the plan to adopt Toni, I decided that accepting Poindexter's offer to take Billy's job was the right choice. I didn't have to tell him anything. He assumed I would take it. I didn't even have to pack. My plan, which came to me during my night of tossing and turning, was to stay in my office, divide up my old job responsibilities between Kelly and Paul Meron and make Billy's office into a real conference room. The truckers could keep their room all for themselves.

I was going to meet with the two of them as soon as I finished my coffee. But when I walked into the bullpen there was a man talking to Kelly. He was Indian or Pakistani and was wearing a well-tailored suit that looked expensive.

"Here he is," Kelly said to the man. "Darwin, this is, uh…."

"Vik Karode, Mr. Burr. How do you do?" He extended his hand.

"Stephanie's friend?" I asked, but I knew. Karode was the criminal lawyer she recommended I contact.

"Yes. Is there someplace we can talk?"

Whatever he had to say, he didn't want to say it in front of Kelly. I couldn't argue with that approach. "Follow me." I led him into my office and closed the door. I was getting a bad vibe. I wasn't due any more good news. This had to be bad. It was.

He sat down in the chair across from my desk and motioned for me to sit down, too. Another bad sign.

"I've learned that the U.S. Attorney has charged you with 12 violations of the RICO statute. He's charging Mr. Rourke on 43 counts. You will be arraigned this afternoon at two p.m. at the Federal Court in Chicago. I am prepared to represent you, or you may choose your own counsel."

Meron was right. Those perfect days don't last. "I thought Stephanie said that there wasn't going to be any indictment. What happened?"

Karode shook his head disgustedly. "Saeed Pahlavi happened. His unhinged rhetoric annoyed and embarrassed the President. And when that happens the shit rolls downhill like a landslide. He chews on the Attorney General who then squeezes the U.S. Attorney and we end up with this bullshit indictment. You are simply collateral damage. Pahlavi is friends with Rourke so if its hands off on Pahlavi then they want Rourke. And you are the road to Rourke."

"I don't have an attorney and if Stephanie recommends you, then I'm fine with having you as my attorney. But why are you here? I didn't think lawyers made house calls."

Karode nodded as if to concede the point. "Stephanie can be, let's say, dogmatic, when she has a strongly held opinion."

"Seems to be the only kind she has."

"Stephanie thought you might not show up if I just called and asked you to come to Chicago to be arraigned. Says you're stubborn. Pigheaded I think was her word."

"Sounds right. So what's going to happen?"

"It's all pro forma. It won't take more than ten minutes. Since we will have the charges in writing, we'll waive the formal reading of them. Mr. Rourke won't be arraigned since he needs to be present. You'll plead not guilty and the judge will release you on your recognizance. They won't even set bail. You should be home in time for dinner."

"Then there will be a trial?"

"God I hope not. Hardly any Federal cases go to trial. This case will be settled with a plea agreement. You have something they want, so we have leverage. But we can talk about that later."

So the roller coaster of Billy troubles continued. I thought about calling Fariba to see if she could get her uncle to shut up, but I decided it was too late for that. I also didn't call Daina. She had a meeting scheduled to secure her appointment as Toni's guardian, and I figured it would be better for her to be ignorant of my situation while that was going on. I would explain this latest Billy development tonight at our family dinner.

"Where do I go?"

"Stephanie would prefer that I drive you. And prefer isn't really the right word."

Karode drove a silver Porsche 911. It looked new, but it's hard to tell with Porsches — they don't change from year to year. "Business must be good," I said, as I settled into the passenger seat.

"Business is good. The government seems to be intent on making everything a crime, which creates a great market for my services."

"How much do those services cost?" I still had my Krugerrands stowed away at home.

"Let's hold off on that discussion until we see what happens today. I'm optimistic, but you never know with this kind of situation."

"What kind of situation?"

Karode shifted into overdrive and the Porsche smoothly accelerated past a line of tanker trucks. "Political," he said.

"You worked with Stephanie for this guy Fitzgerald?"

"Fitzpatrick. Yes. I worked for him for five years. Stephanie thinks very highly of Sean."

"You don't?"

Karode frowned. Slightly. Like a man who worked hard not to reveal too much. "He would sell out his mother if the AG asked him to. His number one guiding principal is to do what is right..." Karode hesitated as he checked the traffic in his rearview. "...for Sean Fitzpatrick."

"Fuck."

"He's got a lot on his plate. This is not a career-maker for anybody. Some other crisis will come up, and getting back at that blowhard Pahlavi won't be at the top of the AG's list any more. That's when Sean will send in one of his assistants and we'll make a plea deal."

The arraignment proceeded almost exactly as Karode had outlined it. Until the end. The judge, Anton Slamkowski, who looked like he could have had a career in the stockyards, if Chicago still had stockyards, was the judge. The bailiff called the case: "*United States v. William Rourke, et al.*" I was just et al, which I guess was a good thing. Vik introduced himself and me to the judge and everyone was invariably polite. Mr. Karode this, Mr. Fitzpatrick that, and lots of Your Honors. Even I was Mr. Burr when I wasn't The Defendant. I stood next to my lawyer with my hands clasped below my belt trying not to look either too confused or too criminal. The only time I spoke was when the judge asked me how I pleaded and I had to clear my throat to say, less boldly than I liked, "Not Guilty."

The judge then asked for a bail recommendation. And that's when the scene went off script. Sean Fitzpatrick stood and buttoned his coat, just like Sam Waterston used to do before he delivered some bombshell. But Fitzpatrick undramatically, without raising his voice or expressing the least bit of outrage, requested that I be held without bail. He added, "The defendant's co-defendant is a fugitive who we believe has fled the country. Moreover this co-defendant has associations with disreputable, check that, unsavory, suspicious international organizations. Mr. Burr has significant resources and is facing decades of prison time. He has the means and motivation to flee."

Karode had clearly not expected that play and immediately responded loudly and formally. "Your honor, this is a surprising request. I'm disappointed in Mr. Fitzpatrick." Karode turned to glare at Fitzpatrick, but Fitzpatrick just looked forward impassively. Then Karode using his folksy, sincere voice started talking about me like we were old friends. Neighbors. "Darwin has no criminal record. Not even a parking ticket. He's married and a pillar of his community. He coaches his daughter's high school basketball team. He does not know where Mr. Rourke is, does not have contact with Mr. Rourke, and has never had association of any kind with Mr. Rourke's so-called unsavory associates. He has surrendered his passport and he has deep roots to his community. Mr. Burr is not, by any stretch of the imagination, a flight risk. Your honor, if the Court wishes, we could bring in witness after witness who would testify to Mr. Burr's integrity. Darwin is anxious to clear his name and when this case comes to trial, he will be vindicated. We request that he be released on his own recognizance."

I thought that was a pretty good speech under the circumstances. I bought it. But Judge Slamkowski didn't hesitate. "Bail denied. Defendant remanded."

I turned to Karode as the Marshals came to take me away. "You were right. He is a prick."

Karode frowned. "Don't say anything. No one is your friend. Trust no one. I'll find out what the deal is. This is fucked up. Hang in there."

Not perhaps the best choice of words.

## Chapter 45
*(Friday, December 2, 2005)*

Federal defendants who are denied bail are held at Federal Detention Center just blocks from the courthouse. There are about twenty floors of "residents," most are waiting for something, bail, trial, plea bargain. I wasn't sure what I was waiting for.

It took them ten hours to process me. I came up with a bunch of ideas on how they could make the process more efficient, but I don't think that was their goal. It was like a slow motion cattle drive. We got herded from station to station, asked the same questions over and over, probed and prodded repeatedly. It sucked. I finally made it through the last station at 3 a.m. They handed me my bedding and one of the guards guided me to my bunk. It was a large room with several long rows of bunk beds.

I was nervous. Apprehensive. Scared. But it wasn't as bad as I feared. Some of the guards processing us were dicks, but most of them just seemed bored. By the time I got to my bunk I was exhausted and fell asleep almost immediately, despite the stuffy close quarters and the din of two hundred inmates trying to sleep.

The daily routine was mind-numbingly simple. Released from our bunkhouse for breakfast — we were offered a sugary wafer and some kind of diluted fruit juice, then it was off to the common room to watch morning soaps until lunch — slimy baloney sandwiches on white bread, then back to the TV and the afternoon talk shows, and finally dinner — another baloney sandwich. No place to exercise. No library. Literally nothing to do.

Family members or friends had to be put on an approved list before I could have visitors. Again, I had a bunch of ways I could have improved their system, but there had been some embarrassing escapes in the last year and I don't think they were interested in making it easier to visit.

Fortunately Daina knew how to navigate the system and with her connections she was able to visit me on my third day in jail.

The visitor center was just like the one on *Law & Order*. A bank of phones with plexiglass between the inmate and visitor. The phones on my side smelled like bad breath warmed over. The handset was sticky. Daina looked grim, but not flustered. She exhibited her usual control. "I met with your lawyer's daughter, Apala. Mr. Karode has large trial. She's young."

What the fuck. "How young?"

Daina shrugged. "She's a lawyer. But young. Maybe 28? She told me she will see you tomorrow."

Not what I wanted to hear. "How did the guardian thing go?" I needed some good news.

Daina smiled and my day immediately brightened. "Went fine. I am officially Toni's guardian." She stopped smiling. "The girls are very upset about you. Toni even more than Astra."

"Tell them I'm okay. I am okay. Just fucking bored to death."

"The attorney needs twenty thousand dollar retainer," she said. "Apala told me many clients take out loan on their houses. I can do that, yes?"

"You don't need to. I borrowed on my 401k when the FBI was threatening me before. There is forty-five thousand dollars in Krugerrands in a tube in my gym bag in the back of my closet. Pay her with those."

Daina looked at me, her head slightly tilted as if to say, "There are a lot of things you haven't told me." But all she actually said was, "Okay. I will get them."

I met with Apala Karode the next day. We met in a room set up for inmates to meet with their attorneys. It was a tiny windowless space, with a plank table where the benches were all bolted to the floor. It had a gaseous, sweaty smell. That odor permeated the whole jail, but it was more intense, harder to ignore in the closed space.

Apala was short and plump with stylishly short, shiny black hair. She was serious and had a quiet confidence. We both knew she was just a placeholder. She was there so I wouldn't think that I had been forgotten by Vik.

"Are you okay, Mr. Burr? Any problems with other inmates?"

"No. It's boring and the food sucks. How do I get out of here?"

She set her briefcase on the table, but she didn't open it. "My father is trying to get a meeting with the prosecutor to discuss a plea. It's difficult at this time of year. The holidays. Lots of yearend legal activities. It doesn't look like he will have a chance to meet before the New Year."

I wanted to yell. Pound the table. Do something. But for what purpose? There were hundreds of us in here, we all wanted to get out. Some of the men had been here for years. Complaining wasn't going to help. "Well that sucks," I said.

"I know. I'm sorry. Thank you for paying our retainer so promptly." Her eyebrows raised slightly, but she offered nothing more about being paid in gold. "My father is convinced they aren't really interested in you. They want Mr. Rourke. If you can cooperate by letting them know where he is, that would favorably impact our plea deal."

"I don't know where he is." That was true. Billy told me he was in Honduras, but he might have lied. "He's dying."

"Excuse me?" Apala's eyes widened.

"He has cancer. I don't think he has long to live."

"That's…I'm sorry I was about to say that was good news. I know he's your friend. I'm sorry for him. If he dies, however, I think they will lose interest in pursuing you."

"Great. If he calls me I'll let him know he should hurry up and die."

I liked Apala. She didn't take my petulance personally. She was unflappable like those Indian customer service people I would encounter on the phone. She opened her briefcase and pulled out my visitor authorization list. "We don't believe it is wise for you to have a visit from Fariba Pahlavi."

My heart pinged when she said Fariba's name. I kept trying not to think about her, but had failed miserably. I thought about her all the time.

"Why?" I asked even though I knew the answer.

"She has the wrong name. If we go to trial, the prosecution will tie her to her uncle, Saeed Pahlavi, and make her part of their conspiracy case. It will get very messy."

"I thought Vik said it would never go to trial."

"We have to prepare for trial. We expect a plea, but we must be prepared for trial. If they refused to negotiate, trial may be a better option for you. It will be my job over the next few weeks to get to know you better. So we can show the jury your many appealing qualities."

"I'm not going anywhere. Stop by anytime you want." Of course at two hundred dollars an hour, it wasn't going to take too long for me to burn through all my Krugerrands.

As she put the visitor list back in her briefcase, she sighed and with a look I had learned to recognize as a prelude to bad news, said, "One last thing, Mr. Burr." She exhaled slowly. "I'm sorry to inform you that AutoPro has terminated your employment. They obviously don't put much stock in the "innocent until proven guilty" concept. I'm sorry."

I would have suggested to her that it's better to deliver the bad news first, but she didn't really have any good news so I guess it didn't matter.

The first thing I thought of when she told me I had been fired, was that I would no longer be able to help coach the girls basketball team. That kind of thinking is clearly an indication of how incarceration had messed with my brain. Of course I couldn't coach the girls team. I was locked up in a jail cell and I was not getting out. Maybe for a long time.

## Chapter 46
(*Wednesday, January 12, 2006*)

The days didn't fly by. With no books or magazines to read, no place to exercise, nothing to do but watch television and with those awful tasting meals full of junk calories, I felt like I'd lost twenty points of IQ and gained twenty pounds of fat.

Apala met with me to discuss my life. She wanted to learn about my "good qualities," so she could help her father to prepare for my defense. She even wanted to know about The Shot. I tried to tell that story like Billy would have, but I was never going to have Billy's flair. Daina visited a couple times a week. She wanted to bring the girls but I didn't want them to see me in here. The team lost the two games they played right after I was arrested. I told Daina the best thing they could do for me while I was in here was play like they played before everything went to hell. They won the next game by thirty points and two days before Christmas they beat Claypool, on their court, by ten points.

Despite Karode's warning to trust no one, I had become friendly with several of the men in my cell block. When life sucks, you look for victories wherever you can find them. The Claxton Eagle Girls basketball team became the most popular team in Floor 6 of the Federal Detention Center.. Reveling in that victory over Claypool with my fellow prisoners was the best Christmas present I could have under the circumstances.

Karode finally had a preliminary meeting with one of Fitzpatrick's assistants to discuss my case. I could tell the moment he walked in the door that it hadn't gone well.

"Sean still has a bug up his ass about this case. They say if we go to trial they will ask for a sentence of twenty to forty years." He waved that off. "That's just posturing. That will never happen." I reminded him that he had been wrong before. He huffed. "Right now their offer is if you plead guilty and tell them where Mr. Rourke is hiding out, they will reduce the sentence to four years. Under federal code, you would have to serve eighty five percent of that sentence. I rejected it as not being even a good-faith offer. They knew I would. Is that okay with you?"

I thought of how old Astra and Toni would be in four years. "Okay." I had a tight feeling in my gut. "So now what?"

"We will prepare for trial. They don't have a strong case and they know it. They will try to delay, hope to wear you down. Sooner or later their number will come down. Unfortunately you are stuck here until that happens. Unless..."

"Unless Billy dies."

He shrugged. "That would be a game-changer. But not something we need to wish for. I understand. I will push for a speedy trial."

The next day I had a visit from Kelly. It's a harrowing experience to visit someone in jail. I was sorry she had to go through it, but it was great to see her.

"They gave Billy's job to that dickwad, Stu Granger. He's so fucking faux nice I want to puke. Made big management points by eliminating your job."

"So now you get to do all of my work. For no more money, right?"

She nodded and frowned. "I'm sorry to be complaining. I'm just nervous. I cried for three days when I heard they'd locked you up." She leaned closer to the glass, as though she could whisper through it. "Are these phones bugged?"

I honestly didn't know, but it didn't seem likely. "No."

She pulled out a photo and held it up to the glass. It was Billy on the beach. He looked great. Tanned and thin, but not gaunt, like when I saw him in Evanston. "He says he's cured. He needs another six months of treatments, but that's just a precaution. He told me that as soon as he's finished this last cycle he will come home. But he wanted me to tell you that if you need for him to come now he will."

"That's great news. That he's better. He looks great. Tell him to stay there and finish the job."

"Are you sure?"

"Billy's our friend, right Kelly?"

A tear rolled down her cheek. "You're a class act, Dar." She leaned over and kissed the plexiglass. "I'll tell him."

It was good news to learn that Billy was…cured? In remission? Whatever had happened to him it didn't look to me like he was going to croak anytime soon. It meant I could stop wishing that if he was dying, that he do it quickly. I hated hoping Billy would die. Now we could go to trial and I would hope Vik Karode was as good as he thought he was.

## Chapter 47
*(Tuesday, February 28, 2006)*

Another of the great features of incarceration is that the authorities open all your mail. I don't know if they read it, mostly they just want to make sure no one is sending the inmates contraband or porn. So any letters sent take an extra week to ten days to get to the inmate. The jail mail policy is another thing on my list of activities I could improve.

I was surprised and unreasonably happy to get a letter from Fariba.

> February 18, 2006
>
> Dear Darwin,
>
> I hope I am not causing more difficulty by writing to you. I tried to visit, but I was not on the list. I understand why. I am so very sorry that you were arrested because of the bellicose actions of my Uncle whom you don't even know.
>
> My heart aches when I think of you locked up. I cannot thank you enough for all you have done for me. The team misses you more than you can imagine. We had a difficult time focusing on basketball after you were taken from us. As you probably know we lost the next two games. But Toni and Astra held a team meeting and told the girls that the best way to help you was to play hard. And Win!
>
> It was truly inspirational. And the team has heeded that call. We have won twelve games in a row and are now preparing for the State Tournament. I wish with all my being that you could be with us for the tournament. I, who does not believe in miracles, am praying for one.

There is much I wish to say to you that I cannot. My heart aches. I will always and forever be your devoted friend. If I can help you in anyway please, please let me.

Your dearest friend,

Fariba

I read that letter a hundred times. And that was just on the first day. I discovered, or perhaps a more accurate word would be "imagined," hidden meanings. Despite my shoddy treatment of her, I believed Fariba still had feelings for me. When I thought about her, my chest ached. But I treasured that pain. Jail is such a numbing experience that pain, heartache, even sadness is better. When I ached for Fariba, I knew I was still alive.

## Chapter 48
*(Thursday, March 2, 2006)*

With the Illinois Girls High School Basketball Championship Tournament and my trial preparation both in full swing, the last couple of weeks provided a welcomed relief from the tedium of jail. The Claxton Eagles won their sectional and marched through the state tournament rolling over their opponents. Only the undefeated Vernon Hills Cougars stood between them and the state title. The championship game would be held on Saturday evening in Redbird Arena in Normal, Illinois.

Jury selection for my trial was scheduled to begin on Monday. For the last three weeks Apala had been working intensely, preparing me for the trial. She told me the prosecution was focusing on Billy's relationship with the specialty suppliers. They intended to elicit testimony from employees of Spartan Engines, L&B Oil Pump, and Jasper Transmission.

"The prosecution will attempt to show that Billy extorted money from those suppliers and that you acted as his bag man."

It was a pretty good theory. Despite Billy's intentions to keep me out of it, I ended up delivering to him the NPC cash. That event would implicate not just me, but also Kelly and Paul.

"They plan to call several AutoPro employees." Apala handed me their witness list. At the top of the list was their star, Wally Weidman, along with Kelly Craven, Paul Meron and Felipe Hernandez. My heart sank. Especially at the prospect of poor Felipe being sweated by that prick Sean Fitzpatrick.

"Do you see anyone on that list who might be a problem for us?" Apala asked.

It was always 'us' when Apala was talking with me. A nice touch. It made me feel like she was planning to accompany me to Dixon Correctional if we lost.

274

"Felipe could be a problem." I knew from all those episodes of *Law & Order* that a defendant was supposed to be totally honest with his lawyer. Tell them everything. Even the bad stuff, like how Paul and Kelly helped me to deliver a quarter million dollars to Billy. But I didn't do that.

"What's the problem with Felipe?"

"Billy charged the roach coach operators rent. He handled it all. They paid him directly. I don't know how much. The week after Billy vanished, I was buying a coffee from Felipe and he handed me his rent money. I didn't know what to do with it, so I put it in the petty cash drawer." There was, at least, an element of truth in my answer.

Apala nodded and made some notes. "Was that the only occasion that happened?"

"No. A few weeks later he tried to pay me again, and I told him we were no longer charging him rent."

"So you didn't take the cash?"

"No."

"That's good. We can use that." She made some more notes. "Why do you think they want the testimony of Kelly Craven and Paul Meron?"

It was becoming sickeningly clear to me that the trial would be ugly. My only chance for acquittal required Kelly and Meron to perjure themselves. Or to have extremely bad memories. And if Kelly broke, and maybe she already had, it would be a disaster for Paul Meron. He hid the cash, he transported Billy, he provided me with a vehicle so I could elude the FBI. He would be screwed along with me.

"I don't know why they want to talk to them."

That afternoon, while I was hanging out in the common area watching *The Young and the Restless,* the guard summoned me. Vik Karode had just come from a pre-trial conference with Sean Fitzpatrick. When I walked into the meeting room, I was surprised to see that he had brought Daina along. She smiled tightly at me, as inscrutable as ever, but Karode's body language — he seemed to be bursting from his expensive Italian suit — suggested he had something interesting to reveal.

"A couple of new developments," he said. "First and most important. I have had indirect communications with Billy Rourke. It's a back channel and I don't want to say anything more about it. But Rourke will agree to return and face prosecution, if the U.S. Attorney drops all charges against you."

I took a long drink from the bottle of water  Vik had provided. How did he find Billy? Or did Billy find him? "Would they do that? Just let me go?"

Karode's eyebrows twitched. "Yes. You could stay out of prison."

"What would happen to Billy?"

"I can't represent Billy. I'm certain he would mount a vigorous defense. Unlikely he could avoid jail time."

There was something more he wasn't telling me. "What's the catch?"

Karode shrugged and looked at Daina. "No catch. They would give you immunity and you would have to testify against him. Just like Wally Weidman. And then you would be free to get on with your life."

I knew there was a catch. "What's the other development, Vik?"

Karode frowned. He was not happy with my obvious lack of enthusiasm for door number one.

"Before I had this outreach from Rourke, I met with Sean Fitzpatrick. And as I predicted, his number has come down. They don't want a trial any more than you do."

I wasn't sure about that. "So what's his number now?"

"Two years. And they'll count time-served here, so that would bring it down to twenty-two months. With good behavior you could be out in a year and half. And it would be at a minimum security facility."

"So I would be out of prison at the end of 2008?"

Karode's brow wrinkled with confusion. "Well yes. But you can be out now. I believe Rourke's offer is sincere. He wants to return. To do right by you."

I wanted Karode to leave the room so I could talk to Daina in private, but I knew that wasn't going to happen. I needed to explain myself without him around. I knew what Daina thought of Billy. "Daina," I said. "Billy's dying."

Her forehead knitted as she processed that news. "How…?"

"He has cancer. The doctors here told him it was hopeless. But you know Billy. He doesn't take no for an answer. He's spent the last six months getting some kind of treatment in another country."

"But—" Karode in usual lawyer fashion wanted to get his two cents in.

"Wait!" I put my hand up to cut him off. "Let me finish, Vik." I continued to look at Daina. "My gut reaction is that he's being treated by a con artist who is taking his money. But he claims he's getting better. He definitely looks a lot better than he did a month ago. Maybe he's in remission."

Daina nodded. "That's good."

"Yeah. It is. Here's the thing. I want us to survive. You and I. But if I sell out Billy to save my skin, we're doomed. I won't be worth anything to you or Astra or Toni. I can't do it. Billy probably doesn't have long to live. I don't want him to spend the rest of his life in some shitty prison." My voice was growing husky. "I'm sorry, Daina. I just…" My chin was trembling. I couldn't get the words out.

Daina reached across the table and grasped my hands. "I understand, Darwin. You are good man. Good father. Good husband, too. You do what you have to do. I stand by you. Always."

Karode sat back in his chair, and rubbed his hand over his head. "Wow. Stephanie was right about you. Both of you." He grinned ruefully. "So you really want to accept the plea,?"

"Yes."

Karode took his papers and stuffed them back into his briefcase. "I will tell Sean that we have a deal. If we hustle, we can get it done today."

"Can I have a week of freedom before I start my sentence?"

"That's not a problem. I'll get you out of here today. You can get two or three months before you have to report. We need to find you a nice minimum security facility."

"I don't want two or three months. I want to be home for Christmas next year. But I want a week. Right now."

Karode had a lopsided grin. "Okay. Might take two weeks, but we'll get it done."

## Chapter 49
*(Saturday, March 4, 2006)*

Redbird Arena in Normal, Illinois had a capacity of ten thousand. It wasn't packed, but the eight thousand rabid fans made enough noise for twenty thousand. Daina and I drove down Saturday afternoon. We didn't tell the girls or Fariba or anyone on the team that I was coming to the game. I didn't want to distract them. I just wanted to see them play one last time. That had been my prayer for the last two months.

Our seats were thirty rows back, on the Vernon Hills side of the court. I didn't want to sit on the Claxton side where I would be recognized. My heart was racing as Toni led the team out of the gangway to begin their warm-ups. I squeezed Daina's hand. There was an apple-sized lump in my throat as Toni slashed to the basket for the first layup. I was an emotional wreck and the game hadn't even started.

"Breathe, Darwin," Daina said.

"Good idea, thanks."

The Vernon Hills Cougars were tall at all positions. Their center, Nadia Zemakova, was six foot six. She was a bruiser with great footwork around the basket. Not as athletic as Toni or Astra, but as my old coach always reminded me, "You can't coach tall." She had dominated the semi-final game, scoring 40 points, and that had included 20 of 21 foul shots. A dominant big man or woman who can also shoot free throws is almost unstoppable.

Almost. I was eager to see what kind of defense Fariba would employ to stop her. She started Astra. No need to platoon for the state championship. There was no tomorrow. She had Marcia contend the opening tap, instead of Toni. It was a savvy call. Nadia controlled the tap easily, but Astra jumped the circle, intercepted the tip, and whipped the ball down court to Toni who had broken for the basket and an uncontested layup.

When Vernon Hills inbounded the ball after the basket their point guard was immediately double teamed by Dede and Astra. Trapped against the sidelines, she made a desperation pass across court that Toni intercepted and took in for another layup.

In the first six minutes of the quarter, Claxton stole the ball in the backcourt five times. On the few occasions that Vernon Hills broke the press and got the ball across half court, instead of settling into their offense and passing the ball into Nadia, who had nearly a foot height advantage on Marcia, they took quick, ill-advised three point shots.

Astra meanwhile was in a shooting zone. She made her first five shots, all three pointers. By the end of the first quarter, Nadia had been shut out and Claxton led by twenty points. For all practical purposes the game was over. At halftime, Claxton led by thirty. When Daina got up to use the ladies room I decided to break my silence and send Fariba a congratulatory text.

I wasn't allowed a cellphone in jail. I looked at the log of texts on my phone and the last text I had sent was to Fariba telling her I'd be at her place in 15 minutes. That was the day I told her I was staying with Daina. After knowing Fariba for four weeks, I had been ready to turn my life upside down to be with her and now here it was three months later, and my life was still spinning out of control.

Hi, Fariba

Miracles DO Happen. I made it to the game (hiding in the Vernon Hills section). Congratulations! The team looks great.

I took a plea. I have a one week furlough and then 18 months in minimum security prison. It won't be so bad. They have a basketball court so I can work on my game. I didn't tell Astra or Toni about the plea yet. I didn't want them to be distracted.

You have done a fantastic job with the girls. You are a true champion. I am honored and humbled to be your friend.

I thought about you all the time while I was locked up. I miss you and I will always love you. Sometimes love has to be enough.

D

It took me ten minutes to compose that text. Astra and Toni would have chided me for my lack of proper text brevity. I didn't figure Fariba would read it until long after the game was over and I wanted my last words to her to be special.

Fortunately the lines for the bathroom were long and Daina didn't make it back to her seat until the third quarter was underway. At the start of the fourth quarter Fariba pulled out all the starters. Claxton had a 40 point lead. The outcome was not in doubt.

She motioned for Toni and Astra to sit next to her. She said something to them and suddenly Toni jumped up like she was going to run back into the game. She stopped at the sideline and stared across the court at the Vernon Hills crowd. Fariba and Astra joined her at the sideline and gently guided her back to the bench. She looked distraught.

The Claxton crowd were on their feet cheering madly as the horn bleated and the game was over. The team rushed on to the court. Someone brought out a step ladder and Astra scrambled up, just as she had done the day Daina had saved her from disaster, and cut down the net. It was a controlled pandemonium, not like when we won years ago, because this time victory was never in doubt. The announcer asked everyone to take their seats so they could award the championship and MVP trophies. Fariba walked out to center court with the team and accepted the trophy for the State Championship. She waved to the fans, flashing that heartbreaking Fariba smile.

The tournament director returned and, holding aloft a the MVP trophy, said, "The Most Valuable Player for the 2006 Girls 3A State Basketball Championship is Toni Wallace!" That surprised no one. Toni had dominated every game and tonight she had been otherworldly.

Toni marched out to center court, frowning the way she did when she didn't understand something. She took the trophy from the director and continued on toward the Vernon Hills side of the court. She scanned the crowd and spotted me — I guess I was cheering more enthusiastically then the remaining Vernon Hills fans. She walked past the Cougars bench and started up the aisle toward me.

The director stood in the middle of the court, mouth agape, trying to figure out what was happening. The cheering had subsided and now a murmur rolled through the stands as Toni marched up the aisle with her trophy.

Daina squeezed my hand and stepped aside as Toni stopped at our row and thrust her trophy at me. "Take it, Coach. You're the MVP."

I had lost my voice. I shook my head no. I didn't know what to say.

Toni glared at me. "Why are you leaving us? We need you. I need you." Her lips trembled.

I took a breath. "It's only for a little while, Toni. I'll be back."

Tears streamed down Toni's face as she pushed the trophy into my chest, her jaw set defiantly.

"Take trophy, Darwin," Daina said. "It is gift from your new daughter."

The announcer was telling the players to remain on the court. But the team, led by Astra had already started up the aisle toward us. I took the trophy from Toni and raised it over my head. "Claxton Eagles State Champions! You girls are awesome!"

If I had known my brief moment of glory was being captured by cellphone video, and in one week would be viewed over three million times, I would have definitely come up with a better line.

Astra, sobbing, made it to my row and threw her arms around me. Toni followed and then Daina joined them. The crowd around us, all Vernon Hills fans, stood and cheered. They didn't know our story. They didn't have to.

Fariba stood a few rows below us, smiling through her tears. I nodded at her and she stepped up and rested her hand on Daina's back. She brushed a light kiss on my cheek and whispered, "You're right. Sometimes it is enough."

I wished Billy could be here. I wanted to hear him tell this story for the next thirty years. The epic saga of how WE had won the state title again. All of us: Billy, Fariba, Daina, Toni, Astra. Darwin.

It was all our victory.

# Acknowledgment

A lot of people have helped me with my this book.

Kendra Joy Witter, Carol Joy Vecchi and Christine Joy have always been willing to read my work and offer intelligent, but kind critiques. A brother couldn't ask for a better trio of sisters.

My lawyer, Jim Clark, read several drafts of BETTER DAYS and provided annoyingly detailed line edits. He also helped me with all the criminal court room procedures and didn't even bill me for his time.

My triathlon coach, Heather Collins, helped me with the coaching dynamics and provided valuable insights on the psyche of female athletes.

I am especially appreciative of my writer-friend Ania Vesenny who has read everything I have written. Ania's favorite word is "cut" and without her help this novel would have been 400 pages

CPSIA information can be obtained
at www.ICGtesting.com
Printed in the USA
FFHW02n2007021018
48671390-52673FF